Uninvited guest . . .

"You won't want to stay," he said heavily.

"Give me the chance." Taylor pressed her advantage.

He shook his head.

"Please, Jason. I need to. I need to try. Don't you see? You've given me so much. I can't stand not to try."

"God, Taylor! I'm not a charity case!" He shoved back his chair, but Taylor was on her feet in an instant. She sensed he was wavering, and she was certain she wouldn't get another chance if she blew this one.

"All right, you can stay. God knows why you want to, but you can stay. For *one* day."

Taylor swallowed. "Thank you."

When he looked at her again, his mouth was twisted in mockery. "Oh, don't thank me yet, Taylor Michaelson. You're a long long way from Hollywood, and I have a feeling you're going to wish you hadn't won this little battle."

Dear Reader:

Romance offers us all so much. It makes us "walk on sunshine." It gives us hope. It takes us out of our own lives, encouraging us to reach out to others. Janet Dailey is fond of saying that romance is a state of mind, that it could happen anywhere. Yet nowhere does romance seem to be as good as when it happens *here*.

Starting in February 1986, Silhouette Special Edition is featuring the AMERICAN TRIBUTE—a tribute to America, where romance has never been so wonderful. For six consecutive months, one out of every six Special Editions will be an episode in the AMERICAN TRIBUTE, a portrait of the lives of six women, all from Oklahoma. Look for the first book, *Love's Haunting Refrain* by Ada Steward, as well as stories by other favorites—Jeanne Stephens, Gena Dalton, Elaine Camp and Renee Roszel. You'll know the AMERICAN TRIBUTE by its patriotic stripe under the Silhouette Special Edition border.

AMERICAN TRIBUTE—six women, six stories, starting in February.

AMERICAN TRIBUTE—one of the reasons Silhouette Special Edition is just that—Special.

The Editors at Silhouette Books

NATALIE BISHOP
Diamond in the Sky

Silhouette Special Edition

Published by Silhouette Books New York

America's Publisher of Contemporary Romance

To the Whidby Island bikers

SILHOUETTE BOOKS
300 E. 42nd St., New York, N.Y. 10017

Copyright © 1986 by Natalie Bishop

ISBN: 0-373-09300-4

First Silhouette Books printing March 1986

SILHOUETTE, SILHOUETTE SPECIAL EDITION and colophon are
registered trademarks of the publisher.

America's Publisher of Contemporary Romance

Printed in the U.S.A.

Books by Natalie Bishop

Silhouette Special Edition

Saturday's Child #178
Lover or Deceiver #198
Stolen Thunder #231
Trial by Fire #245
String of Pearls #280
Diamond in the Sky #300

NATALIE BISHOP

lives within a stone's throw of her sister, Lisa Jackson, who is also a Silhouette author. Natalie and Lisa spend many afternoons together, developing new plots and reading their best lines to each other.

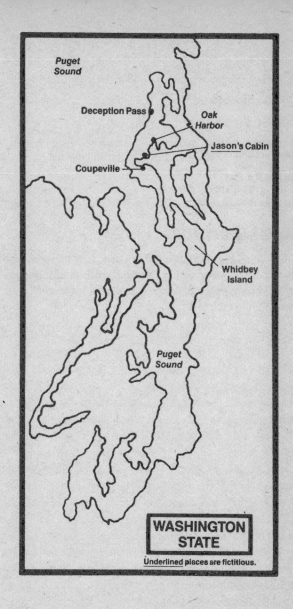

Puget
Sound

Deception Pass

Oak
Harbor

Jason's Cabin

Coupeville

Whidbey
Island

Puget
Sound

**WASHINGTON
STATE**

Underlined places are fictitious.

Chapter One

Everyone had told her she was making a terrible mistake.

Taylor Michaelson turned her face to the salt sea spray and leaned against the rail of the ferryboat. A pale lemon October sun broke through the gray skies, picking up amber highlights in her burnished blond hair and leaving a dazzling streak sparkling on the rough waters of Puget Sound.

Taylor sighed. The feel of the ferry chugging undaunted toward the shore of Whidbey Island, the sense of adventure that came as she saw the Washington mainland slip behind, the beautiful vista of silver skies, yellow sunshine and forest-green ocean waters: all of it together couldn't displace the misgivings she felt inside.

Ross Corley, Taylor's agent, had been the first to let her know how foolhardy her plan was.

"For God's sake, Taylor," he'd said in his precise diction, straightening the vest of his three-piece suit. "You leave now and what's left of your career will be ruined. Chasing down Jason Garrett is foolish and pointless. The man wants to be left alone, so leave him alone. What can you do that others haven't, anyway? Nothing. Take it from me: if you want to act, you've got to stay in Hollywood, stick with what you're doing and let the Jason Garretts of the world fight their own demons...."

Taylor had tried to argue with Ross. "I owe that man my career," she pointed out in a soft but determined voice. "Jason Garrett is the only reason I've had any success at all. You know as well as I do that I was sinking in that first role. I was terrible—scared and frozen! Jason took the time to teach me things about acting that would have taken me years to learn on my own."

Ross hadn't achieved his present success by being bullied by his clients. Taylor's words fell on deaf ears. "Well, that's the best reason I know of to stay, then," he said brusquely. "You've got too much to lose now. Don't throw it all away! Jason Garrett would tell you the same thing if he were here."

Taylor had argued long and hard with Ross and in the end had decided to ignore him entirely and follow her instincts. Jason Garrett, after a brief and brilliant Hollywood career, had suddenly packed it all in and headed, with his wife and three-year-old daughter in tow, to Whidbey Island, one of the many islands scattered throughout Puget Sound and along the Washington coast. Taylor had only recently learned that he was still there—two years after the storm and quarrel she'd witnessed during the filming of *Queen of Diamonds*, the last episode of the *Diamond Girl* trilogy, the series she and Jason had starred in together.

Between then and now, tragedy had touched Jason's life: his wife and daughter had been killed in a terrible accident. Taylor could well understand the emotional trauma Jason had suffered, yet even so, she was horrified that he was still a recluse; that just wasn't the style of the Jason she had known.

Taylor had gone to Phil Walker next, a psychologist friend of Jason's who had known him years longer than Taylor had.

Phil was, if possible, less encouraging than Ross.

"Taylor," he'd said with a sigh, stroking his trim salt-and-pepper beard, "Jason Garrett needs help. Not the kind of help you can give him. Professional help. I've been to Whidbey Island once already. Jason..." Phil cleared his throat, his mouth tightening in remembrance. "Jason threw me out. Literally. He pushed me out the door and told me to go and...well, never mind. Let's just say he was very explicit."

Taylor was stunned. Professional help? Could she and Phil be talking about the same man? Jason Garrett, though certainly imbued with an artist's mercurial temperament, was one of the sanest men she knew. In a town where reality and fantasy blended, sometimes becoming indistinguishable from one another, Jason had always had his feet planted firmly on the ground, his emotions kept under strict rein. Taylor knew Jason had resented her selection as the *Diamond Girl* trilogy's leading lady— she was a dismal amateur in comparison to his expertise!—yet Jason had been extremely patient and helpful. She'd seen him lose control only once—that day in Camara de Lobos—and even then he'd pulled himself together within minutes when he had realized Taylor was watching him. It was impossible to imagine Jason being in the kind of shape Phil was describing.

"Don't go to Whidbey, Taylor," Phil had advised as she was leaving his office. "You'll regret it."

Regret it. Taylor bit her bottom lip. Maybe she already did regret it a little. She was crazy to think she could help him if Phil Walker hadn't been able to. What was she to Jason, anyway? A friend. A casual acquaintance. A woman who admired and, yes, maybe even idolized him, but she was hardly equipped to deal with the kind of man Jason had apparently become.

Taylor inhaled a lungful of sharp sea air and shook her head at her own incredible optimism. Why had she ever thought that she might make a difference? Just because she was eager, empathetic and truly concerned for Jason's welfare didn't mean she was qualified to help, yet she knew in her heart she couldn't back out now.

The bow of the ferry edged toward the dock, the ferrymen working quickly to release the chain across the gate. They wore gray slickers with fluorescent orange hoods, equipped for the worst kind of weather during the quick twenty-minute voyage. Today, however, the wind was benign, little more than a brisk breeze ruffling dark green waters. Taylor shoved her hands deep inside the pockets of her jacket, her collar turned up at the nape. She stared across the churning wake and tried to think positively. This had been her decision, one she still believed in even though she was riddled with anxiety. What's the worst that could happen, anyway? she rationalized to herself.

Jason might throw you out, too.

Taylor made a face, then squared her shoulders and tightened her resolve. She could live with that. No pain, no gain, she thought wryly.

Once Taylor had decided to ignore Ross's and Phil's advice, there was one person left she had needed to see:

Meredith Maddox, current head of Maddox Production Company, a woman who had been closely associated with Jason both personally and professionally for years. Meredith knew Jason better than practically anyone, maybe even Phil; Meredith's sister had been Jason's wife....

Meredith's dark brows had arched with skepticism, however, when Taylor had outlined her plan. "Look, Taylor," she'd said with a grimace that drew lines in her otherwise flawless skin, "your altruism is commendable, but Jason isn't in any frame of mind to listen to anyone. Phil Walker tried, you know, and he got thrown out bodily." She sighed and lit a cigarette, shaking her head at the waste. "I'd do anything to get Jason back to Hollywood. He's sensational; the public loved him in those films. They loved you, too, of course, Taylor," she put in diffidently, then swept on before it was necessary for Taylor to comment. "I'd like to do more *Diamond Girl* pictures, with both you and Jason. Let's face it, right now Jason Garrett's bankable—he's only been out of the spotlight a couple of seasons. But if we wait much longer..." Her voice trailed off gloomily.

"I just want to make sure he's all right," Taylor stated clearly. "If there's anything I can do, I want to do it."

To make certain Meredith understood her motivations, Taylor had then swallowed her pride and committed what Ross would have termed "professional suicide"—she admitted her failings to an important producer. "Jason guided me through those films," she told Meredith. "He taught me to act. Without him I was just another ex-model with delusions of being an actress. He made me an actress. He made me be the best that I can be."

Meredith was silent so long that Taylor had counted thirty of her own frightened heartbeats. She'd virtually tossed her career at the producer's feet, and only much later did she remember that Meredith had been the one who hadn't wanted Taylor for the *Diamond Girl* trilogy in the first place.

What it was that Meredith had really concluded on that day three weeks earlier, Taylor still didn't know. But eventually, in a curious voice, Meredith had asked, "You really mean this, don't you?"

"Yes."

The producer's attitude had subtly changed. "Then let me be frank, Taylor," she'd said. "If you go to see Jason, I'd like to ask a favor. You see, I would like Jason Garrett back in Hollywood. I want to star him in several new films." Her dark eyes lifted to Taylor's troubled amber ones. "You and he were great together; the *Diamond Girl* trilogy is proof of that. In fact, I'd like to make more *Diamond Girl* pictures. If you can get Jason off that island and back to work, I'll draw up a contract for three more films—starring both of you."

Taylor had been dumbfounded. She could only stare at the petite dark-haired woman who wielded so much power.

"Those films made terrific revenues," Meredith had continued. "I know more films will do just the same— no, *better*. And you, Taylor Michaelson, will find yourself a full-fledged star."

Taylor finally found her voice. "That's a very generous offer, Meredith, but I can't guarantee I'll succeed. Jason may not want to come back. I just want to try and help him, that's all."

"And you will," Meredith interjected hastily. "Jason's been on that island too long. It's unhealthy to mourn Lisabeth's and Kerri's deaths this long. He needs to get back in the mainstream, and if you can do it, Taylor, you'll be helping both him and yourself, too. I grant you, your chances of success may be small." She shrugged and looked discouraged for a moment. "The film offer is just added incentive for both of you. Oh, by the way, I understand from Ross that you've been writing a screenplay along the *Diamond Girl* lines. When you get back from Whidbey I'll be happy to take a look at it...."

The ferry horn blasted, shattering Taylor's uncomfortable reflections. She ran her fingers through the thick strands of her hair, and after a last troubled look toward the Washington mainland hurried down two flights of stairs to the ferry's lowest deck. She climbed into her rented Toyota, waited for the ferryman to wave her through and swallowed against a tight throat.

Meredith Maddox certainly didn't pull her punches; she wanted Jason and she was willing to use Taylor to get him. What Meredith didn't understand was that Taylor had no intention of doing her bidding. She would never coerce Jason into returning just to further her own career. As far as Taylor was concerned, Meredith Maddox, Ross, Phil, the whole Hollywood scene—none of it mattered. All that mattered was Jason, locked away on an island, his world in turmoil, living the life of a recluse, forsaking everything and everyone he'd ever known.

Taylor's fingers flexed around the steering wheel. She slid her car into gear as the first of the vehicles drove onto the Whidbey Island ramp.

"Oh, Jason," she whispered, her heart thudding with something like fear. "I hope they're wrong. I hope I'm not making a terrible mistake."

Barely more than a giant's step from the mainland, Whidbey Island was about fifty miles long, dotted with small towns and was a great tourist attraction during the summer. Taylor drove onto the two-lane highway that bisected it, trying without much success to control her racing pulse. Now that she was here her heart was in her throat. She hadn't seen Jason for two years. *Two years!* And though she'd worked opposite him for many months, she wasn't certain he would greet her with anything more than the politeness of strangers.

If he was even polite.

Taylor heaved a deep sigh, looking through the window at the sleepy farmland edging each side of the road, the weathered homes small and charming, the pace almost out of another century compared to the rush and frenzy of Los Angeles.

She was gripped by a curious nostalgia as she drove along. Her own childhood had been scattered, moving from town to town, house to house, always one step ahead of the bill collectors. She'd traveled from one end of Los Angeles to the other but had never really put down solid roots. As much as she loved her actor father, she recognized now that he'd been too much of a vagabond to settle down. Taylor's mother had realized that much sooner and had left them both.

Resolutely pushing those thoughts aside, Taylor drove northward, periodically consulting her map, glad there was only one major highway to follow. Whidbey Island was long but narrow, at points less than two miles across. Jason's house was about halfway up the island, where the eastern shore curved into a sickle-shaped bay.

She found the rutted lane to his house without difficulty. As she turned in, her vision limited by tall, stately firs and densely packed pine trees, Taylor's heart began to pound. What would he think of her, coming all this way just to see him? She'd sensed Jason had liked her, though at times, especially toward the end of their last film together, he'd seemed so distracted that she'd wondered if he even remembered whom he was with.

Taylor let out a slow breath as her car nosed through the trees into a clearing. A small cottage was perched on a gentle knoll at the edge of the sound, and Taylor caught a glimpse of vivid sunlight glinting on the restless water beyond.

She stepped from the car, somehow dreading and anticipating at the same time this moment of truth. Her whole trip could be for nothing, and she would find out within the next few minutes. She would also find out just what kind of shape Jason was truly in.

She walked to the door, inhaling and exhaling several times to calm her nerves, listening to the sharp cry of sea gulls as they swooped down to skim just above the water. Puget Sound was saltwater, an arm of the Pacific Ocean that reached east between Washington and British Columbia, then extended downward, halfway through the state of Washington. Whidbey Island, the San Juan Islands and a myriad of other tiny islands were sandwiched between the two sides of Washington's mainland, but Taylor felt the isolation of the area keenly. She seemed light-years away from the world she lived in.

The paint on the cottage door was peeling as Taylor knocked sharply several times. Gray shingles covered the outside walls, and the structure was capped with a cedar shake roof, currently carpeted with pine needles. The smell of smoke filled her nose and she could see a gray plume rising from the river-rock chimney.

To her surprise, a middle-aged woman opened the door. "Yes?" the woman asked, eyeing Taylor warily but in a friendly fashion. She held a broom in one hand, and underneath a faded apron the line between her bust and waist was indiscernible.

Taylor swallowed and smiled. She searched the woman's face for some clue to the state of the household, but other than polite interest there was nothing to read on that plump countenance. "I was looking for Jason Garrett," Taylor explained. "Is this his home?"

The woman nodded, her sharp eyes examining Taylor critically. "But he isn't here right now."

"Oh." Was that relief she was feeling? Taylor issued herself a stern warning and gathered up her courage. "When will he be back?"

"I'm not sure. Sometime later. Are you a friend of his?"

The woman's suspicions sounded in her voice. Taylor thought she was probably leery of Jason's friends after the treatment Phil Walker had received.

"We used to work together," Taylor answered evasively.

"Ah! You're the girl!" the woman exclaimed. She moved her imposing frame back a few inches and invited Taylor inside. "I recognize you now. You did films with him. Of course, when Jason moved into the cottage we didn't know at first it was Jason. But my daughter's a fan, and when she finally figured it out, it like to blew her mind!"

The woman laughed with a hearty robustness that did a lot toward easing Taylor's anxieties. "My name's Maxine," she said, dusting her hand on her apron then extending it to Taylor. "I live two houses down, and try to keep order around this place." She stopped suddenly and gave Taylor a mock-fierce look. "You're not gonna try to talk Jason into something he doesn't want to do, are you?''

"I'm Taylor Michaelson," Taylor said, shaking Maxine's hand. "And I don't think it's possible to talk Jason into something he doesn't want to do."

"Good. That other fellow didn't do him any good at all."

"Phil Walker?"

Maxine wrinkled her nose. "All full of self-importance and gobbledygook. He tried to impress me with his vocabulary, but I don't impress easily. Where are your things? Aren't you planning to stay a few days?"

Taylor was a bit nonplussed by Maxine's forthrightness. "I, uh, was going to check with Jason first. I haven't seen him in several years, not since we worked together."

Maxine's smooth forehead creased, and she gave Taylor a quick look. "He's not the same as he was before his wife and child were killed," she admitted reluctantly.

Taylor sighed. "That's why I think it would be a good idea to talk to him before I just...move in. Where is he? Is it possible for me to find him?"

"Oh, yes," Maxine turned away, whisking at some nonexistent dirt with her broom. "He's at his favorite afternoon haunt—the Tidewater."

"The Tidewater?" Taylor repeated woodenly. The grimness in Maxine's voice made Taylor's spine tingle.

"A local bar in Coupeville. Just go back the way you came. You'll see the town. And you'll see the Tidewater."

A feeling of doom came over Taylor. Jason? Spending his afternoons in a bar? Her plan to charge to his aid suddenly seemed as ill-conceived as everyone in Hollywood had predicted. "Do you think I should go to the

Tidewater, or just wait for him here?" she asked awkwardly.

"If you wait here, you'll be waiting a mighty long time," Maxine said with a heavy sigh. "I don't know what your relationship to Jason is, but if I were you, I'd go get him. What he needs is a friend—a *real* friend—not the kind like I've been seeing, if you know what I mean."

Taylor wasn't sure she did. But since Maxine had to be referring to Phil Walker, she silently thanked the forces that had made Maxine believe Taylor was different.

Though she'd never been the type of person to pry, Taylor felt desperately in need of a little more background information. Tentatively, because she didn't want to upset her budding friendship with Maxine, Taylor said, "I haven't seen or spoken to Jason since he left Hollywood. I sent a card when I learned about the accident, but it came back unopened."

"Ahhh . . ." Maxine nodded sadly.

"I'm afraid Jason might throw me out, too."

Maxine studied Taylor once again, and Taylor had a mental image of what the housekeeper must have seen: unusually serious yet slightly exotic amber eyes, golden shoulder-length hair streaked by the sun, high cheekbones, wide mouth, lithe frame, full bustline. Taylor was almost too short to be a model and had mainly done head shots—photos of her face and shoulders. It had been a career thrust upon her by her long-distance mother, one she'd reluctantly followed until her father, probably in petty retaliation, had steered her toward acting. But at least acting had given her room to grow, though in all truthfulness Taylor had found she enjoyed writing—her own career choice—best.

"Jason Garrett's not the man you remember," Maxine said with certainty.

The smile Taylor had been trying to dredge up died completely at Maxine's tone. "Why do you say that?"

"He's very, very..." She searched for the right word, and Taylor could hear her own uneven breathing in the hush that followed. "Bitter," Maxine came up with finally, her face reflecting sorrow for a friend. "He's bitter. He can be...unbearable."

Taylor's misgivings turned to out-and-out dread. "Thank you," she said with difficulty, turning toward the door.

"You're not like his wife then, are you?"

"His wife?" Taylor asked blankly, not understanding the woman's meaning. "Well, no. I don't think so. I'm just an acquaintance of Jason's," she added with a sense of unreality.

"That's what I figured." Maxine nodded, satisfied. "Take care," she said, then walked off in the direction of the kitchen.

Taylor watched Maxine leave, her mouth suddenly full of cotton. If she'd deluded herself about the severity of Jason's problems, Maxine had opened her eyes the rest of the way. It was plain that Jason was in trouble and that Taylor was in way over her head. But there was no backing out now.

The Tidewater was a two-story clapboard building whose second floor was at street level. The lower floor was at water level, and except for sturdy barnacle-covered wood pilings showing beneath its structure when the waves receded, the whole building looked as if it could easily slip into the sea.

Taylor opened the door and stepped into a small anteroom that served as a lobby for the upstairs restaurant. Faint country and western music filtered from the stairwell to her right, and she surmised the bar must be below.

Slowly she walked down the narrow steps. As the music grew louder she recognized Charlie Rich's "Behind Closed Doors," and she found herself standing in a small shag-carpeted room with black barrel-backed chairs. Taylor looked around the place with growing horror. This was where Jason was? It wasn't exactly sleazy, but it had little to recommend it besides a mahogany bar with a curved nautical design, and even that was nicked and dulled from too much use and not enough care.

Taylor stepped further inside, catching the stares of several men in oil-stained work clothes. She scanned the room anxiously for any sign of Jason, but couldn't see him anywhere. To Taylor, every occupant of the room looked exactly alike.

It took a great deal of willpower for her to ignore the appreciative whistles and knowing laughter that followed her as she walked toward the bar. Her back was stiff, her features frozen, her face flaming by the time the woman barkeep deigned to interrupt her conversation with a burly male customer seated at the end of the bar and came to greet her.

The barkeep had red hair tinged with grey, secured in a ponytail by a rubber band. "Can I help you?" she inquired, her world-weary eyes scanning Taylor from head to toe.

Though Taylor was in jeans, she was patently overdressed. Her pants were tucked into short dress boots of soft gray suede, her mint-green blouse and wool sweater coat looking like the last word in sophistication compared to the checked cotton blouse, well-worn jeans and cheap metal belt of the woman behind the bar. Even the tousled cut of Taylor's hair didn't quite fit in. She stuck out like the proverbial sore thumb.

"I'm looking for someone," Taylor said, smiling, her eyes searching the other patrons, trying not to meet the admiring male gazes that were sliding her way. The Tidewater's only other saving grace was the floor-to-ceiling windows that circled the back of the building. Puget Sound was literally at the back door; the view was exquisite.

The woman's brows rose suspiciously. "Oh?"

"I'm a friend of Jason Garrett's," Taylor explained, taking the plunge. "Do you know him?"

"Sure." The barkeep and the man at the end of the bar exchanged a look that Taylor couldn't interpret.

"Hey, Rita," one of the customers called out. "How about another one over here."

The red-haired woman didn't answer, but she grabbed a frosted mug and put it under the tap. Taylor's nerves stretched as she waited. Her fingernails dug into her palms. Jason was nowhere in sight.

Taylor was at the point of turning to leave when the red-haired barkeep suddenly said, "He's over there," her hand pointing vaguely toward the windows.

Taylor focused on the lone man sitting at a corner table. This was Jason? She didn't recognize the man slouched in the chair, his back turned to her, his gaze focused somewhere on the sun-dappled waters. A battered Stetson covered his head, long straggles of brown hair brushing against the collar of a dark suede, fleece-lined jacket. He wore dusty jeans, and his long legs were stretched out on another chair, his feet encased in thick boots. A plaid cuff poked out from the arm of his jacket, and after one startled glance, Taylor was certain the woman must be mistaken.

The red-haired woman offered no further clue. "You want a beer?" she asked in a bored tone, and Taylor, still not believing her eyes, hesitated only briefly before saying yes.

She perched on one of the black Naugahide bar stools, studying the man carefully. It could be Jason, she thought with a sinking heart. The hair was the right color, the build similar. She couldn't see his face, so it was difficult to tell, but with another glance around the room Taylor determined that he was the only man who came close to the right description.

She licked her lips and slid off the stool; every step she took was filled with trepidation. But as she approached she realized the woman had been right. Something about him struck a familiar chord. Hesitating, Taylor stepped to his right side, seeing the aristocratic nose and brooding, unhappy mouth beneath the broad brim of his hat. It *was* Jason!

Taylor's jaw slackened in disbelief. In one moment, her doubts about coming both dissolved and crystallized. She knew now that she'd been right to be worried, to want to help him. Jason would never have gotten himself into this kind of shape unless something was eating him alive. Yet at the same time Taylor was filled with despair; her chances of any kind of success were remote.

As she looked at Jason, seeing his lackluster slouch, the fingers curved around an empty beer mug, Taylor realized he was dead drunk. Her heart went out to him. Back when she'd known Jason, he'd never drunk alcohol at all. His wife, Lisabeth, had been rumored to have a drinking problem, and Jason, because of that or possibly something else, had never drunk anything stronger than club soda in Taylor's presence.

With more courage than she'd thought herself capable of, Taylor walked straight up to him. She ignored the curious eyes of the other patrons and stood next to Jason's table, waiting for him to look up. She had absolutely no idea what to say to him now that she was there.

The Stetson tipped backward and Jason, his incredibly blue eyes squinting against the glare off the water, suddenly stared at her full in the face.

Hope sprang to life in Taylor's breast. He wasn't as far gone as she'd originally thought! He was clean-shaven; his gaze, though slightly muzzy, definitely focused on her face; his mouth was still a fascinating blend of masculinity and sensuality, quirking with disbelief, lips parting in surprise to display a set of straight white teeth.

Heart hammering, the smile on her lips as tremulous as her insides, Taylor called on her acting talents—the talents Jason had helped her to develop—and managed to drawl, ''Well, hello there. Is it Jason Garrett, or Jesse James?''

Chapter Two

Jason stared at her in bewilderment. "Taylor?" he asked hoarsely.

"How are you?" she inquired as Jason made an attempt to straighten up, his long legs unwinding, feet dropping to the floor with a dull thud. Taylor swallowed and tried not to let him see how shocked she was by his appearance. It was hard to believe this cowboy was the impeccable actor she'd known in Los Angeles!

His gaze dropped, narrowing on the empty glass mug. "I'm fine," he said shortly. "Can't you tell?"

Taylor heard his underlying sarcasm—or was that merely the effect of too many beers? He shot her a look that was distinctly hostile and asked flatly, "What're you doin' here?"

Taylor managed a smile. "Well, I think it's pretty obvious: I came to see you."

The woman barkeep brought Jason another mug of beer, picking up the empty one without a word. She scraped some of Jason's change from the table, gave Taylor a look that could have meant anything from sympathy to smugness, then turned back to the bar.

Taylor sat down gingerly in the chair Jason's feet had vacated, hardly encouraged by the deep frown that settled between his brows. She should be glad, she supposed, that he was as congenial as he'd been. By the looks of things, he'd already put in a long shift at the Tidewater and had no intention of leaving in the near future.

She sipped her beer and examined him surreptitiously as he stared out the window at the bright waters. Except for the disillusionment in his face, and a new gauntness, Jason looked just the same: the same thick brown hair, the same determined jaw, the same thick-lashed blue eyes, the same tough build and strong character. But the easy humor was missing from around his eyes, and his mouth looked as if it hadn't really smiled in a long, long time.

"How did you find me?" he demanded tersely, reaching for his beer.

"I learned from Meredith Maddox where you were," Taylor answered, curbing the urge to aid his unsteady hand in its search for the glass mug. "And I learned from Maxine about the Tidewater."

Jason turned, his expression blank. "Maxine told you where I was?" At Taylor's nod, his face turned thunderous. "Well, how did you bribe her? She isn't easily fooled, that woman."

"I didn't bribe her," Taylor said, affronted.

"The hell you didn't."

Taylor blinked rapidly. This antagonistic man wasn't the Jason she remembered! With a feeling bordering on panic, she wondered if her memories had dimmed and softened what kind of man he really was.

But no. All she had to do was remember Jason's unselfish kindness to her when she'd been drowning in that first *Diamond Girl* film. She would never forget his patience, his understanding, the depth of his commitment to making the film the best it could be, making Taylor the best *she* could be. She'd idolized him then, and did still, but his hostility now was new and discouraging.

"Who sent you?" Jason demanded. "Phil? Clifton?" He made a show of snapping his fingers but no sound came. "I bet it was my sweet sister-in-law, Meredith."

Taylor looked at him in distress. "I came on my own."

He laughed mirthlessly and shook his head, taking a deep draft from his mug. "You're a terrible liar," he told her flatly. "Go home."

Taylor gritted her teeth. She hadn't forgotten that Lisabeth Garrett—Jason's wife—had been Meredith Maddox's sister, but she was surprised that Jason's hostility seemed to extend to Meredith too. Taylor had wondered why Meredith hadn't tried to talk Jason into coming back to Hollywood, but now, after witnessing his current state of mind, Taylor could see it probably wouldn't have helped in any case. Meredith, intelligent woman that she was, probably already knew the effort would have met with poor results.

Jason's reference to Clifton brought up a whole host of memories for Taylor. She had a sudden sharp vision of that bitter quarrel she'd overheard during the filming of *Queen of Diamonds*. Jason had been arguing with Clifton Maddox, Meredith's husband, head of Maddox Productions until a mild stroke had forced the seat of power to be transferred to his wife. Jason had been lashing and vicious, Clifton white-faced and full of bottled-up fury. The two men, always close friends, had said things to each other that had made Taylor's blood run cold. The rift, as far as she knew, had never been repaired, and Jason's disparaging remarks now seemed to suggest that was still true.

"I'm not leaving until I've had a chance to talk to you," Taylor said after several moments. "And I'd prefer it to be when you're sober."

For just an instant he smiled, giving Taylor a much-needed glimpse of his former self. Tiny webs of lines crinkled engagingly beside his eyes, and his mouth curved sensually, displacing the dispirited man in front of her with the vibrant one she'd known so long ago. He looked, for that moment, as if his innate sense of humor would rescue him. She could see amusement lurking in his deep blue eyes, could hear it in his voice as he drawled sexily, "Sorry, Taylor. I can't oblige. What you see is what you get, and it's *all* available."

She smiled. "If it's so available, why is it being wasted here?"

The moment passed. Taylor could see the sparkle of humor in his eyes fade as he subsided into a deeper slouch, and she mourned for the Jason that had been.

"Go play Angel of Mercy with someone else," he rasped harshly. "I don't give a damn."

"If you think I came all the way here just to be turned away, think again," Taylor said with a firmness that even surprised herself. "Rudeness won't get rid of me."

"Then what will? Why don't you tell me now so we can put an end to this and get it over with."

His gaze slid over her indifferently; then he fixed his eyes on the water once more, yanking his brim down over his forehead.

A gull landed on the piling of a broken-down pier and Taylor concentrated on it, trying to assuage her feelings of frustration, annoyance and concern. "It looks to me like all you want to do is sit around and brood," she accused, her temper getting the upper hand.

"What's it to you?" he growled.

Taylor was exasperated. "Maybe I just care about what happens to you."

He swore under his breath.

Taylor took a big gulp of her beer, nearly choking on its bitterness. She marveled at the way she was speaking to him, the way he was speaking to her! They'd never had words. Never! And she never could have imagined herself in such a position before, was having trouble believing it now.

She sucked in a deep breath and put in doggedly, "Other people care about you, too."

Jason slowly tilted up his brim with one finger, his blue gaze less focused. But his voice was remarkably clear as he said, "Your naiveté astounds me, Taylor."

"It seems to me, you're the one who's cut himself off from his friends, Jason, not the other way around."

"Friends!" He spat the word out as if it had a bitter taste. "Go back to Hollywood, Taylor. It's where you belong."

"It's where you belong, too."

Anger pierced through the numbness of the alcohol he'd consumed. She could see it in the rigid line of his jaw, the sudden fierceness in his eyes. "Don't tell me what's right for me!" he snarled. "I know. *I know!*" He inhaled unsteadily. "Now get the hell out of here. I don't give a damn why you're here. Just get out."

These last few words were ground out through his teeth. Taylor couldn't help the hurt that welled inside her, even though she shouldn't have expected any better treatment. Hadn't Phil warned her? Hadn't Ross, and Meredith? If she'd had any doubts, she didn't anymore. Jason didn't care about her motivations or feelings at all; he just couldn't wait to be rid of her. Abiding by normal social graces had been dispensed with long ago, she thought with an inward grimace. This Jason Garrett was raw and primal and equipped with weapons that could seek and find all of Taylor's weak points, laying them bare, hurting her in ways no one else could, if he chose to.

And he chose to. It was in his face, his eyes, the stern determination of his chin. She could practically see the warning: *If you stay here, beware. I'm going to hurt you like you've never been hurt before.*

"You need anything else?" Rita asked as she walked up to their table, oblivious to the awkward silence.

"No," said Jason grimly.

"Yes," Taylor disagreed. "Another beer, please."

Jason glowered, his blue eyes burning with a dangerous flame. "Make it two," he said, reaching in his pocket for some change.

Taylor beat him to it. She handed the woman several bills and slid amber eyes in Jason's direction. "My treat," she said in cool challenge.

He snarled something beneath his breath, then leaned his head back, eyes closed, mouth a grim line. He was furious with her—with the whole damn world, it appeared. She didn't really blame him. If he'd forced himself into her private world, she'd probably be just as angry.

But even as she watched him, Taylor could see his anger disappear beneath the weight of a great sadness. Her chest hurt at the unhappiness that drooped the corners of his mouth and made his shoulders slump in defeat.

She wanted to comfort him but knew he would resent her for it. Instead she paid for the beers and, taking a cue from Jason, stared out the window across the sound, seeing, yet not seeing, the beautiful gray-lavender of gathering twilight.

At length, Jason exhaled a deep breath. Taylor didn't swing her gaze to meet his. She just waited.

"What are you really doing here?" he asked, his tone somewhat resigned but still wary. She noticed that he hadn't yet picked up his new mug and considered that a good sign.

"I told you. I wanted to see you."

"Why?"

She raised her brows and turned to him, looking askance. Jason glowered and moved an impatient hand. "I forgot," he said sarcastically. "You *care* about me. Like hell, Taylor. Since when did you become so fond of me?"

Taylor's answer stuck in her throat. She'd always been fond of him. She'd even, she could admit with squirming honesty, had a terrible stars-in-her-eyes crush on him. The love scenes they'd done together had left memories in her mind that refused to fade. They'd been billed as a couple, gone out together—strictly for publicity—as a couple, and had suffered the usual round of gossip and rumor as a couple. Of course she cared about him! How could she not? Even in his current debilitated condition, Jason was an extremely attractive man.

But attraction was as far as it went. Taylor had always known her intense feelings about Jason were the result of fantasy—a beautiful, intangible, butterfly-fragile fantasy that was all of her own making. Jason, after all, had been married then, and Taylor, like everyone else, knew how much Jason Garrett had loved his wife.

He took her silence as an answer to his question. "So...I was right. You came because of something else." He looked vaguely amused. "What did Clifton offer you for coming to see me, hmm? No, no." He wagged his finger in front of her nose as she opened her mouth. "Shhh." His finger touched her lips. "Let me guess. A part. A part in a new movie. A *leading role!*"

His voice had risen until several heads turned in their direction. Taylor was paralyzed. She couldn't answer him, couldn't deny the accusation. Though her reasons for coming to Whidbey stemmed from real concern for his well-being, Taylor could hear Meredith Maddox once again, as if she were speaking to her now.

If you can get Jason off that island and back to work, I'll draw up a contract for three more films starring both of you.

Taylor unconsciously licked her lips, still feeling the warm imprint from Jason's finger. "I came because I wanted to," she said slowly and truthfully. "Clifton Maddox didn't contact me."

"Pah." Jason turned away in disgust.

"Clifton isn't...head of Maddox Productions anymore, you know," Taylor said diffidently.

Jason reached for his beer, downing most of it in one long draft. Taylor watched, swallowed, then added, "Since his stroke, Meredith's taken over control."

She didn't know what kind of reaction she'd expected from him—none, most likely. She'd just assumed Jason had to know about Clifton's health problems, rift or no.

So Taylor was completely unnerved when Jason's blue eyes focused hazily on hers, a line forming between his brows as he asked blankly, "What did you say?"

"Clifton Maddox had a mild stroke eighteen months ago. Meredith was the natural successor, so she's been—"

"Stroke?"

Jason's face drained of color so quickly that Taylor grew alarmed. She started to rise but strong hands suddenly crashed down over her arms, pinning her to the chair.

"Say it again! My God! What are you talking about? What are you *saying*?"

"It was a mild stroke." Taylor's voice managed to work, but her heart was pounding. "Really. He's nearly completely recovered, but he's been taking it easy with business."

Jason stared into her eyes as if searching for a lie. Then he collapsed into his chair, looking dazed. "I didn't even know."

"No one could contact you," Taylor reminded him gently.

Jason heaved a deep sigh and wearily rubbed his forehead. "When did you say it happened?"

"A year and a half ago."

"Dear God." Jason shook his head. "You're telling me the truth on this? You're not lying, are you?"

"I wouldn't lie about a thing like that," Taylor choked, wounded.

"I meant about the seriousness of the stroke, Taylor! For God's sake, I don't think you're that much of a ghoul."

Taylor couldn't speak. She just shook her head and tried to collect her thoughts. She felt as uncertain and vague as Jason undoubtedly did at that moment. Suddenly, all she wanted to do was tumble into bed and forget everything and everyone, including Jason. It had been a long, long day; one fraught with too many anxieties.

"Damn my fogged brain," Jason swore through his teeth, giving Taylor new hope that he wasn't as far gone as she'd thought. For a few moments she allowed herself to believe that her news about Clifton had shaken Jason so much that it had turned him off alcohol. He shoved the mug aside, swept off his hat and raked unsteady fingers through his hair. She saw his throat constrict and her insides twisted in anguish. She wanted so desperately to help him, to get him back on the right track!

Then Jason pulled out a wad of bills and tossed them on the table. Taylor looked at them with total lack of understanding until Jason said, voice full of challenge, "If you're going to stay, you'd better start drinking. I'm not leaving for a while."

A rock formed in Taylor's stomach as Jason called to the red-haired barkeep. She looked numbly at the amount of money on the table and saw the futility of the evening ahead. She could count over fifty dollars without even trying. Jason was preparing for an all-out binge.

Taylor drove Jason's mud-spattered Jeep carefully down the narrow road that rimmed the sound. She was unfamiliar with the gears, and every bump threatened to yank the wheel from her hands. She dared one glance at Jason, slouched loose-boned in the seat. If he hasn't passed out yet, she thought dispiritedly, it's just a matter of time.

Taylor sighed. Her eyes felt gritty, her throat tight. It hadn't been easy seeing Jason drink himself into oblivion, but she couldn't have left him even if she'd wanted to. Still, it had torn her apart to watch him and had shattered all kinds of illusions.

Jason had only made it part way through the stack of bills before Rita had cut him off. Unfortunately, the damage had already been done. It was a miracle of balance that he'd made it up the stairs at all, let alone all the way to the street without assistance. But when he had insisted that he was perfectly capable of driving himself home, Taylor had intervened. Jason had glared at her, but was by then incapable of stopping her. He had climbed, after several attempts, into the passenger side and had fallen immediately into a silent stupor that Taylor had considered a blessing.

Taylor had left her car parked in front of the Tidewater, hoping that crime in Coupeville was as meager as its population. And now she was considering what to do with Jason when she got back to his cottage, and what to do about herself. She already knew he'd resent finding her there in the morning.

She rounded a corner, seeing the glimmering water through a stand of tall firs, then glanced again at Jason, whose heavy breathing indicated he had slipped into unconsciousness. Taylor's chest felt constricted; in a way she was sorry she'd seen him like this.

Phil Walker had been right: Jason did need help. But Taylor had no doubts about his sanity; it was the dual effects of too much time and too much beer that had eroded the man he'd been.

Taylor wrenched her eyes away from him, but his image persisted in her mind. He was so different now, so completely foreign, not the man she'd grown to know so well. With a feeling of looking back on a past life, Taylor remembered the Jason from before, the one who'd helped her so much during those last few weeks working together on *Queen of Diamonds*, their third and final film. . . .

Maddox Productions had decided to film in Camara de Lobos, a small fishing village on Madeira Island off the coast of Portugal. It was May, and the days were warm and pleasant, the nights cool. The hotel, chosen for both accommodations and backdrop, was little more than a renovated hostel, and it was filled to overflowing. The Madeiran natives all walked around in bemusement at the sight of crazy Americans who worked at all hours and asked for the strangest things.

The island itself, the summit of an underwater mountain chain, was a steeply sloped paradise: sheer cliffs plunging into turquoise water, jagged black volcanic peaks brooding in shrouds of mist, terraced hills, banana trees, a profusion of brilliantly colored and scented flowers. White stucco houses with red tile roofs were clustered and stacked in villages by narrow roads that wound up the steep mountain slopes.

Taylor, who knew no Portuguese, was relieved that many of the hotel employees spoke English and also French. But Jason, to Taylor's immense surprise, knew enough Portuguese to make himself understood and had struck up a friendship with several of the more adventurous Madeiran locals, youths who hung wide-eyed around the fringes of the shoot. He even managed to talk Clifton Maddox, head of production, into hiring a few of them, and Taylor could hear the excitement in their rapid-fire Portuguese as they eagerly leaped to every task. She could also see the growing respect and admiration for Jason in their eyes, and ruefully realized that she probably looked much the same way.

They had been filming for about three weeks when, after a particularly long day, Clifton Maddox announced at dinner, "We're going to do the balcony scene again before we go on. It's just not right."

The whole crew groaned, and Taylor's eyes dropped to her plate. The balcony scene had been shot twice already, that day and the day before. It was her fault that it had to be done again. She hadn't been able to get the timing right for the quick repartee that was supposed to pass between the two central characters, Jake and Julie Diamond. The director, a man much better at creating images and scenes than pulling out human emotions, had been impatient, and Taylor had automatically turned to Jason for help. He'd worked with her on the lines, but by the time they were prepared to reshoot, the light had faded. Needless to say, no one had been happy, and all Taylor's self-doubts had returned a hundredfold.

Clifton waved away the grumbling and sat back down. Taylor shot a guilty glance across the hotel's small, quaintly bare dining room to where Jason was sitting. Apart from a certain somber grimness around his mouth, he gave no sign of his thoughts. But Meredith Maddox, seated next to him, was not so controlled. Her lips were pulled into a thin line of annoyance.

Taylor barely tasted the rest of her *lapas*, a local specialty that was a kind of mollusk prepared with garlic and butter. She was holding up production, and she felt terrible. She decided that the only way to get through tomorrow's filming was to go back to the well one more time—she would ask Jason to go over the scene with her alone.

Taylor waited until nearly nine o'clock to walk the three flights to the top floor, where Jason's room—and that particular balcony—were located. Her timing was purposeful. Jason called Lisabeth, his wife, every evening at eight. Taylor had no wish to interrupt him, especially since she'd heard that Lisabeth had recently been ill, accounting perhaps for Jason's unusual preoccupation since he'd arrived in Madeira.

She was standing in the narrow, whitewashed hallway outside Jason's room, her hand poised to rap, when she heard angry voices from within and noticed belatedly that the door wasn't completely shut.

It was Clifton's voice she heard first.

"...damm fool if you don't accept," he was growling angrily. "You're throwing your career away! Don't think that because of friendship I won't sue, because I will!"

"Do whatever you have to," Jason answered flatly, but there was a steel challenge beneath the words.

"I will! I'll fight you with everything I've got if you try to leave, Jason." Clifton's voice took on a deadly edge as he added, "And I'll make sure you regret it."

Taylor was frozen in shock, too embarrassed to betray her presence now, too transfixed to move.

"The trouble with you, Clifton, is you can't see the forest for the trees!" Jason lashed back. "There are a lot of things in life more important than making films, things you should keep better control of!"

"What's that supposed to mean?"

"Oh, hell...nothing." Something in Jason's tone caused Taylor to quiver with apprehension. She sensed Jason trying to tell Clifton something without really saying it, and it left her feeling cold inside.

"I'm getting out," Jason said tautly. "As soon as this picture's over."

"*Why?*"

"Because I have to!"

"You mean because of Lisabeth," Clifton threw back scathingly.

Jason inhaled sharply. "Among other things," he muttered, his footsteps sounding on the creaking hardwood floor. He was moving toward the door.

Taylor backed away, horrified that she might get caught in her innocent eavesdropping. She turned blindly in the direction of the stairs. She'd never heard Jason and Clifton argue before; their friendship was too close for them to lose control of their tempers. The emotion packed into those few angry words frightened her. She determined she would talk to Jason later, maybe tomorrow.

But suddenly Jason was in the hall, Clifton at his heels. Taylor got a good look at their faces and felt a distinct shock. She was glad their anger was not directed at her.

"Taylor!" Jason stopped abruptly when he saw her. He turned back to Clifton, then looked again at Taylor and lifted his shoulders, as if by doing so he could shrug off his rage. But storm clouds still filled his blue eyes, and Taylor wished her timing hadn't been so inopportune.

"I'm sorry, I think I've caught you at a bad time," Taylor said lamely. Clifton's expression was stony, his immaculate white hair in frantic disarray, his lips white. Jason seemed only slightly more in control, but with an actor's ability he was able to veil the fury she'd heard in his voice.

"You were looking for me?"

"Yes." Taylor glanced at Clifton, but the older man neither smiled nor acknowledged her in any way. "I was wondering if you had some free time...to go over the balcony scene. But if you don't, it's all right."

"No. That's okay." Jason inhaled deeply then let out a slow breath, one hand rubbing his neck.

"I need to talk to you now," Clifton put in meaningfully.

"Later," Jason countered. He gave Taylor a lopsided smile of apology. "Something's come up that's got Clifton dancing on his toes." To the infuriated production head, he added, "I'll stop by your room when Taylor and I are finished, but we need to get that balcony scene right first."

Clifton could hardly argue, but he gave Jason a menacing scowl before tramping off toward the one and only, and often temperamental, elevator.

Taylor didn't reveal what she'd overheard; she didn't understand it anyway. In a slightly numbed state she followed Jason back to his room, her curiosity simmering. Was Jason giving up acting? Why? Because of Lisabeth?

But her questions were forgotten as Jason took her back inside his suite-cum-location site. He ignored the paraphernalia left by the crew and began working with Taylor, telling her when her expression wasn't up to par, helping her add just the right inflection to her words, perfecting her timing and delivery.

"Jake and Julie love each other but they're trying to one-up each other," Jason said for the umpteenth time. "Jake doesn't really want her to help in his investigation. Julie exasperates him; she's too pretty to be so smart. He tells her he would really like her at home in the kitchen, taking care of a couple of kids, the perfect wife and mother..."

Taylor was nodding, seeing Julie through Jake's eyes, when Jason suddenly trailed off. Taylor looked up, her breath stopping at the look of deep unhappiness that had invaded his face. But it was quickly masked, and Jason went on as if nothing had happened. "But Jake really wants more in his wife; he just doesn't know it. He wants an equal, a partner, someone to share with. It's just that sometimes Julie's enthusiasm about being an amateur private detective gets in his way.

"She, on the other hand, understands him perfectly. She also knows what *she* wants—to help solve the mystery. He's the expert, but she's got the savvy." Jason's expression was wry as he thought about Julie Diamond. "She's the shining star in this picture, not Jake," he told Taylor. "The scene on the balcony epitomizes it all. It's Julie deadpanning Jake all the way. She listens to all his objections, she nods, she even offers a few humble comments. She lets him think he's won."

Taylor was rapt. She thought, not for the first time, that Jason should turn his talents toward directing; he was head and shoulders above the man Maddox Productions was paying.

"But the whole scene's got to be believable," Jason extolled firmly. "Jake's no fool but Julie's got to fool him. Only when his back is turned, when the camera comes in close, does Julie give away any hint of her true feelings. She's amused, satisfied, but not in a mean way; it's all just an extension of how much she loves him. She's got to look...like *that!*"

A smile had been hovering around Taylor's lips, and at Jason's exclamation it became an out-and-out grin. "That light touch you keep telling me about. It's all a frame of mind," she said softly.

"Exactly. And you're perfect for the part, Taylor. Don't let anyone ever tell you otherwise."

She was dumbfounded by his praise; he'd never said anything remotely like it. "Thank you," she said uncertainly.

"Come out on the balcony and we'll go through it word by word."

For two hours she played Julie Diamond under Jason's expert guidance. By the end of that time she was tired and freezing, the night air penetrating her thin cotton blouse, raising goose bumps on her bare arms. As if realizing it for the first time, Jason brought her back inside and shut the door, cutting off the sea breeze and the fragrant scent from the purple flowers of the jacaranda tree.

"Here, drink this," Jason said. "It'll warm you up like nothing else."

It was Madeira wine, a slightly syrupy, sweet and pungent wine that was drunk like a cordial. Jason handed her a small thimbleful of it, taking none himself.

It slid down Taylor's throat like fire and instantly took the chill off. "Thank you...I think," she said with a smile, turning to leave. "I'm sorry I took so much of your time," she said, realizing the late hour. She regarded him with rueful eyes. "It seems like I'm always apologizing. You've helped me so much."

Jason's eyes were narrowed on the crystal decanter of wine. "You've helped me too, Taylor," he said cryptically. "You'll never know how much."

She was still trying to figure that out when he led her over to the couch and sat down next to her. Taylor felt a tingle of awareness that left her breathless. Her eyes were questioning as they studied his grim face.

"I'm giving up acting," he said in an odd voice. "At least, I'm giving up Hollywood, and at this point they're one and the same. I'm sorry." His blue eyes looked into her confused amber ones.

She couldn't imagine why he was apologizing to her, and it showed in her face.

Jason's jaw worked. "Clifton wanted to do another picture—another *Diamond Girl* picture—with the two of us," he explained. "I'm bailing out and he says he won't replace me. In other words, I've cut you out of a part."

"It's all right," Taylor immediately wanted to set his mind at rest. She owed him so much already.

"Maybe someday I can make it up to you."

"Don't worry about it." Taylor gave a nervous, dismissing laugh. "You've done more for my career these past few years than I have myself. I should be thanking you!"

Jason's gaze softened. "Don't be so hard on yourself. You've got the talent, it's there. It's just raw." He glanced at his watch and made a face, then said, "You'll get it perfect tomorrow, I guarantee it."

Jason's prophecy had come true. Taylor sailed through the balcony scene the next morning, earning applause from the rest of the cast and crew. Each word, each move, each touch had been choreographed the night before, and when Julie finally told Jake she would do as he asked, Jason bent his head so that Jake could give Julie an affectionate, husbandly kiss.

What Taylor felt at that moment was just that: affection. Affection for Jason; affection passing from Jason to her. He pulled back from her an instant later his hands on her shoulders, his blue eyes smiling into hers. The breeze lifted strands of her hair, painting them against an azure sky. All around was sea and sunshine and white stucco and a look between two people that was forever captured on film.

That moment of film was made into a picture—a frozen instant that wound up gracing magazine covers, posters and television commercials. For months Taylor saw it everywhere she went, long after the filming was completed and the film released, long after Jason had taken off for Whidbey Island, long after Lisabeth and Kerri had met their terrible deaths.

The publicity had generated a flurry of film offers for Taylor, but she'd turned them all down. She'd been typecast by the industry as Julie Diamond, but she found it impossible to accept any such role that didn't have her playing opposite Jason.

Ross screamed at her, her father said he was disappointed in her and her career took a steep nosedive. As a way to come to terms with herself and what she wanted, Taylor took up writing, and after several attempts to divorce herself from Julie Diamond entirely, she decided the best purge would be to write Julie out of her system.

Taylor had spent a year preparing *Diamond in the Sky*. It was nearly finished. But until Meredith Maddox mentioned it, Taylor hadn't had much hope of having it read by a producer. Now, it seemed, anything was possible.

Except that Jake Diamond—and the actor who'd played him—didn't exist anymore....

The Jeep was parked next to the cottage, its nose facing the sound. Taylor listened to the engine slowly tick and cool, wondering once again what had driven Jason from Hollywood in the first place, what had caused that unusual animosity she'd seen in Clifton Maddox's face. Was that what was keeping him on Whidbey, causing the pain? Or was he, as Meredith had suggested, still mourning for his wife and child?

Jason stirred slightly, heaved a sigh, then slid sideways, his head nestling against Taylor's hip, his hand curving around her thigh.

Taylor looked down at the intimate gesture in alarm, then amusement, then with a certain degree of tenderness. She opened her door and gently slid away from him, wondering how in the world she was going to get him inside.

The answer came in the form of a brisk, icy wind. It rolled off the cold waters of the sound and penetrated the interior of the Jeep. While Taylor shook Jason's shoulder, the frigid air seeped inside his collar and down his neck. He came to groggily, and Taylor ended up half-hauling, half-pushing him toward the porch. Her teeth chattered while she vainly searched his keys for the one that would fit the lock. Jason, weaving on his feet, suddenly plunged toward the door.

"Wait! I haven't got it—"

Taylor's words were cut off as Jason's fumbling hand twisted the knob and the door swung inward, nearly toppling him over. He straightened and moved with a kind of drunken dignity toward the short hallway, disappearing around the corner.

Taylor wondered if he cared, or even knew, whom he was with. She unzipped her coat, worried about the sanity of leaving a place unlocked even on Whidbey, then stood blankly in the center of the room, not sure of what to do next.

For a start, she went back outside to Jason's Jeep and grabbed her bag, which she'd transferred from her car to his. She scurried back inside and turned the lock behind her. Years of living in Los Angeles couldn't be forgotten in one night, no matter how benign the surroundings, she mused ruefully.

Taylor found a blanket shoved into the top shelf of a tiny linen closet and made herself a bed on the couch, then changed into a floor-length robe to sleep in. A fire still glowed softly in the river-rock fireplace, but it was the only source of heat, so Taylor heaped it with logs before settling in for the night. Then she closed her eyes and tried, with limited success, to forget about Jason and fall asleep.

After twenty minutes of tossing and turning, she uttered an angry sound directed solely at herself, threw back the blanket and decided to check on him to assure herself once and for all that he'd made it to bed all right.

She found his room at the end of the hall. The light was still on, and he was lying face up on the bed, still completely dressed. Even in sleep his handsome face was lined with anguish, deep grooves furrowing beside an unconsciously sensual mouth, his forehead creased in unhappiness. Whatever was bothering him was buried deeply, affecting him even during his alcohol-numbed sleep.

Taylor swiftly removed his boots and tugged the top comforter back, managing to get him covered. Then, with a final lingering look, she turned out the light and left, trying to forget the pain she'd seen written cruelly across his face, trying to forget her own disillusionment, and trying, most of all, to forget that things would certainly be no better when Jason awoke tomorrow morning.

Chapter Three

Taylor awoke early, eyes flying open at the sensation of being watched. She sat up and saw Jason standing in the open doorway between the cottage's small living room and the hall.

"Good morning," she said diffidently, self-consciously running her fingers through the tousled waves of her golden hair.

Jason, apart from a bruised look around his eyes and a pallor beneath his tan, looked not much the worse for wear. Still dressed in the wrinkled clothes he'd slept in, his hair uncombed, his face shadowed with beard, he nevertheless exuded that male sensuality and strength Taylor had always been attracted to.

"I want you out of here by ten," Jason stated flatly.

Taylor regarded him moodily. She'd hoped she would have a chance to talk to him at least for a few minutes before the war began again. "Could I have a shower first?" she asked. "Maybe something to eat?"

"There isn't anything to eat. Maxine hasn't gone to the store yet."

At this bit of information, Taylor perked up. "Maxine does your shopping?"

Jason scowled. "Sometimes," he answered tersely. He rubbed his palm across his chin, but even from across the room Taylor could see the fine tremor in his fingers.

Taylor stood up and folded the blanket, her wine-colored robe reaching to her bare feet. "It takes me a while to get started in the morning," she told him over her shoulder. "Why don't you take a shower first, and I'll finish getting my things together."

Jason didn't answer, but after several moments she heard him turn and leave. Minutes later she heard the shower running.

With a small smile she walked to the kitchen and checked through cupboards to see just what really was available. She'd pulled a classic Julie Diamond on him—letting him think she'd surrendered when in fact she'd barely begun to fight.

Last night she'd felt hopeless. There seemed nothing she could do for him, nothing he would let her do. But today, seeing a sober, if unrepentent, Jason Garrett, she'd glimpsed the man she'd known before. And Taylor had never been the kind of person to give up without a fight.

She found a half-full can of coffee and, after searching carefully, an age-old coffee pot that looked as if it hadn't been used for years. The coffee was cheerfully perking when Jason suddenly appeared in the kitchen. He was shirtless, his faded jeans slung low over his hips, a snowy white towel draped around his neck. His dark hair still glistened with water drops as his eyes took in the domestic picture Taylor made.

"What are you doing?" he asked stonily.

"Making coffee. Want a cup?"

"No . . . thanks."

Taylor found a blue enamel cup and filled it with steaming coffee, conscious of Jason standing directly behind her left shoulder. It made her very aware of her appearance, self-conscious to the extreme, yet she knew Jason couldn't care less about what she looked like.

She sat down at the small circular kitchen table and cupped the mug in both palms, blowing across the top. "How often does Maxine go shopping for you?" she asked.

"Often enough."

After a brief hesitation, Jason pulled down another cup and poured himself some coffee. He stared into its dark depths for a long time, neither drinking nor setting the cup down.

"Not often enough to do you any good, apparently," Taylor observed, noticing the outline of his ribs. "By the look of it, you don't eat much of anything."

Jason set the cup down with a clink that spilled coffee over the counter. He flung her a dark look then disappeared into his bedroom, returning a few minutes later wearing another flannel shirt. Taylor kept her silence, very conscious that Jason's new leanness did nothing to detract from his masculine appeal.

In an act of defiance, he went to the refrigerator and opened a beer. Taylor's brows pulled into a frown as she heard the twist-top release with a soft *fffft*, but she maintained a steady silence.

"Think it's too early in the morning to drink?" Jason challenged.

"Did I say it was too early?"

"You thought it."

Taylor feigned disinterest. "Your diet leaves something to be desired, but if you've got a death wish I can't stop you."

"Now that's the first thing you've said that I agree with!"

Taylor stared straight ahead, ignoring the angry blue eyes boring into her. But when she met his eyes again, his gaze was dark and moody.

"What do you really want, Taylor?" he asked somberly. "What are you after?"

"Nothing." She shrugged. "Your welfare, perhaps."

Jason's mouth twisted. "I'm doing just fine without you."

Taylor gave him a cool glance. "So I see."

Jason's eyes narrowed, but after a moment or two he walked to the table, turned a chair around, then straddled it, arms folded across the back, eyes trained watchfully on Taylor.

"You say Meredith's running Maddox Productions now?" Jason asked.

So that, at least, had piqued his interest. Taylor nodded. "I understand it's only a temporary position. You'd have to ask her yourself."

"I don't talk to Meredith."

Taylor's smile was tight. "That's self-evident."

For the first time Jason gave her an assessing look, not just the angry glances he'd thrown at her since deciding she was some kind of Hollywood emissary. "Is that a comment on my life-style?" he asked sardonically.

"Maybe."

"Well, you can save it. I'm doing what I want to do. It's no one's business but my own."

As Taylor digested this, Jason leaned forward, the chair tilting on two legs, as he thrust his handsome face very close to hers, staring her down. Taylor tried not to react, but the little pulse beating in her throat gave her away.

"I'm not crazy, y'know," he said mildly. "Although Phil Walker would probably tell you I'm deeply depressed. Maybe I am. So what? Who the hell should care about it but me?"

Taylor saw the challenge written in his eyes. She licked her lips and said, "Isn't that kind of a selfish attitude? Especially when other people care about you."

"There you go again!" Jason exploded, his weight dropping the chair back with a crash. "The trouble with you, Taylor, is you're working from faulty assumptions. People don't care about others unless they want something from them." He regarded her carefully controlled face and added scathingly, "Except you, of course. *You* care about me."

Taylor could have pointed out that he obviously cared about Clifton, but she kept her silence. Whatever had caused his deep burning anger wasn't going to be erased by a few well-chosen barbs, and she'd learned that arguing with him could be disastrous.

But after long moments, Taylor began to feel uncomfortable under his stripping gaze. It was as if he were going to force her out of his life by sheer will. Sticking out her chin, she stared back at him, intent on not being cowed.

"You really care about me?" he asked quietly.

Taylor tried to hide her surprise. She didn't trust the shift in the conversation but answered with a silent nod.

"Then why don't you sleep with me? It's been a long time since I've had a woman, and frankly, I've always thought you were attractive. An hour or two in bed with you would probably do wonders for my poor, crushed spirit."

Taylor bit back the gasp of hurt that threatened to escape. Jason just regarded her blankly. He was baiting her for all he was worth, and only the pain she saw buried deep in the azure depths of his eyes kept her from slapping him.

"You really know how to be a bastard, don't you?" she choked out, wounded. "You've got it down pat. And I'll admit, it hurts."

Jason's mouth turned into a thin line. "Phil couldn't take the heat, either."

Taylor yanked her gaze away from his. A terrible pause ensued. She was torn by feelings of rage and distress, her throat raw and hurting, tears building behind her eyes. But she refused to buckle under to his tactics—that would only weaken her position.

"What happened?" Taylor asked with false lightness. "Did you proposition Phil, too?"

She heard Jason's swift intake of breath and mentally congratulated herself. If he was intent on getting rid of her, she certainly wasn't going to make it easy for him.

Jason growled something she couldn't hear and settled back further into his chair, his expression dark. Taylor realized he had barely touched his beer and decided he'd only pulled it from the refrigerator to test her reaction.

"I would love to have been a little mouse in the corner when you had your argument with Phil," Taylor added, sipping her coffee. "It must have been blistering."

She thought she saw the corners of his mouth lift in a reluctant grin, but a moment later his lips were drawn tight, his expression stern. "Phil had it coming," he said testily.

"Mmm." Taylor felt a moment of victory. He was actually talking to her!

"That man tried to psychoanalyze me to death. I couldn't say anything without Phil asking, 'What do you mean by that, Jason. Is that what you really think?' It's a wonder *he* didn't drive me crazy."

Taylor smiled. "That's the price you pay for knowing a psychologist personally."

"Well, I've put it behind me now," Jason said firmly. He rubbed the base of his neck with his palm. "And what do I have to do to get rid of you?"

His tone was merely curious. Taylor considered it a real improvement over his seething anger. She said with potentially self-defeating honesty, "I'll admit, like everyone else you know, I'd like you to get back in the mainstream again. However," she added quickly, seeing him move sharply in his chair, "if you don't want to, fine. I can't—and wouldn't try to—force you. But I'd like to stay on Whidbey for a few days and plead my case—"

"No," he interrupted flatly.

"—and then if you want me to leave, I'll go without another word."

"Taylor—"

"What are you afraid of, Jason?" she cut him off heatedly. "Think I'll be able to change your mind, after all?"

"No!"

"Can't stand the challenge? Afraid the lure might be more than you can resist?"

His blue eyes were simmering with rage. "You don't understand any of it!"

"That's right. And maybe that's why I'm so persistent." Taylor was being reckless, totally overstepping all the careful social bounds. But she sensed it was working. "I'll give you a choice: tell me what's eating you alive, or let me stay—just a few days. After that I'll leave. I promise."

Jason struggled with himself, the impact of her words making his brow break into a sweat. He opened his mouth, and for a moment she actually believed he might tell her, but then a deep shudder wracked his frame and his teeth clenched together. Cords stood out in his neck, and she felt his pain come to her almost in physical waves.

He inhaled a long, unsteady breath and let it out again. His blue eyes were bleak with some terrible inner vision. "You won't want to stay," he said heavily. "You won't."

Taylor pressed her advantage. "Give me the chance."

He shook his head.

"Please, Jason. Even if you don't want any help, please let me stay." She bit her lip and gambled. "I need to. I need to try. Don't you see? You've given me so much; I can't stand not to try."

"God, Taylor! I'm not a charity case!" He shoved back his chair, but Taylor was on her feet in an instant. She sensed he was wavering and she was certain she wouldn't get another chance if she blew this one.

"One day," she begged. "I can't leave until I get my car, anyway. Just give me the rest of the day and then decide."

"I've already decided."

"Then change your mind! One lousy day, Jason, please..."

Taylor looked at him through wide, beseeching eyes, feeling his conflict, sensing he wasn't as immune to her compassion as he let on. He passed a hand across his eyes, pressed his temples, then said gruffly, "All right, you can stay. God knows why you want to, but you can stay. For *one* day."

Taylor swallowed. "Thank you."

When he looked at her again, his mouth was twisted in mockery. "Oh, don't thank me yet, Taylor Michaelson. You're a long, long way from Hollywood, and I have a feeling you're going to wish you hadn't won this little battle."

Taylor drove with Jason back to Coupeville to get her car, feeling as drained as if she'd just finished the Boston Marathon. Her victory would turn to ashes if she couldn't get him to listen to her, but at least she'd won herself some time.

Jason had reverted to a waiting silence after giving her the okay, and seeing that talk was out of the question, Taylor had used the time to take a shower, wash her hair and change into her clothes. Now she was dressed in more appropriate Whidbey Island garb—a pair of jeans and a forest-green turtleneck sweater.

In Coupeville some of Taylor's newfound hope disappeared when Jason left her at her car with a terse, "I'll see you later," and headed in the direction of the Tidewater. Taylor watched him bleakly. So this was how he was going to keep out of her way today; she should have known.

Deciding she couldn't take another afternoon like the one she'd spent yesterday, Taylor used the time to do some grocery shopping. Then she drove back to the cottage, making a mental note to drag Jason out of the Tidewater by force if he hadn't returned by five.

Which was all very well, she thought grimly, if she could just figure out how to do it.

Maxine was at the cottage when Taylor returned. The wonderful smell of beef stew wafted from the tiny kitchen, and some of the raw October cold that had chilled Taylor all day seemed to disappear just at the scent of it.

"You're still here," Maxine said with surprise.

"Not by Jason's choice, I assure you," Taylor admitted wryly. She liked Maxine and hoped, since the woman seemed on fairly close terms with Jason, that she might become Taylor's ally.

Maxine chuckled, taking several large bags from Taylor's arms. "It's no more than I expected. That's one headstrong man!"

"Amen," Taylor said. Then she asked curiously, "Do you do all his cooking?"

"No, just now and then. I know how much he likes stew and so I make it whenever I can." Maxine shot Taylor a look. "He could use some meat on his bones."

Taylor nodded in silent agreement.

"He does his own cooking, mostly," Maxine went on, putting groceries away, "but sometimes I help him out. He's rather limited. You didn't have to buy all these groceries; I was going to the store myself this afternoon."

"It's all right. I needed something to do. Jason's . . . at the Tidewater."

"Ahhh . . ." Maxine sighed.

"Will he—does he usually—come home before dinner?"

Maxine regarded her sympathetically. "It's hard to know. Sometimes. Depends on how upset he is."

"Upset?" Taylor couldn't imagine him any more upset than she'd already witnessed.

"There's something inside him that's killing him," Maxine said. "And he's letting it."

Taylor was horrified. Maxine's words sounded like the crack of doom. "Do you have any idea what?"

"No." She reached for her coat, then turned down the stew to a slow simmer before walking to the door. "But I do know he wasn't like this when he first got here, when his wife and child were still alive. Then he was just angry, and he didn't talk to anyone but his family. But after they died . . ." Maxine shook her head slowly to and fro, worry creasing her brow. "But what he's going through isn't just simple mourning, mind you. It's something else, but he won't let anyone know," she added with a heartfelt sigh.

Taylor stared at the door after Maxine had left, throat dry, heart pounding. She began to realize fully for the first time what an impossible task she'd set for herself. Maybe Phil Walker had been right. Maybe Jason did need professional help, someone who could help him face whatever terrible forces were tearing him apart. Someone other than Taylor.

But he wouldn't let anyone else near him, and Taylor was running out of time.

Taylor waited until nearly six o'clock. Her five o'clock deadline had come and gone, and she was still locked in indecision. Should she go after him? Should she wait? Time was ticking by, and she'd done nothing more constructive than edit the first fifteen pages of *Diamond in the Sky* for at least the fifth time.

She shoved the manuscript back into its manila envelope, unable to concentrate. Then she prowled around the cottage, checking on the stew, pacing across the plank-wood floor, tossing another log on the fire. She'd give him until seven, Taylor determined, hating herself for putting off the inevitable, knowing she wouldn't be able to convince him of anything he didn't want to be convinced of.

At ten to seven she heard his Jeep rumble into the driveway, and she breathed a silent prayer of thanks. Now the decision was out of her hands, and she waited in chest-tightening apprehension to see what kind of state he was in.

To her relief, and complete amazement, Jason walked in stone-cold sober. He raised his eyebrows at the look on her face, and Taylor quickly hid her expression.

"Maxine must have been here," he said, smelling the beef stew. He tossed his Stetson into a chair and stretched, drawing Taylor's eyes to his lean chest.

"You expected a drunk, didn't you?" he said without rancor, his lips quirking at Taylor's look, his expression too knowing.

Embarrassed, Taylor dropped her eyes, unable to come up with an answer.

"Well, I thought about it," Jason said, smiling sardonically. "But then I figured you wouldn't be able to perform your miracles and would probably beg for an extra day. For the record, I'm not interested in seeing you after tomorrow morning, but you've got the rest of the evening with me, so go ahead. I'm ready for any and all your ministrations."

Taylor was nonplussed. Jason dropped into the faded corduroy rocker across from the couch and regarded her with a smug grin, looking infuriatingly pleased with himself. But it was a vast improvement over the man she'd met yesterday, and Taylor inclined her head toward the kitchen. "All right. How about some food first?

My mouth's been watering for that stew ever since I got home.''

Jason stared at her for several moments, then lifted his shoulders indifferently. ''Suit yourself.'' He got up and walked into the kitchen, and Taylor, after a slight pause, followed.

He pulled two bowls down from a shelf and started setting the table. Taylor was relieved, if a little leery, of his sudden affability. But it was light-years ahead of yesterday, and she wasn't going to spoil the moment unless she had to.

She'd managed to toss together a salad during her hours of worrying about when, and if, Jason would return, and now she placed it in the center of the table along with a loaf of sourdough bread and a jar of Maxine's homemade crabapple jelly.

Taylor ate hungrily, savoring every bite. She had only had time for a cold sandwich while she was out grocery shopping, and the hot stew was a balm to her tired mind and body.

In contrast, Jason barely touched his food. He set his spoon down, tasted the crusty bread, put it back on the plate and heaved a sigh, pinching the bridge of his nose. Then he scraped back his chair and paced the small confines of the kitchen.

Taylor didn't say anything. She concentrated on spreading Maxine's jelly over her slice of bread and waited for Jason to fill the silence.

''I'm going to have a glass of wine,'' he told her flatly, as if expecting some criticism. Then, as an afterthought, he added reluctantly, ''Would you like a glass?''

Taylor shook her head, defeated. Then a moment later she decided that Jason's offer had been something of an olive branch and said instead, "On second thought, yes, please. I'd like one very much."

"You don't have to be so polite, Taylor," he replied tautly.

She felt her expression change before she could school her features. Unable to speak, she dipped her head, trying to hide behind the curtain of her hair. She didn't want Jason to know how much he could hurt her with a few unkind words.

Jason swore softly, yanked a long-stemmed glass from a cupboard and filled it with ruby-red wine. "I just don't deserve it," he said through his teeth, handing her a glass, then tipped up his own before she could respond. After he'd downed half the glass, he seated himself opposite her, heaving a tired sigh.

Taylor picked up her glass, sipping carefully. "You know what I think," she said softly, screwing up her courage. "I think you're trying awfully hard to be obnoxious."

His smile was cold. "And succeeding?"

"Without question. But I don't think it's easy for you."

"Really." He was sardonic. "You know something, Taylor, you're even worse than Phil. At least he's a professional."

Taylor flushed. "I wasn't trying to—"

"Sure you were." Jason wouldn't release her gaze from the condemnation of his. "That's what this whole visit is about. Don't kid yourself, Taylor." Jason's voice was scathing. "Your motives are all the same."

"I don't know why it upsets you so much that people want to help you, whether you want it or not. At least we're not apathetic! Even if you don't agree with us, surely you can see the logic!"

"Dear God!" Jason clapped a hand to his forehead. "You *are* worse than he is! And the hell of it is, I think you believe your own propaganda."

Taylor's lips compressed. "This isn't getting either one of us anywhere."

"Well, well. You finally see my point."

"Jason—"

"Don't, Taylor." With a fervent shake of his head he cut off the entreaty in her voice. "It's no use. I won't listen." He was actually trying to be kind, not antagonistic. He was speaking the truth; he just wanted her to save her breath.

Taylor licked her lips. "It hurts me to see you like this," she admitted in a low voice.

A look of pain crossed Jason's face. "I don't know how I can make it any clearer," he said hoarsely. "I don't want help from anyone. You, Phil, Clifton…" His brows pulled into a frown. "I've got some…problems to work out," he admitted, his jaw working. "But I can do it on my own."

That glimpse of Jason's vulnerability was almost Taylor's undoing. She had the strongest desire to touch him, to wipe away the tension in his face, smooth the lines of pain. For that one moment she forgot to hold back her feelings, and unknown to her they were written across her face.

Jason inhaled swiftly. He looked away, focusing on her overnight bag. "You can sleep in the spare bedroom tonight. It's not much, but it's infinitely better than the couch. I'll take your things in."

The moment passed. Taylor looked down at her empty plate in defeat and embarrassment. What was wrong with her? The more of herself she let him see, the more open she left herself to his cruelty... though he hadn't been cruel just now.

"Thanks," she said weakly. "I'll do the dishes."

He looked as if he were about to say something else, his eyes darkening for a moment, his attention focused somewhere near her mouth. Taylor managed to keep her lips from quivering, but her heart beat deeply and unevenly. Then Jason shook his head, picked up her partially opened bag and retreated down the hall, leaving her the task of cleaning up.

Taylor slid her hands into the soapy water, her thoughts chasing one another as she washed each dish. She was running out of time. There were bare hours left until her twenty-four-hour deadline was up and she was forced to leave.

And then what?

Taylor sighed. She didn't want to think about giving up and leaving Jason now, not after she'd seen him. How could she just pack up for Los Angeles knowing what kind of state he was in?

She finished cleaning up and waited for Jason in the living room, watching the moon-bright rippling water of the sound through one of the paned windows, wondering what was taking him so long in the spare bedroom. She didn't really care if he came back to Hollywood or not, she realized with a tiny pang of surprise. Not if he was happy. Not if living on Whidbey Island was what he truly wanted to do. If he could convince her of that, she would leave with no regrets.

Well, almost no regrets. Taylor made a face, searched her feelings and realized there was an ember of—what? Compassion? Affection? *Love?*—burning for Jason. She'd never let herself face it before, but she faced it now.

She found it a bitter pill to swallow to think she might never see him again.

If she just had a little more time!

She heard him come into the room before she turned around, and something about the way his footsteps sounded, something about the ominous way he suddenly stopped, something about his erratic breathing, made the hairs on her nape instinctively rise. Emotion was radiating from him at the same dangerous level in intensity it had been earlier, and as Taylor turned around, Jason demanded through his teeth, "What the hell is this?"

He was holding a manila envelope, stretching it out to her as if he couldn't bare the touch of it. With a sinking heart she recognized the package containing her manuscript. The flap was open, and Taylor realized he'd already looked inside.

"It's what I've been doing since you left town," she said with a weak laugh. She was embarrassed that he'd found it. "It's a screenplay, along the lines of *Diamond Girl*."

She could scarcely believe his reaction. He was livid. His knuckles were white where he gripped the envelope. He took two steps toward her, then stopped, his free hand clenching and unclenching, his furious gaze traveling from her to the burning logs in the fire, then back again. For one horrifying moment she thought he was going to toss it in the flames, and she took a step closer to him, her eyes frightened.

Her movement decided him. With a stinging curse he threw the whole package at her feet, white pages scattering in all directions.

"You care about me, all right," he snarled viciously. "With the kind of real feeling and depth that come straight out of Hollywood! Well, you're going to have to look elsewhere for a meal ticket, Miss Michaelson. I'm through taking care of leeches!''

''Wha-a-t?'' Taylor was trembling.

''I'll be damned if I'll help you! Go find another sucker. You're the one who needs to have her head examined if you think you can talk me into backing your lousy script by telling me how much you *care* about me! God! You make me sick!''

Taylor's stomach felt as if it had been kicked. Jason glared at her, his blue eyes filled with rage and pain. Then he wheeled around, kicked furiously at a hapless page that had fallen on his boot, strode to his bedroom in stiff-backed rage and slammed the door with a reverberating crash that echoed to the very depths of Taylor's soul.

In stunned misery, Taylor collapsed on the couch. She couldn't believe what had just happened. Good Lord, how was she ever going to win his trust now?

Chapter Four

How far is it to Deception Pass?" Taylor asked the attendant behind the counter of the all-night convenience market and service station. Sunlight slanted through the wide windows of the storefront, adding some much-needed atmosphere to the sterile cubicle while cutting the glare from the fluorescent bulbs.

The attendant screwed up his face as he handed Taylor a Styrofoam cup of coffee and her change. "About twenty miles. It's at the north tip of the island."

"Thanks."

Taylor walked back to her car, gloomily noticing that beautiful weather had finally come to Whidbey now that she was being forced to leave. The sun was high and bright, tiny wisps of white clouds sailed through a crisp blue sky and a cool, nippy breeze replaced the slicing wind.

Taylor started the engine, pointed the nose of the car toward the northern tip of the island and tried not to think about what a failure she'd been.

Unfortunately, her failure was foremost in her mind. Even with Jason's condemnation of the night before, Taylor had optimistically hoped for a chance to explain, to tell him he was wrong in thinking she had ulterior motives for trying to find him. She had only wanted to see Jason happy. She'd tried to tell him as much this morning but had gotten no further than, "Good morning," when he'd delivered his ultimatum.

"Don't try to explain," he'd warned tersely. "Don't say anything at all. Just pick up your things and leave."

He'd come in from outside just as Taylor was pulling her boots on, his arms loaded with freshly cut logs. He piled them on the hearth and dusted his hands, then crossed his arms across his chest as his gaze pinned Taylor.

But Taylor couldn't just meekly acquiesce. Seeing Jason so much like she'd remembered him in the past—his hair windblown, his face flushed from the brisk air, color heightening his gaunt features, eyes a brilliant blue—had made it impossible for her to turn and walk out.

"I can't," she'd told him honestly. "I can't just leave."

"You'll have to." Without another word he picked up her bag and carried it outside to her car. Then he opened the driver's door, tossed the bag inside, stepped back and waited. Eventually, Taylor could no longer hang back and pray for divine intervention; she had to get in the car.

"I don't want to go," she murmured, eyes turned beseechingly to his.

"I want you to go." Jason closed the door, his expression plain and determined, his mind clearly made up.

So Taylor had been forced to drive away; there was really no other choice. But as she had driven northward, intending to cross back to the Washington mainland over the bridge at Deception Pass rather than catch the ferry at the south end, she'd sunk deeper and deeper into depression. At the town of Oak Harbor she'd stopped for a cup of coffee, hoping caffeine would revive her flagging spirits.

It helped, but not a whole lot. She just couldn't work up any enthusiasm about going home.

Home. Taylor shook her head and tried to clear her mind. What was home? A one-bedroom apartment with a view of more one-bedroom apartments. A career that invited more rejection than acceptance. A group of acquaintances who couldn't be called friends. A good-natured, derelict father. A supercilious agent. A lot of unpaid bills.

Taylor sighed. She had to face facts—there was really nothing left for her in Los Angeles. The only person who'd ever cared enough about Taylor to win her loyalty lived right here on Whidbey.

Taylor got almost to the bridge before she made a U-turn and pulled her car into a rest stop. She couldn't leave now. She just couldn't!

She sat in a haze of indecision for what seemed like hours. She berated herself for being the worst kind of masochist, then berated herself some more for being a quitter. She didn't know what she wanted, but she knew it had something to do with Jason.

With resolution, but not that much hope of success, Taylor drove back toward Jason's cottage. She was still trying to think of some way to convince him to let her stay when her mind filled with other memories, one in particular.

It was while she and Jason were filming *Diamond Girl*, the first film of the *Diamond Girl* trilogy, and one in which Taylor had first been introduced to Jason. They were on a soundstage rehearsing lines, and Taylor had just begun to realize what an amateur she was. Jason had been coaching her until her head was swimming with advice, and she was overwhelmed by the enormity of what she needed to learn. Her performance went from bad to worse, plunging from mere mediocrity into total disaster.

"Don't fall apart, Taylor," Jason had warned harshly. "It's self-indulgent. Nobody has time to cater to your whims. If you're in over your head, swim harder. You'll hate yourself if you give up now."

"I'm not sure I can handle it," she'd answered, swallowing her pride.

"You can handle it if you want to."

"You're so sure of yourself, Jason," she'd returned. "I'm not."

"Taylor, it's all a matter of just wanting to bad enough. That's all." Jason had smiled then. "Never, never, *never*, give up."

Now, thinking back, Taylor's mouth curved into a wry smile. Never give up. How many times had she remembered his advice? How many times had she gained strength just by recalling his words? Countless. Taylor had learned to live by those three words; they were the key to whatever success she'd had.

And she would heed them now, she determined, speeding past the fir trees that lined the road, her resolve tightening with each passing mile.

"You may be sorry you ever uttered those words, Jason Garrett," she murmured softly. She wasn't about to give up. Not while he was in trouble. Not while he needed her. . . .

The cottage was unlocked when Taylor returned. She opened the door with trepidation, even though Jason's Jeep was nowhere to be seen, and took several deep breaths as she walked inside. The air was still, the room quiet as a tomb, dust motes floating lazily in the streaming sunlight from the living room windows. The pervading sense of peace confirmed that Jason was not at home, but Taylor was hardly encouraged by his absence. There was only one place he could be.

The Tidewater. Taylor bit into her lower lip, wondering if she had the courage to face him there. Jason would hardly worry about what he said, or whom he said it in front of, and Taylor wasn't certain she was up to the inevitable scene that would come when he found out she intended to stay on Whidbey. Yet, she wasn't eager to put off the confrontation, either.

She climbed back into her car and drove straight to Coupeville. She walked briskly to the door of the Tidewater, fought to control her mounting uneasiness as she stepped down the narrow stairway, held her breath as she scanned the occupants of the bar, then felt vague surprise when she realized Jason just wasn't there.

Neither was Rita, the bartender, it seemed. A hefty man with huge jowls and graying hair was wiping down the bar, and he looked up when Taylor walked in.

"Can I help you?" he asked with a wide, friendly smile.

"No. Thank you. I was looking for someone, but he's not here."

She left before any other questions could be asked, drove aimlessly around Coupeville for a while, then, when she found no sign of Jason's Jeep, finally gave up and went back to the cottage. The same heavy silence greeted her. With a feeling of being an intruder, Taylor stowed her bags in the spare bedroom, threw another log on the fire, fixed herself a sandwich and settled down for a long wait. Her apprehension heightened every time she thought she heard Jason's Jeep pull into the driveway, but hours passed and no one came. The cottage didn't have a telephone, and Taylor became keenly aware of how cut off she was from the rest of the world.

Eventually her apprehension gave way to worry. Where was Jason? At Maxine's? Did he know anyone else on the island? Had he left the island?

There was no one she could contact to find out. She wasn't even certain where Maxine lived.

Seized by the fear that Jason had taken off for parts unknown, Taylor gave up pacing the room and strode to his bedroom. She searched through his drawers and found all his clothes still there. At least, she thought with relief, he hadn't abandoned the cottage altogether.

She was shutting the bottom drawer when she saw the corner of a picture frame sticking out beneath his carelessly folded jeans. It was face down, and as Taylor pulled it out carefully and turned it over, her skin broke out in goose bumps.

It was a little girl. Taylor knew, even without the hazy memory of seeing it before, that it was a portrait of Kerri, Jason's daughter. She looked a lot like her father, except her hair was a much darker shade of brown, nearly black like her mother's. But the shape of Kerri's eyes and mouth was all Jason.

Taylor's throat went dry. She felt a terrible, aching sadness. She remembered now that the picture had been in Jason's hotel room in Madeira; he'd taken it with him wherever he went.

Unexpectedly Taylor's eyes filled with tears. She carefully slid the picture back into place and shut the drawer.

She couldn't stay in the cottage after that. She walked outside, found a path along the rim of the sound and followed it blindly. The wind was once again picking up, and a gust of frigid air blew in off the water. Taylor tucked the collar of her coat tightly around her neck and jammed her bare hands deep within its pockets, ignoring the finger of cold air that still got beneath her hair and ran down the nape of her neck.

A third of the way across the bay she could see a line of bright yellow buoys and wondered what their purpose was. But Taylor's thoughts were too absorbed by other issues to dwell for long on anything else.

Kerri's picture had hit Taylor viscerally, making her feel—really feel—some of what had been torturing Jason for two years. It was so unfair! If it had been she, Taylor wondered, and not Jason who had lost a child, could she have survived as well as he had?

And Jason had lost a wife, too, Taylor reminded herself grimly. A wife, moreover, that he'd been deeply in love with. It was a crippling double blow, one that many wouldn't be able to ever recover from.

Twilight was falling as Taylor reached a small clearing where a wooden bench was positioned to provide a fantastic view of the bay. She sat down, huddled inside the warmth of her jacket and watched as night fell over Whidbey, tiny dots of light on the other side of the bay winking on almost simultaneously, as if directed by some master switch.

It was peaceful on Whidbey, the only sounds from the gulls and the lapping water. The loneliness of the place added to Taylor's melancholy, and she tried to thrust her unhappy thoughts aside and think about the future. But the mood prevailed, and Taylor found herself thinking about Jason and Kerri, and somehow that reminded her of the loneliness of her own adolescence.

Her father had broken promise after promise to her. After Taylor's mother departed, she was left in the sole care of a man she loved, but who was more of a child than she was herself. He was an actor, but he didn't have the diligence and dedication it took to succeed at his profession. And every time Taylor truly needed him, he just wasn't there. If she begged him to attend some school function that was important to her, he always promised he would, then never showed. Eventually she learned not to ask.

It wasn't that Sean Michaelson didn't love his only daughter; it was that he was incapable of responsibility. Taylor had worked odd jobs all through school to bring in needed money, and her father had only worked when the whim took him. It was no wonder that Taylor's mother had been appalled when Taylor called her to say she'd decided to become an actress, following in her father's footsteps. Yet even Loretta Michaelson had turned a blind eye to the problems besetting her child; she'd never offered one penny of support.

Taylor had lived from one meal to another, a desperate life that had, nevertheless, not stolen her creative talent. Now, when she could, she sent her father money, and though he loudly and profusely objected to living off his daughter, he always took the offering. As for her mother, other than the time she'd pushed Taylor into modeling, she'd remained pointedly out of touch, dropping a ''see-you-soon'' card in the mail at Christmas and, if she remembered, another at Taylor's birthday.

Taylor had learned her independence early; she'd had to. The few romantic relationships she'd managed had died on the vine, and she'd never really gotten close to anyone else. In fact, Jason was the only man—the only person!—she'd ever trusted completely, and that was what accounted for her determination to help him now, come hell or high water.

The damp cold seeped up from the wood bench and Taylor stood up, chilled. Maybe Jason was back now, she consoled herself as she headed down the path.

As she neared the cottage, she met Maxine walking from the other direction. "Well, hello," Taylor greeted her, happy to see a friendly face. "I didn't know you lived so close to Jason."

"Right over there," Maxine answered with a wave, returning Taylor's smile. "Right at the curve of the bay. I have a bed-and-breakfast house. Didn't Jason tell you?"

Taylor shook her head. "No. But then, Jason hasn't told me much of anything."

"You're still here though." Apparently Maxine found that as amazing as Taylor did herself.

"Not with Jason's consent," Taylor admitted ruefully as they walked up the steps to the cabin together. "He kicked me out this morning, and I'm afraid sparks are going to fly when he finds out I'm still here." Taylor glanced somewhat fearfully toward the windows, but no light could be seen within. It seemed that Jason still hadn't returned.

Maxine's plump face pulled into a grin. "Good for you. But if the going gets really tough, you have a place to stay. Okay?"

"Thank you." Taylor's relief showed on her face. "I may be there before you know it."

"Oh, no. I think you'll manage somehow. Just like Julie handles Jake."

Taylor was surprised. "You've seen . . . our . . . films?"

"My daughter dragged me to one," Maxine explained. "In Seattle. But it was worth it. I got to see a different man than the one here."

"Yes . . . well . . . Jason was just playing a character," Taylor explained, fearing Maxine had taken the Jason on the screen as the man he used to be. He might not be the same man Taylor had known before, but he was never cool, nerves-of-steel Jake Diamond.

"Oh, I've known Jason for years," Maxine said, blowing Taylor's theories to smithereens. She nodded fervently at the look of incredulity that crossed Taylor's face. "Oh, yes. Jason's grandparents lived on Whidbey. He used to spend his summers here. I've know him since he was a little boy. That's why he bought this cottage, to have a place to escape to."

"I didn't know." It seemed there was a lot about Jason that Taylor didn't know.

"We couldn't believe it when he became an actor," Maxine went on, her smile touched with pride. "And a successful one too! He lived a charmed life, all right, until—"

Maxine broke off with such suddenness that Taylor looked around herself anxiously, certain that Jason must have come home.

Maxine's mouth pulled into a grim line. "Well, never mind. It's not good to speak ill of the dead. I'd better get to cleaning."

Taylor was dumbfounded. It was obvious Maxine was referring to Lisabeth. From all reports Taylor had ever heard, Lisabeth Garrett was loved by everyone who knew her, especially her husband. Taylor would have given a lot to know exactly what Maxine had meant by those cryptic words, but she couldn't bring herself to press her. She knew enough about gossip to know it usually wasn't founded in truth; everyone involved in the film industry had been targeted at one time or another.

Maxine insisted on starting dinner, even though Taylor assured her that she'd be happy to take over the chore. She needed something—anything—to keep herself busy.

"Trust me," Taylor begged. "I need something to do."

Maxine fussed for a few moments more but finally took pity on Taylor. "All right. I'll leave you to the spaghetti sauce," she agreed, wiping her hands on the dish towel.

"Perfect. I may not be the world's greatest chef, but I'm terrific with spaghetti."

After Maxine left, Taylor finished preparing the meal, but she decided to hold off on cooking the pasta until she saw the whites of Jason's eyes. She tried not to watch the clock while she worked, but when the meal was as ready as she could get it, she found herself with time on her hands.

Eight o'clock. Taylor picked up her manuscript and attempted to work on the first scene. *Diamond in the Sky* started in Madeira, picking up where *Queen of Diamonds* left off. The first scene was in a small cafe where Jake and Julie Diamond are approached by a beautiful woman who insists on telling Jake his fortune, all the time nervously looking over her shoulder. Jake, at Julie's prodding, reluctantly accepts. The woman tells him point-blank that he has seventy-two hours to live, then leaves before either Jake or Julie can recover.

Taylor knew the plot was right, but something was missing in that first scene that she just couldn't put her finger on. She read it over again but ended up frustratedly thrusting the manuscript back in its folder. Where was Jason?

Time crawled.

At ten o'clock Taylor cooked the pasta and sat down to eat. Jason didn't know she was there, she reminded herself. He had no idea a meal was waiting for him.

By midnight Taylor had cleaned the kitchen until it shined, stacked the fire for the night, swept the hearth, read yesterday's newspaper from cover to cover and worked out some dialogue for a scene in *Diamond in the Sky* in which Jake shows up three hours late and Julie's in a panic.

Taylor went to bed, her stomach tied in knots. She was certain, later, that it was the longest night she'd ever spent in her life. She tossed and turned restlessly, getting up just before dawn to take a shower and wash her hair. She made a pot of coffee and tried to think positively and not let her nagging worries about Jason's safety take over her reason. Jason had, after all, expected her to be back in Los Angeles by now. He had no idea that she was waiting for him.

Still, it seemed impossible not to worry that he had not come back at all. Where could he be?

Without a telephone Taylor couldn't even get hold of Maxine. She wondered if she should try to find Maxine's cabin and tell her...what? That Jason hadn't come home for the night? It was hardly Taylor's place to alert the neighbors, but what if he was injured?

Dawn was breaking in breathtaking streaks of hot pink and mauve over the sound, when Taylor, her gaze focused unseeingly on the horizon, heard Jason's Jeep rumble into the driveway. Her heart leaped. He was all right! She could hardly contain her relief, but as his booted feet sounded on the steps she pulled herself to-

gether and steeled herself for the inevitable confrontation. By now he had to have seen her car.

The door was flung open and Taylor involuntarily took
a step backward. The smile that was hovering on her lips
fell at his appearance. He was wearing the same clothes
he'd had on yesterday, and it was obvious he hadn't taken
them off since. Her heart sank as she realized he must
have been on an all-night drunk.

"You're still here?" he asked incredulously, the back
of his hand rubbing the stubble on his chin.

Taylor blinked. She'd been wrong! He was sober.
"Yes, I'm here. And I've been half out of my mind with
worry about you. Do you often stay out all night?"

Jason's jaw dropped for an instant before he managed
to control his reaction. Then he clamped his mouth into
a firm line. "Good God," he said in disbelief. "You
expect me to report to you?"

"No." Color swept up Taylor's neck as she realized
how presumptuous she'd sounded. "I was just worried,
that's all," she said lamely.

"Why are you still here?" Jason's gaze narrowed
warily.

Taylor took a deep breath. At least he wasn't yelling at
her . . . yet. "Because I couldn't leave with things the way
they were between us."

"Between us?" Jason repeated slowly, and Taylor felt
another wave of heat stain her cheeks. Then he shook his
head as if he couldn't believe what he was hearing, let out
a deep breath and said, "I need a cup of coffee."

Taylor hurried to the kitchen and poured it for him.
She saw the weariness in his face as she handed him the
blue enamel mug, and for a moment Jason's eyes held
hers, his brows drawing into a frown of displeasure.

"And here I thought you'd gone on the afternoon ferry," he said wryly, still watching her as he sipped his coffee.

Taylor shook her head. "No. I headed north, to Deception Pass—"

"North?"

"Why, yes, I thought it might be quicker..." Her voice trailed off in alarm. Jason had gone white; coffee threatened to spill from the mug he held in his suddenly trembling hands. Stunned, Taylor reacted without thinking. She cupped his hands with her own, steadying him, feeling the turbulent emotions churning within him.

"Jason, what is it?" Taylor asked, alarmed by the beads of perspiration that stood out on his brow.

Inhaling a shuddering breath, he attempted to get hold of himself. "Nothing," he said in a strangled voice.

"Don't shut me out, Jason," she pleaded. "Tell me something!"

Her urgency seemed to touch him as nothing else had. His jaw tightened and he gritted his teeth. Then he said with a half laugh, "See what two days of sobriety does? I think I'd rather be drunk."

Taylor stared into his deep blue eyes. Maybe there were sides to Jason she knew nothing about, but there were certainly sides to him she understood very well.

"Well, at least you haven't lost your talent as an actor," she said evenly. "But you can't fool me, Jason. Your trembling has nothing to do with sobriety. It's emotion."

She was still holding his hands, and he was doing nothing to push her away. She watched as whatever terrible memory she'd inadvertently brought to mind faded and he slowly relaxed. But still she didn't let go of him.

Instead she looked him straight in the eye and said, "Tell me why I shouldn't drive to the north."

Jason looked away and said tersely, "You really know how to push your luck, Taylor."

"That's right. I'm as bad as Phil Walker. I believe my own propaganda." Her smile was tight. "It's something to do with Lisabeth, isn't it?"

Jason flinched. "I suppose that wasn't too hard to guess." Lines formed beside his mouth. "Yes, doctor, it's true. Lisabeth's car plunged into the sound just around the curve of the bay. I was there when it was pulled out. They were, of course, both dead."

Though she'd half expected the explanation, his recital was chilling. She ignored the sarcasm with which he'd spoken and said in a whisper, "I'm sorry."

As if he suddenly realized she was still touching him, Jason pulled his hands from hers, measuring her with his eyes. "Answer me a question, Taylor," he said.

"Anything."

He frowned. "Why are you here, really? What's the kicker? Is it because of your screenplay? Do you want me involved with it somehow? Tell me the truth . . . now."

Taylor swallowed, leaned against the counter for support and arranged her thoughts carefully. "I want to answer you, but I'm certain you either won't believe me, or you'll start raging at me again."

Jason set down his mug with extreme care and regarded her through narrowed eyes. "Go ahead. I feel like the fatted calf already; you might as well finish the job."

"My screenplay has nothing to do with you," Taylor said firmly, deciding to plunge in. Jason looked skeptical but he kept quiet, and Taylor added, "Except that you were the obvious inspiration. I understood Jake and Julie Diamond's relationship because you helped me to understand it, and so the romance in my story was easy to write.

"If it has a flaw," Taylor went on, focusing on the top button of his shirt so she didn't have to face the censure that was sure to be in his face, "it's the mystery aspect. I think it's pretty good, but some things just don't quite seem to work. My agent already has a copy, but I thought I'd bring mine along on this trip to see if I could work out the flaws."

Jason shifted his weight from one foot to the other. "That doesn't explain why you came here in the first place."

Taylor sighed inwardly. He had convinced himself the screenplay had something to do with him, and nothing she could say would change his mind. And, in a remote way, he was connected to it. Taylor's conscience pricked her as she remembered Meredith Maddox's promise to read her story.

"Don't get angry, Jason," Taylor said, "but I really did come here because I was worried about you. Writing the story did bring you to mind, and when I found out you'd spent the past two years on Whidbey—" Taylor's mouth turned down "—grieving…well, my decision was made."

"I'm not grieving," Jason denied tersely.

Taylor's brows rose. She'd just seen proof positive to the contrary. "What would you call it, then?"

"Voluntary escapism! Just because all of you find Hollywood such a wonderful place doesn't mean I do."

Their brief truce was apparently over. Well, she'd been lucky to get even that. "Then the death of your wife and daughter has nothing to do with your present situation?"

Jason's shoulder had been leaning against the refrigerator door. At Taylor's brutal words he jerked upright, his cheeks paling. "Damn you," he muttered savagely.

"I'm not telling you something you don't already know," Taylor said, feeling a little guilty that she was taking advantage of the vulnerability he'd shown her.

She looked at him through troubled, eloquent eyes. "The Jason Garrett I knew before wouldn't have run from Hollywood just because he didn't like it there. That Jason Garrett loved to act. And he would have put up with all the garbage just to work." Taylor swallowed, unable to hold his tortured blue eyes any longer. "I don't know what brought you to Whidbey," she added painfully, "but I think the accident is what's making you stay."

The silence that stretched between them crashed around Taylor's ears. Jason's tension vibrated through the room. In a swift movement his palms captured her shoulders, yanking her closer to the anger flaming in his eyes.

"I didn't ask for you, Taylor Michaelson!" he ground out hoarsely. "I don't want to listen to you spouting your theories about me."

Her chin came up. She had so little to lose that she wasn't going to let him bully her into backing down. "You started this discussion," she pointed out.

"I don't give a damn!"

"You just don't like hearing the truth!"

Jason's breath came out in a rush. He glared at her, but Taylor refused to drop her eyes. They dueled silently for several moments.

Jason wanted to shake her. His hands tensed around her shoulders with that intention. Damn her! Damn the whole bloody lot of them!

Her eyes were the color of molten gold. Why hadn't he ever noticed before? he wondered. Then he was engulfed by a huge wave of pain, and he felt his strength drain from him, misery blinding him.

"Jason?" Taylor was alarmed at the sudden change in him. She instinctively put her arms around him for support, sensing, rather than seeing, him sway.

His breathing was ragged, torn. Giving in to a moment of weakness, he pressed his forehead against hers. "Don't talk to me," he murmured. "I don't want to talk."

Taylor's chest was tight and hurting. She wished she could absorb some of his pain. "I'm sorry," she said softly. "I'm so sorry."

He tried to disengage himself but couldn't. "It's not what you think."

"It doesn't matter," Taylor assured him. Her hand rubbed his back in commiseration, a part of her offering comfort, a part conscious of the well-defined muscles beneath his shirt.

"I don't want sympathy, Taylor. I can't bear it."

She could readily understand that. "Oh, Jason," she whispered. "I just want you to be happy."

His cheek was now pressed against hers, his arms around her as tightly as hers were around him. Taylor realized with a pang of awareness that for all the times she'd been in his arms, this was the first time there'd been any real feeling between them as people. She should probably draw back, she supposed, but she was unwilling to. He was reaching out to her and, oh, she wanted so much to give!

She felt his mouth brushing against her hair. Her pulse pounded in her ears. In all their love scenes together, Taylor had always felt Jason's detachment and concentration; he had undoubtedly felt hers. But this was something new, something elemental. She tried to speak, but the words lodged in her throat. Her eyes fluttered closed, and a soft gasp escaped her as his lips touched her lobe.

"Jason..." she moaned.

His arms tightened. She hadn't meant it to sound like a plea; she'd hoped to say the words that would provide a cold dash of sanity. But somehow she'd sounded willing and urgent, and she had no idea how to change things now.

"Are you going to run from me, Taylor?" he muttered. "Don't run from me."

"I can't... I couldn't..."

His thighs were pressed urgently against hers, straining. The edge of the counter was cutting into her, but she felt no pain. Then his palm captured the slope of her jaw, and his mouth came down on hers.

It wasn't the first time she'd kissed him, but it was definitely the first time he'd kissed her with this gripping intensity. Taylor's legs felt weak at the quick motion of his tongue, the demands of his lips. He gathered her to him with a closeness that left little doubt about his state of desire.

The kiss went on and on. Taylor's senses swam. Her hands clung to him, her hips moved against his, her hair tangled within his palm. The very touch of him thrilled her in a wild, exciting way, and her mind went completely blank to all the reasons she should beware.

Then abruptly it was over. With a deep groan, Jason pushed her away, his eyes very blue, still brilliant with desire, but filling rapidly with apology. He raked a hand through his hair and took a few uncertain steps away from her. "God, Taylor. I'm sorry."

She instantly had a mental image of herself: tousled hair, swollen lips, pleading eyes, heaving chest. She wanted to bury her face in her hands and hide.

"Taylor..." Jason's uneven voice cut her to the bone. She turned away, blindly seeking escape.

"I'm fine. I'm okay," she said in a voice unrecognizable as her own. "It was just a release of emotion. It's okay."

Jason made a deprecatory sound directed solely at himself. His breath whistled between his teeth. "You've got an answer for everything, don't you?" he said bitterly.

Not hardly. In those few terrible moments she had realized the truth of her feelings: she loved him. And it nearly killed her to accept the fact that her future would be without him.

But the situation was obvious to Taylor now. Jason hadn't spent the past two years on Whidbey for nothing: he was still in love with his dead wife. And she was a fool to let her emotions get tangled up with a man who couldn't love her back.

Jason stepped back, ran a hand around his neck and looked around the room as if he longed to escape. "I'm tired. I haven't been to bed all night. Look, don't try so hard to save me. I'm okay. Really. What problems I have, I need to work out on my own."

"Don't tell me to leave again," Taylor said through stiff lips. "Please."

"God, I don't know what you want!" he exploded. "Stay if you want! Stay!"

And with Jason's surrender ringing in her ears, Taylor watched him stalk off toward his bedroom. The door closed, but this time without the furious slam of the night before. This time it was shut softly, with purposeful and pointed care, as if Jason was determined to prove he was back in control.

Jason sagged against the bedroom door the instant it closed behind him. His head throbbed. His throat ached. He couldn't believe what had just happened! He was more appalled at himself than at Taylor, though inside he felt a searing anger that had no particular direction.

"Damn."

Jason closed his eyes, his hands clenched into fists. He could still feel the yielding warmth of Taylor's skin, the taste of her on his lips. His reaction to her was totally unexpected and unwelcome, and he was more eager than ever to get rid of her once and for all.

So why'd you invite her to stay?

Swearing under his breath, Jason thrust himself away from the door, walked unsteadily across the plankboard floor and flung himself facedown on the bed, groaning deeply. At times he wanted to die. He should be dead, he reasoned. He should have died with Lisabeth and Kerri.

He rolled onto his back and stared at the fir-beamed ceiling. Damn Taylor! Damn Phil! Damn the whole rotten Hollywood community! His palms closed into impotent fists, and he raged inwardly at all the injustices he'd been forced to bear.

He didn't want to think at all.

After long moments, his pulse returned to normal—or at least as close to normal as it could, considering Taylor was in the other room and determined to "save him from himself."

Jason clenched his teeth together. He didn't believe for a minute that that was the real reason she'd come. There was her screenplay to consider, and even though Taylor had never struck Jason as the type who'd use a friend selfishly, it was hard to believe her interests were totally altruistic.

So why was she here? And why was she so insistent on staying? And most of all, why had he let her?

Jason groaned again. Taylor's attempts to help had forced him to remember scenes that still broke him into a cold sweat. He could feel the slap of Lisabeth's palm across his face, the hard pelt of gravel spewing from beneath her tires, the agony of watching her low-slung car career around the curve at breakneck speed. Jason's pulse pounded in his ears, and he took several deep breaths, trying to shut the images from his mind. He couldn't remember; he wouldn't let himself. He remembered enough in his dreams as it was.

Phil had told him it was unhealthy to repress the past, that hiding the accident in his subconscious was killing him. But Phil didn't understand. Jason could recall every detail of that night without even trying. It wasn't a matter of unhealthy repression—the problem was, he *couldn't* forget.

And Taylor. Why hadn't he forced her to leave? Her staying would do neither one of them any good. Jason was at a loss to understand his own motives where she was concerned, but inside he felt a deep uneasiness. He didn't want her around. He didn't like thinking he cared about her at all. But holding her and sharing with her had, for one glorious moment, blotted out the past. He'd wanted her, in a way he hadn't wanted anyone in a long, long time.

But to let her know... That would place a power in her hands that Jason couldn't afford, and he'd already given himself away! Jason hadn't looked at another woman since Lisabeth's death; he'd had no desire to get that close to a woman, any woman, ever again. But now...?

Taylor's image was sharp in his mind, the feel of her imprinted on his very soul. It had been a lot easier dealing with Phil, Jason had to admit; but then Phil had had neither Taylor's determination nor her womanly shape. From the moment she'd walked up to him at the Tidewater, Jason had been aware of Taylor's soft curves, the gentle scent of her feminine perfume, the natural grace with which she moved. He'd known Taylor for years, yet now something had changed, and being near her brought on a physical reaction that made him grind his teeth in frustration.

He had to get rid of her, and as he lay staring at the ceiling, exhaustion overtaking him from his sleepless night of aimless driving, he devised a plan. It was fairly simple, really, and he had no doubt about its effectiveness. A faint smile of regret touched the corners of his mouth as he planned how to make her life so miserable she'd be forced to leave.

And then he could finally be left in peace once more.

Chapter Five

Hello? Ross?" Taylor twisted in the narrow confines of the telephone booth, putting a hand over her free ear in an effort to hear more clearly. "Are you there?"

"Taylor?" Ross Corley's voice sounded faintly surprised. "Where on God's green earth are you? Not Los Angeles."

"I'm still on Whidbey Island, in a phone booth in Coupeville. I thought I'd check in and let you know that I'm still alive and in one piece."

"What about Garrett? Have you seen him?" Ross sounded interested.

"Well, yes." Taylor felt a twinge of conscience as if she were about to give some of Jason's secrets away, but his attitude this past week had convinced her that she owed him nothing anymore. Jason had been abominable, letting her know in no uncertain terms that since she was staying at the cottage, and since he found her reasonably attractive, she should be having an affair with him.

He'd been utterly serious about it, approaching her later in the evening after he'd announced she could stay. Taylor's relief at being allowed to remain had turned to dismay when Jason walked into the living room and announced, "If you plan on staying here, there are a few ground rules."

His tone of voice had made her uneasy. Gingerly, she had set aside the manuscript pages she'd been working on, afraid the situation might deteriorate just by having it in plain sight. But apart from a brief, dark scowl, Jason had ignored her screenplay, his gaze centering on Taylor.

"Name them," she said, returning his stare.

Jason's skin tightened briefly over his cheekbones. "No more talk about Lisabeth . . . and Kerri."

Swallowing, Taylor nodded. She had no wish to put him through that pain again unless he was willing himself.

"Second, I don't want any preaching about my lifestyle. It's the way I've chosen to live, so leave it."

"I haven't preached yet; I don't intend to start now."

The stubborn tilt to her jaw seemed to amuse rather than annoy him. She saw a brief flash of humor lighten his eyes, as if he were enjoying some inner joke—perhaps one at her expense. However, Taylor was too happy with her progress for the day to worry unduly, so she just smiled back at him.

Jason then walked the rest of the way to the couch and dropped down beside her with that masculine grace that Taylor found so attractive, his thigh resting lightly against hers. Trying to look casual about it, Taylor put some space between them. The memory of his passionate kiss was still fresh in her mind. Like a broken record, it kept playing over and over again, and she found herself liking what she'd felt far too much.

To her shock, Jason had next trailed a finger along her thigh. Taylor's eyes flew to his face, but his expression was hardly encouraging. There was serious purpose in the slant of his mouth, the determination of his chin. The meditative way he was examining her lips brought on a wave of heat that left Taylor feeling weak.

"You didn't ask me where I was last night," he said softly.

"That was your business." Taylor's breath had shortened. The fingertip drawing lazy circles on her thigh burned through the fabric of her jeans. What was he doing?

"Well, I'm going to tell you where I was. I spent the night at Rita's."

The barkeep? Taylor couldn't prevent her gasp of shock. The excitement of the moment receded under a wave of revulsion. It had never occurred to her that Jason might be with another woman, certainly not the Tidewater's red-haired Rita! She felt an intense pang of jealousy that had no place, and, knowing her face had become a mirror to her feelings, Taylor struggled frantically for some kind of self-control. But an ache was spreading through her limbs, a knifing pain that tightened her chest and constricted her breath.

She yanked her gaze away from Jason's, suddenly remembering the look that had passed from Rita to the man at the end of the bar when she'd mentioned Jason's name. Yes, Rita knew Jason. Yes, Jason spent a lot of time at the Tidewater. Yes, it was possible he was telling the truth....

"But, y'know," he said conversationally, "you're a very beautiful woman, Taylor, and I think I'd rather have you in my bed. If you're so hell-bent on staying, I can't see any reason why we shouldn't enjoy each other. What would you think about that?"

Taylor stiffened, reacting before she thought. "I think it's a terrible idea! I'm not . . . I couldn't . . ." To her fury and embarrassment she began to tremble, and Jason, his hand still making forays down the length of her thigh, could feel it. Realizing belatedly what a mistake it had been to let him see her discomfiture, Taylor added tightly, "If you're trying to shock me, you'll be glad to know you've succeeded."

"Ahhh, Taylor." One hand had somehow wound its way into her hair. She felt the tug on her scalp as his hand pulled her to him, and her heart pounded. The situation was getting away from her and she had no idea what to do next.

"Let go of me!"

"I just wanted to recheck your response. This morning you felt willing enough, but I was afraid you might have changed your mind." A feather-light kiss dusted her temple. "It's hard for me to believe you're saying no now," he murmured.

Taylor clenched her teeth together. "If this is a ploy to get me to leave, it won't work."

His laugh was low and husky, and a shiver skimmed up Taylor's spine. "I don't want you to leave anymore," he admitted, and she watched with frozen disbelief as his mouth came closer to hers.

"Stop it, Jason . . ."

She twisted away but strong arms held her fast, a hard mouth searching and finding hers, pressing against her lips with an abandon that both thrilled and alarmed her.

Her chin was captured, Jason's thumb sensuously rubbing the slope of her jaw. Taylor thrust her hands against his chest, but the hard beat of his heart was something she hadn't meant to discover. Inside she was beginning to melt—she could feel it! And it was dangerously erotic, dangerously seductive. Her pulse raced insanely, her skin burned for his touch, her mind went numb to everything but the excitement of his insistent, stimulating caress.

"Taylor." Jason's breath was warm near her ear. She felt the damp probing of his tongue, the tender bite on her lobe. She heard the moan issue from her own throat and felt raw disbelief. She'd never been this excited before, had never been so expertly aroused. She'd never had the time to have a love affair, hadn't met a man worthy of one—until Jason—and when she'd met him he'd been married.

"Jason, I can't," she said breathlessly. Thoughts of Jason's marriage brought back some presence of mind.

"Wrong, Taylor. You can. You will..."

His other hand had crept beneath her sweater, and she was powerless to stop its slow, measured progress to her breasts. They swelled in anticipation, the skin utterly sensitized to the texture of her wool sweater and the warm possession of Jason's fingers as they tentatively explored, then firmly molded the straining peaks. She moaned in delight, her eyes fluttering closed.

Again his mouth brushed against hers, and her lips parted involuntarily, a soft sigh escaping her throat. Jason took her soft utterance as one of submission, and his mouth closed over hers possessively, urgently, his tongue warmly finding the sweetness within, drawing it out, but offering more sensual pleasure than it took. Taylor couldn't move. She was drugged with desire and a beautiful sense of wonder at the whole unbelievable state of affairs. She could do no more than grip the hard swell of his upper arms, silently battling her own need to capitulate, knowing innately that by giving in she would surely lose, yet not wanting the shattering, wild emotions running through her veins like liquid fire to end.

Jason's breath was hot and ragged. He wrapped one leg over hers, forcing her down on the couch until the bared skin of her back made contact with the soft corduroy ribbing.

"No..." Taylor made a last, feeble effort to escape, but beautiful bubbles of excitement were sweeping through her bloodstream, tempting her, driving her onward until the shifting of her own hips belied the plea of her lips.

"Yes." Jason's head was bent in concentration as he pulled her sweater above her breasts. Weakly, Taylor saw the dark buds of her nipples straining through the sheerness of her bra, then gasped as she felt the hot, shocking warmth of his mouth closing around one tip.

He moved against her in a way that made his intentions obvious, and Taylor, her legs and arms tangled up with his, her skin quivering at the magic his tongue was performing at her breast, tiny moans of pleasure issuing from her own throat, was unable to get her limbs to obey the commands of her brain. She couldn't let it go on. She couldn't! She was a fool to have let it go as far as it had, yet she was overcome by a sensual lassitude, a slave to her own passions.

"Jason..."

His hands were holding her hips in a way she dimly recognized as a means to ready her. She wanted to warn him about her inexperience. It seemed the sensible thing to do. But she was whirling from the stroke of his touch, and the words jumbled in her mind.

"It's all right, love," he murmured huskily. "Just a little longer. Be patient." His mouth began a dangerous foray downward, dropping wet kisses on the trembling skin of her stomach, as his hands came around to find the snap of her jeans.

What finally penetrated Taylor's senses was his assumption that *she* couldn't wait. From mindless submission, she suddenly awoke to the horror of the situation. What in the world was she doing? This crazy lovemaking was not only destructive to her state of mind, it had probably torn her credibility to shreds!

Taylor made a strangled sound and started struggling in earnest. Jason, sensing her new determination, released her instantly, as if he too were relieved that she'd finally managed to say no and mean it. Taylor's sense of shame went bone deep. He'd never even been totally involved! she realized with a jolt. She'd just *been* there. Available.

He was looking at her with unreadable eyes, his lips still swollen sensuously. Taylor felt the heat in her face, and she knew no amount of acting experience could help her rearrange the look of disaster imprinted there. She was horrified with herself, quaking inside and out.

"I take it that, at least for the moment, your answer's still no," he said with devastating lack of passion.

Taylor could hardly believe his tone. If she'd harbored any hopes about what his lovemaking had meant, she didn't anymore. Pure and simple sex is what he'd said he wanted, and Taylor, against all logic, had nearly given him just that!

She could hardly get her voice working. "You were testing me, weren't you?" she accused shakily. "You were just testing me!"

Jason laughed ruefully, disengaging himself completely from the warm tangle of their entwined bodies. "You know better, Taylor. It's difficult for a man to hide his reactions, and you're certainly aware of mine."

She swallowed. His reaction was physical, he was telling her, something entirely removed from emotional involvement; she shouldn't be naive enough to confuse the two. Angry and ashamed, she felt some explanation for her behavior was necessary. "Jason, I—"

"Well, think it over," he cut her off, swiftly getting to his feet. "I'm ready and willing whenever you change your mind, or—" he looked back, his eyes glowing dangerously "—whenever you can admit that you want me, too. Just don't take too long, Taylor. I'm not a patient man."

Taylor had been too stunned by her own reactions to give much thought to Jason's words. But later, when it became obvious that Jason's only interest in her was because she was an attractive female, when she realized the only topic he was willing to discuss was sex—specifically sex between the two of them—and when his visits to the Tidewater became even more frighteningly regular, a means to block her out, Taylor had begun to burn with resentment. Damn the man! He was a master at attacking her self-respect, and Taylor was half-inclined to give up her foolish campaign and make a beeline for southern California.

Calling Ross had been a decision made after five unbearable days, a way to vent her own miserable frustrations. Yet even now she was reluctant to leave Jason. She cared too much about him for her own good, she realized defeatedly, and even though he was deadly determined to make her life utterly miserable, she couldn't leave yet.

"Well, is Garrett as messed up as Phil Walker seems to think?" Ross asked curiously, after Taylor had explained that she was staying at Jason's cabin.

Taylor looked through the glass of the phone booth, across the street to the front of the Tidewater where Jason's Jeep was parked. "No. He just wants everyone to leave him alone."

"But you're still there."

Ross's voice was full of intrigue, and Taylor sought to set the record straight. "Not because Jason wants me to be," Taylor said forcefully. "But I'm not willing to admit defeat yet."

"Good Lord, what on earth do you hope to accomplish? If the man doesn't want you, leave. Think of yourself, Taylor. The longer you stay away, the more damage you're doing to your career. Sweetheart, it's disintegrating before our eyes."

"That's why I called, Ross," Taylor interrupted. "I've been working on my screenplay while I've been here, and I've worked out almost all the bugs. If I can, I'll send it to you in a few days."

"If you can?" he inquired sardonically. "Look, Taylor. Forget the screenplay. There's been a cattle call for that new prime-time soap opera and I put your name in on the off chance you'd be back from Timbuktu."

"Ross, I can't do it. I don't know when I'll be back."

"What's holding you there?" he demanded. "If Garrett doesn't want your help, come home. I know he means a lot to you. I know you feel you owe him everything, but honey, you've got to make it on your own now and let him do the same."

Taylor closed her eyes and pressed her lips together. She couldn't explain her feelings to Ross any more than she could to herself.

"Give up this insanity and get back to L.A. I'll schedule your screen test for next Thursday. Oh, and Taylor, maybe you should give Phil Walker a call and tell him about Garrett. It might make him feel better. I think he's honestly concerned."

"No screen test, Ross. Sorry." Ross made some attempts to convince her, but Taylor closed her ears. She wondered if she should take his advice about Phil Walker, however. The man was a close friend of Jason's, whether Jason would admit to it now or not.

"Taylor, *think*," Ross implored.

"A few more days, Ross. That's all." A few more days would be all she could stand anyway! "I'll call Phil, though," she added before she hung up. "It will make him feel better to know that Jason is not suicidal. And I'm sending you my screenplay whether you want it or not." Some imp within her provoked her into adding, "Meredith Maddox made some noise about it when I talked to her."

"What? When?" Ross's voice sharpened. "She called about your screenplay?"

Taylor laughed silently at Ross's predictability. Business always captured his full attention. "I don't know if she was serious or not, but she said she'd like to see it."

"Wonderful. Great." Taylor could practically picture him rubbing his palms together. "Send it to me as soon as you can."

"I haven't been guaranteed a sale, Ross," Taylor reminded him, growing sorry that she'd brought it up. Meredith's words hadn't been all that encouraging.

"Taylor!" Ross's voice held a note of profound discovery. "Is this why you've gone to see Garrett?"

"What do you mean?"

Taylor was vaguely disturbed, but Ross was on a train of thought that made perfect sense to him. "You want him in the picture. What a package that would be: Jason Garrett, Taylor Michaelson and a *Diamond Girl* screenplay. It will sell sight unseen!"

"You're getting ahead of yourself, Ross," Taylor said desperately. "I haven't asked Jason anything about the screenplay. I wouldn't! And I'm an unknown writer. No one, certainly no one at Maddox Productions, would take a chance—"

"Yes, they would. They *will*." Ross was positive. "Send me the screenplay as fast as possible. I can get Meredith to sign you to a contract."

"Ross, listen to me!"

"Why, Taylor Michaelson, I never knew you had it in you," Ross said, laughing. "Garrett will never know what hit him."

It was impossible to talk to Ross. Taylor wasn't certain whether he really believed what he was saying or if he was just needling her. Either way it was imperative that she correct the impression.

"Look, Ross, you don't understand. I didn't come to Whidbey to get Jason to sign on for my screenplay. That's not it at all. Even if I had, he wouldn't do it."

"Whatever you say." He sounded amused.

"I mean it, Ross. I don't give a damn if Jason ever comes back to Hollywood. And you can quote me on that."

Her urgency fell on deaf ears. "Sure, sure. I believe you." His voice said he patently didn't. "Stay as long as you like, Taylor. You never know—" silent laughter thrummed beneath his voice "—you might do Jason Garrett some good. Send the screenplay down. I'll be looking for it."

Taylor hung up and found her hands were shaking. She was surprised at her reaction until she realized it stemmed from fear. If Ross said anything to *anyone*, it was possible his words would find their way back to Jason. Taylor groaned inwardly at what he would think of her then.

"Now you're borrowing trouble," she muttered, but she couldn't quite shake off the feeling of uneasiness.

She searched through her purse for her address book, looked up Phil Walker's phone number and dialed it with a sense of impending doom. Phil had been adamant about the insanity of her decision to see Jason; even good news about Jason wouldn't change his mind where she was concerned.

Phil, as it turned out, was with a patient and could not come to the phone. Taylor was relieved that she didn't have to talk to him, and after giving Phil's secretary her name and the promise that she would call back later, she hung up. Then she slid open the door to the phone booth and stepped into the crisp, late-morning air.

She stood on the sidewalk for a full minute, wondering what in the world to do next. Her presence on Whidbey was superfluous; Jason had told her as much, and he'd made it clear by his actions too—unless, Taylor reminded herself grimly, she was willing to fall into bed with him. Then, according to Jason, she would have a purpose.

Taylor walked down the street, forcing herself not to give the Tidewater more than a cursory glance. If he wanted to drink himself into oblivion, she couldn't stop him. But she'd be damned if she'd watch his destruction.

There was a section of Coupeville along the waterfront, several blocks north of the Tidewater, that had been renovated into quaint gift shops and tiny eateries.

Taylor headed in that direction, stopping at a small bakery for a cup of coffee and some hot cinnamon bread.

The situation between herself and Jason, Taylor reflected as she blew across the top of her coffee, was all the more discouraging because she *did* want to make love with him. She ached to, with new, wild feelings that had sprung upon her unexpectedly. They made a mockery of all her good intentions to come and "save" Jason, and made Taylor face facts about herself that she didn't quite like.

She was falling in love with him. Or maybe—and this was the hardest to admit—she'd been a little in love with him all along. Those months of working together had been some of the best of her life, and now she knew it wasn't just because of the part she'd been given. It was because of Jason.

It was frightening how much she was attracted to him. But Taylor wanted him emotionally as well as physically, and with Lisabeth still such a great force in Jason's life, she knew she couldn't have both. And so she would have to accept neither.

Taylor drove back toward Jason's cabin in a state of depression. The week had been emotionally wearing, Jason's continual insinuative remarks taking a deep bite out of her self-respect. She was certain his words were meant to force her into leaving, but knowing that didn't make them any easier to take. It was doubly worrisome because of her own traitorous desires—desires Jason knew about—and Taylor thought she'd go crazy just waiting around the cottage one more afternoon for Jason to come home and have the whole scenario begin again.

At the last moment, Taylor veered away from the drive into Jason's cottage and steered her car farther north, almost to the sickle curve of the bay. Maxine's house was down one of the long, limb-canopied lanes, and Taylor turned into the first, determined to shake off her mood and talk to someone. She needed to see a friendly face, and once Taylor had seized on the idea, she clung to it like a lifeline for a drowning woman.

As soon as she turned Taylor saw she'd guessed correctly. A creaking wooden sign suspended from a wrought iron frame declared: Bed and Breakfast. Taylor drove into a small clearing, parked her car and looked around with admiration. Maxine's home was a white clapboard two-story house with forest-green shutters. A lawn now overgrown with barely tamed shrubbery swept down to the bay. There was actually a porch swing rocking gently in the ever-present breeze, and as Taylor stepped from the car she was overcome by a wave of envy. Surprised, she searched her feelings and realized this Norman Rockwell picture was everything that had been missing in her life. As humbling as it was to admit, she envied Maxine, envied the people in the world like her. They had something she could never attain; it had passed her by, and the gift of her beauty and success couldn't quite take its place.

A full-grown collie came bursting around the white fence, barking loudly, hurtling full speed in Taylor's direction. Though unafraid, Taylor prudently flattened herself against the car until she saw the collie's tail begin to fan enthusiastically.

"You're a great big fake, aren't you?" she said, bending down to scratch the dog's ears, trying to evade its wildly excited tongue and muddy paws. She was laughing by the time Maxine came through the front door, shooing vainly at the dog.

"Gretchen! Get down!" Maxine grabbed hold of the dog's collar, only her ample size keeping the dog from dragging her toward Taylor.

"She's beautiful." Taylor smiled and dusted off her jeans.

"She's a pain in the neck but she's part of the family." Maxine patted the collie's side affectionately. "Was there something you wanted, Miss Michaelson?"

Taylor shrugged, feeling awkward. "A cup of coffee, maybe? Unless you're busy, of course."

Maxine's face broke into a grin. "You need someone to talk to," she said, nodding several times. "Go on, Gretchen." She let go of the whining dog, which broke into excited barking upon hearing the scolding chatter of a gray squirrel, its tail flicking back and forth, as it hung precariously from the tip of a bending fir limb. Gretchen jumped and whined and barked, twisting frustratedly beneath, just out of reach. Taylor had to admire the squirrel's nerve.

"Come in the house," Maxine said. "I just finished making a pot of soup for Jason. You can save me a trip."

"I'd be happy to take over the cooking while I'm here," Taylor told Maxine for perhaps the hundredth time, but the older woman just waved that notion aside.

"Oh, good heavens, no. Why, you never know; you may be leaving tomorrow," she said with startling candor. "No sense in me getting out of the habit."

Maxine's kitchen was a blend of old and new: painted white cabinets whose well-worn corners revealed avocado green beneath, a claw-footed scarred oak table, gleaming new white Formica countertops, an ancient oven that shone with cleanliness and, above it, incongruously, a black glass microwave oven whose timer was dinging softly as they came inside.

A girl of around fifteen with short black hair was carefully pulling a bowl from the microwave oven. She turned as they entered and did a classic double take at the sight of Taylor.

"Sarah, this is Miss Michaelson," Maxine said by way of introduction.

"It's Taylor, please." Taylor smiled at the girl and was rewarded with a wide grin in return.

"My husband's asleep," Maxine said as she poured a cup of coffee from the pot on the stove. She tested it herself, found it suitable, then poured another cup for Taylor, adding as she handed it to her, "He works graveyard at Crenshaw's, and Sarah's staying all night with a friend in Seattle tonight, so I'd be more than happy for the company."

Crenshaw's, Taylor learned later, was a bottle-manufacturing company that employed Maxine's husband, Tom, and many of his friends. Maxine ran the bed-and-breakfast house almost single-handedly, and though she complained about business falling off in the winter, Taylor got the impression she was relieved and content just to take care of her own family—and Jason.

"You play Julie Diamond," Sarah said, seating herself opposite Taylor. "I've seen all your movies. Are you and Jason going to do another?"

Apparently Sarah had no real idea of what Jason's problems were, and Taylor wasn't about to bring them up now. She just smiled and said, "Not in the near future, but you never can tell."

"How long have you known Jason?" she asked, eyeing Taylor with the critical scrutiny Taylor had had to get used to from fans who met her in the flesh.

Sarah's question brought all Taylor's memories to the fore with bittersweet poignancy. "I met him when I was nineteen, almost twenty. I did a screen test for *Diamond Girl*, never believing in a hundred years that I'd actually be given the part. Jason had already been cast for the male lead, and when the producers saw our test, they gave me the job.''

''Wow.'' Sarah's eyes were wide.

In reality, getting the part had involved a great deal more. Clifton Maddox had raved about Taylor's fresh, clean-scrubbed quality, clasping her in a huge bear hug as soon as she had walked into the screening room after the production company had viewed her test.

''You're perfect!'' he'd boomed out, looking around the room for support. Several people nodded in agreement, several looked openly disapproving, but the majority just kept their expressions blank. Clifton's artistic nature couldn't handle the careful civility. ''Don't you think so?'' he challenged everyone within earshot.

Taylor's embarrassment had been acute. She'd longed to escape, but Clifton had made his choice and he wanted everyone to know it.

Jason had been the first to answer Clifton. His blue eyes had ranged over Taylor's face, searching her expression as if he expected to read what was in her mind. Then he'd smiled, that sensual curve of lip and flash of white teeth that had brought him such quick fame.

''It was a great test,'' he admitted softly, and Taylor glowed inside. It *had* been a good test, but only because Jason had taught her how to relax. She wanted to tell him as much, but before she could speak, Meredith Maddox stood up.

''No offense, Miss Michaelson, but you might as well know how we all feel right now.'' She turned to her husband and said pointedly, ''I would rather have someone with more name recognition for the part.''

"Pah." Clifton dismissed her with a sharp jerk of his hand. "The public's tired of the same old faces. Give me someone new who has vitality, energy, mobility!" His infectious mood caused some reluctant smiles to break through on everyone but Meredith. "And you're it, babe." He chucked Taylor under the chin affectionately. "It's a great face," he said. "A great face. We'll use it."

Meredith had flushed, subsiding into silent anger, and Taylor had worried that she'd inadvertently made an enemy. But it turned out that Meredith, once the decision had been finalized and all the contracts signed, accepted Taylor as whole-heartedly as her husband had.

Thinking back, Taylor realized just how much she owed to both Clifton and Meredith as well as to Jason. They'd gambled on her, and now Meredith was willing to gamble on her again, if she could talk Jason into coming back to Hollywood, which at this point was a very big if indeed.

"I think Jason should go back," Maxine said as Taylor fell silent. Both Taylor and Sarah looked at her.

"What?" Taylor asked. It was as if Maxine had read her thoughts. Yet even Taylor wasn't completely certain Jason would be happier in Hollywood. How could Maxine be?

"I think Jason should go back to moviemaking," Maxine repeated, her broad face serious. "Don't you think it would get him back on track? Isn't that why you're here?"

"No. I'm just a friend—as I said."

"Well, sure. But he needs a job to get him over the brooding. I kinda hoped you'd be the one to make it work."

So that was what was behind Maxine's bonhomie. She'd seen Taylor as the savior Phil Walker had tried, and failed, to be, and Taylor realized with sinking defeat that she would disappoint Maxine, too, if she packed up and left now. Maxine was expecting success.

Thinking she needed to let Maxine down gently, Taylor said with a sad smile, "Jason left Hollywood for reasons unknown. The accident was something else entirely. Even if he got over that, I don't know that he'd want to go back. I don't think anyone could talk him into going, no matter how much they wanted to help."

"I know why he left," Sarah said matter-of-factly.

Taylor turned to stare at her. Apparently the girl was perfectly serious.

"Really," Sarah went on, bobbing her head enthusiastically. "One time I overheard him and his wife arguing about going back. Jason was really mad. He told her that she was weak and Hollywood made her weaker, and if she went back he'd take Kerri away from her forever."

"Sarah!" Maxine was shocked. "You shouldn't eavesdrop on people!"

"I was just walking along the bay!" Sarah protested. "They were shouting at each other. I couldn't help but hear."

Sarah subsided into injured silence, dipping into her soup. Taylor picked up her coffee cup with unsteady hands, imagining the scene Sarah had described so clearly. She remembered Lisabeth's illness while they'd been filming in Madeira and Jason's preoccupation with his wife's health. Was that the weakness he'd referred to? It made no sense. Why would Jason be angry about it, and why would he blame it on Hollywood? Unless . . . Lisabeth's weakness had been her rumored alcoholism.

"How long are you staying with him?" Sarah asked, somewhat subdued.

"Not much longer, I'm afraid." She laughed ruefully. "He already thinks I've overstayed my welcome."

"You know you can come here if the going gets rough," Maxine offered again, and the friendliness in her face convinced Taylor she was truly welcome.

"Thank you." Taylor was also sincere. "I really appreciate it, but I think I'll probably go home before that becomes necessary."

Maxine clucked her tongue and looked thoughtful. Taylor glanced at the wall clock and realized she'd been gone quite a while. Not that it really mattered, she had to admit, since Jason couldn't care less where she was or what happened to her.

"Are you anxious to get back to him?" Maxine asked, rising. She picked up the cups and asked with her eyebrows if Taylor wanted a refill.

Taylor shook her head. "No, thanks, and no—" she laughed in irony "—I'm not anxious to get back to him."

"Has he been awful?" Sarah looked intensely interested, her natural ebullience returning in force.

"Let's just say he's tried to be...difficult," Taylor tempered, and they all three broke into smiles.

"He can be a beast when he wants to," Maxine put in, ignoring Taylor's refusal and pouring her another cup. She sat back down at the table with a fresh air of camaraderie, and Taylor found it impossible to escape, nor, she realized with faint surprise, did she want to. Maxine and Sarah's friendship mattered a great deal to her, more than she would have thought possible in such a short space of time. And she couldn't bear the thought of leaving this warm kitchen for the frigid battleground she would be facing at Jason's.

"Stay the rest of the afternoon," Maxine encouraged. "Give Jason something to think about besides himself. It'll do him good."

Sarah's eyes danced. "Mom!" she admonished, obviously surprised by a side of her mother she'd never seen.

Maxine waved a plump hand. "Jason Garrett's just a man. He needs to realize what a good thing he's got in Taylor."

"Our relationship's not quite like that," Taylor protested.

"Doesn't matter." Maxine sighed knowingly, a smile as old and wise as time crossing her lips. "It will be if you want it to."

Taylor was shocked into silence that Maxine had read her feelings so accurately. Before she had time to come up with a suitable reply, Maxine said, "Don't give Jason Garrett another thought until tonight. You can spend the afternoon with us, the night too, if necessary, but you know that."

Their genuine eagerness to pull her out of her blues made Taylor feel a gratitude that nearly brought her to tears. She scolded herself for her propensity to fall apart at the least little kindness. A life without stability, roots, a loving bond, had left her amazed when someone offered so much without reservations.

"I'd love to stay," Taylor said, and Maxine and Sarah chorused their delight.

They both moved their chairs in closer, and Sarah leaned forward on her elbows. "Tell me what it's like to be a movie star," she said breathlessly.

Taylor hid a smile and began to explain that she was far from being a star, and that most of what she did was plain hard work. Sarah, she could see, simply didn't believe her. Taylor spent the next few hours answering question after question, drinking coffee and even accepting a slice of Maxine's applesauce cake, enjoying the peacefulness of a sun-filled afternoon on Whidbey, letting herself be swept away by the soothing country tranquility.

At seven-thirty Taylor pulled into Jason's driveway, both glad and uneasy when she saw his Jeep parked beneath one of the heavily boughed trees. She walked quickly across the fir-needled gravel path and gave a sharp rap before opening the door.

Jason was nowhere to be seen. It figures, Taylor thought resignedly, placing Maxine's food on the counter and stripping off her jacket against the blast furnace heat from the fire.

She didn't bother calling for him. She'd learned the best way to handle their wary coexistence was to make no demands and just try to keep her emotions cool and unaffected, a daunting task at the best of times, but a necessity with Jason. Any crack in the armor and he was ready to shoot with both barrels.

Taylor put the sandwiches inside the refrigerator, poured the soup into a saucepan and turned on the burner. Whatever Jason was paying Maxine, Taylor reflected as she stirred the soup, it wasn't enough. The woman's good-natured help and fabulous cooking were more than he deserved.

"Well, well, there you are."

Taylor nearly dropped the spoon at the sound of Jason's voice. It took considerable will for her to pull her expression into order and glance back at him with only mild interest. She kept right on stirring the soup, concentrating carefully on making perfect little circles, telling herself that the sudden racing of her heart was from surprise, not the sight of his lean body propped against the kitchen wall.

"And here I thought you'd run out on me," Jason added sardonically. She felt the weight of his gaze between her shoulder blades and strove for a lightness she didn't feel.

"With all my clothes still here?" The soup was starting to bubble, so Taylor turned down the stove. "Not on your life."

"Hmm."

It was nice to know that his extended visit at the Tidewater hadn't affected him too much; the brief glimpse she'd allowed herself had confirmed that his eyes were clear, his expression sharp and slightly mocking. In fact, he had managed to keep sober most of the time she'd been on Whidbey, Taylor reminded herself. Then, again, Jason had always been a consummate actor. It was entirely possible that he'd been fooling her on that, although she'd been searching for telltale signs.

"Maxine made some soup and sandwiches," Taylor said. "I spent the afternoon with her and brought them back with me."

"You spent the afternoon at Maxine's?" Jason repeated slowly.

"Uh-huh. You want some soup? I'm not really hungry. We ate late."

Taylor ladled Jason a bowlful, then retrieved the plate of sandwiches. She set the table without looking at him, then eyed the space between him and the corner of the table, wondering if it was possible to squeeze by without touching him. His long legs were blocking the way, and she would have to step right over them to escape. She decided it would be more dignified to wait.

"I'm not really hungry either, but I'll probably suffer endless nagging unless I sit down and eat," Jason observed wryly, straightening. He regarded her broodingly for a moment, then stretched his arms over his head, revealing taut, steel muscles and, where his sweater gapped, the board-flat expanse of his abdomen. Taylor looked away instantly, annoyed by the tingle along her nerves. She was even more annoyed by the perceptible twitching of Jason's lips; he knew what she was feeling!

"I'm not the nagging sort," Taylor said flatly.

He raised his brows, and Taylor regarded him defiantly. "You certainly have a one-track mind," Jason reminded her, "and I think the two go hand in hand." He took a seat at the table, allowing Taylor passage around him.

"What makes you think I have a one-track mind?"

"You're still here, aren't you? A less single-minded person would have left long ago."

Taylor turned her back on him and walked to the kitchen door, where she leaned against the jamb and stared into the living room. There was something about his soft mockery that scraped her nerves raw—the fact that there was an element of truth in everything he said, she supposed.

Her screenplay lay on the coffee table, and the sight of it depressed her, reminding her of her promise to mail it to Ross. It also reminded her of how ineffective she'd been in helping Jason. Maybe she should just give up, she reasoned defeatedly. Jason would probably do handsprings if she left.

He ate in silence, and Taylor did her best to ignore him. For the first time since she'd arrived she began to give serious thought to the length of her stay. When should she leave? Tomorrow? The next day? Next week? Next month? It seemed incredibly foolhardy just to take each day as it came, hoping for a miracle. At some point she was going to have to face her uselessness and go home.

Jason put his dishes in the sink and turned on the taps. "Do I detect second thoughts?" he asked, slanting her a look.

"More like third or fourth," Taylor admitted.

"Ah-ha. The lure of Hollywood rears its ugly head."

Frustration made Taylor's voice sharper than usual. "It's a case of finding out that my skin isn't as thick as I thought it was. You know how to be truly awful."

Jason feigned surprise. *"Moi?"*

"I thought I could stand it. I really thought I could. But I had no idea." Taylor shook her head. "You won't talk to me . . . unless it's about sex," she added witheringly.

"One of my favorite subjects," Jason agreed placidly.

"And you've made it more than plain that I'm not wanted here and that I couldn't help you even if I were."

Taylor inhaled deeply, her eyes serious. "Maybe I'll leave tomorrow," she said, surprising both herself and, apparently, Jason. His eyes widened, his nostrils flared briefly, the skin stretching across his cheekbones. Then a second later his face was a mask of control, and Taylor wondered if she'd imagined his reaction.

He lifted his shoulders indifferently, brushing past her into the living room. "That's what I've been telling you to do all along," he said sardonically. "At least you're finally listening."

Taylor remained stubbornly silent. She looked into his handsome, sensual face and refused to let the defeat she felt be revealed.

"You're sure you're not interested in a quick one-night affair, no strings attached?" Jason queried, the tiny lines incised by his mouth turning to quirks of humor. "We'd both enjoy it—well, at least I would—and you're so damn uptight that you could use some...uh... relaxation."

Taylor's gaze was cold. "You're not going to bait me tonight, Jason. Okay, I admit it. I made a mistake coming here. You didn't want me, and I was so certain I could help that I hung on anyway. Well, you can start counting your lucky stars; I'm leaving tomorrow."

She punctuated the end of their discussion by sitting down abruptly on the couch, reaching for her screenplay. To hell with him, she seethed inwardly. Let him stay up here all by himself. Let him rot. She didn't give a damn.

Deep inside, Taylor was very aware that she felt entirely different toward Jason, but it did her battered pride good to nurse her anger, and she spent several moments devising ways to cut him down a notch or two.

Jason's mockery vanished. He stared at her unblinkingly, until Taylor could feel his gaze ripping its way into her heart. Then, when her nerves seemed about to snap, he turned abruptly away, heaping wood on the fire with more energy than was really required. He muttered something she couldn't hear—and which, she was sure, she was lucky she couldn't hear—then rocked back on his heels and stared at the tiny flames that curled around the mossy fir, turning it briefly into a red inferno before the moss burned to ash.

Taylor held her screenplay clenched in her hands. She'd been looking at it unseeingly for a long time, feeling vaguely aware that something wasn't quite right, when she finally realized with a stinging shock what it was. The papers were stacked in perfect symmetry, the edges of the manuscript clean and defined. It hadn't been that way when she had left this morning; the pages she needed to rework she'd specifically pulled out a half inch for easy retrieval, leaving the edges uneven.

"You read my screenplay," she said in stunned disbelief.

The muscles in Jason's back bunched together. Taylor felt a wave of betrayal and anger wash over her, followed quickly by embarrassment. She hadn't told him not to read it and she'd left it in plain sight, yet the knowledge that he'd spent the afternoon over her story felt like a terrible invasion of privacy.

Jason glanced around and saw the tightness in her face. "Shouldn't I have?"

"No. You should have asked first!"

Taylor was dying inside, remembering certain phrases she'd written about Jake and Julie Diamond. In light of her new and strange relationship with Jason, she wondered what he would make of it.

"Sorry. You weren't around to consult. I was bored and restless and—"

"Why didn't you just spend the rest of the afternoon at the Tidewater?" Taylor cut in scathingly. "I thought that's where you were!"

Jason stood up slowly, running his palms down the sides of his thighs to dust off the dirt. When he looked at her, the sensuality in his expression started her heart beating unevenly.

But Taylor was too angry to respond to his allure. She'd put up with an awful lot this week, and she intended to give as good as she got. "If you're bored and restless, there's always Rita. I'm sure she'd be a lot more entertaining than my screenplay."

He glanced toward the pages tortured between her fingers. "Not necessarily," he said enigmatically.

"Really." Taylor was disbelieving as she tossed the screenplay onto the coffee table.

A log slid off the stack in the fireplace, sending a shower of sparks up the chimney, and Jason quickly shoved it back into place with his boot. Taylor glared at him mutinously for several moments and belatedly came to a conclusion she should have reached before.

"You lied to me about Rita, didn't you?"

Jason didn't answer.

"When I first saw you at the Tidewater," Taylor went on with growing conviction, "you told me you hadn't been with a woman in a long time, yet later you deliberately tried to make me think you were seeing her." His jaw grew tight, his stony expression making her realize she was right, and for some reason this last deception hurt worse than all the rest. "It was all a lie. Just another miserable trick to make me give up."

Jason sighed. "Actually, I'm amazed you believed it at all."

"You bastard," Taylor said tonelessly. "You really don't deserve the attention you get."

Jason's expression darkened but he nodded. "You're right."

"I should have kept on going when you threw me out the first time. Where were you all that night? I spent a lot of useless hours worrying about you."

Jason flexed his shoulders. He wasn't used to being dressed down, and he didn't like the feeling. But he liked Taylor's opinion of him even less, and he answered tersely, "I was driving."

"All night? I would have thought you'd have planted yourself at the Tidewater."

With a muttered imprecation, Jason demanded, "Hasn't it occurred to you yet that you've upset my routine?"

"I'm sorry," Taylor answered, her anger spilling into her voice.

His eyes regarded her with a kind of smoky soberness, and the air grew thick with charged emotions. "Do you know how hard it is to leave you here?" he grated suddenly. "To spend my afternoons anywhere else, knowing that you're waiting at the cabin? It's an image that haunts me, Taylor, and to be honest, I came back this afternoon with the intention of doing something about it—one way or another. But fortunately, all I found was your screenplay."

Taylor's throat constricted. She was suddenly sorry she'd forced this argument. "I don't know...what you mean."

"The hell you don't." Jason crossed the room in two swift strides, and stood directly in front of her, the coffee table the only barrier between her and his anger. "I've been trying to get rid of you, to be so blasted obnoxious and rude that you'd leave of your own accord. But it backfired, love." He laughed shortly. "Now that you finally want to leave, I don't want you to go."

Taylor blinked in astonishment.

"That's right. In a small way, you've won. The way you look, the way you are..." His gaze dropped over her, heavy-lidded. "It's done things to me. I don't think I can let you go now, Taylor Michaelson."

Taylor's lips parted but no words came. Her heart was thudding in her rib cage so heavily that she feared he could hear it. Was he serious? She had to believe he was!

"And this—" his arm swept down, indicating her screenplay "—this is incredibly good for the kind of story it is. You were right. You do understand Jake and Julie.''

Taylor's mouth went dry. She was certain she hadn't heard him correctly. Incredibly good? Had he really said that?

Jason's hands were at his hips, every muscle tense. ''So aren't you going to say *anything*?'' he demanded fiercely.

Taylor swallowed. ''I...uh...what?'' She could feel herself trembling. ''I don't know what to say. You've...stunned me.''

He considered her for long, glittering moments, his blue eyes boring into her in a way that made her insides quiver. She'd thought he couldn't surprise her anymore; but he'd just knocked her feet out from under her with a double blow, first admitting his desire for her, second praising her screenplay.

Taylor found another shock yet in store when he picked up the screenplay, his brows knitting in concentration, his voice saying quietly, ''There are a few places that need extra work, however. The first scene especially.''

Advice? Though Jason had always been willing to help her in the past, Taylor was dumbfounded that he would attempt to now. She was still reeling from the attack his first words had made on her senses, and now this....

A pulse was alive in his jaw, giving credence to the fact that she did affect him in some way. ''Would you like some ideas?'' he asked, watching her.

Taylor pulled herself together. ''Sure,'' she said thinly, then cleared her throat and tried again. ''Any and all advice would be appreciated, especially—'' she added with a return of humor ''—Jake Diamond's.''

Jason scowled. His thoughts were on some path of their own that she couldn't follow. "Jake's a better man than I am," he muttered.

"Jake's not a man at all, he's a character," she protested, surprised.

Jason's hand clenched. "Taylor..."

She'd been looking at the screenplay, her gaze focused on the result of her labors caught in the powerful grip of his hands, but now she glanced up again. His gaze was so intent that Taylor could do little more than stare right back, aware of delicious and potentially dangerous sensations alive within her, conscious of the tight-skinned strain on his face.

"I'm sorry," he said vaguely after the moment had stretched to eternity. His gaze hovered briefly on her lips; then it dropped to the screenplay.

Taylor felt as if she'd been through a war. Sorry for what? she wondered. Making her life miserable? Wounding her? Reading her screenplay? She didn't know what was happening between them, but apparently it wasn't one-sided. Jason wanted her—wanted *her*—and Taylor's emotions were running wildly in all directions. To realize she had such a profound effect on him was like taking a will-sapping drug. She felt pliable, weak, filled with yearnings, and if Jason chose that moment to push her, Taylor knew she would have no resistance.

Jason's blue eyes rose to hers. He saw the flush that had colored her smooth skin a rosy pink, the faint trembling of her lower lip, the beautiful anticipation that glimmered like molten gold in her eyes. The effect she had on him paralyzed him, and it was difficult to dredge up the reasons he couldn't touch her.

But then he remembered Lisabeth and sanity slowly returned. Getting involved with Taylor would only com-

plicate matters more than they already were, and with an
iron effort of will, he pushed his desire for her aside.

"Do you want to go over the first scene?" he asked in
a fairly normal voice.

The change in her was instantaneous and disastrous.
Embarrassment flooded through her, and a shaft of pain
that echoed in his own heart filled her eyes. She wrapped
her arms around herself, anger and resentment passing
across her face in quick succession.

Well, you finally did it, pal, Jason told himself. *She
won't forgive you this one.*

"Yes, let's," Taylor said woodenly, putting a visible
cloak of control over her emotions.

Jason felt regret way out of proportion to the situation. He wanted Taylor. He ached for her. But he was
frightened of what she could do to him. He'd learned a
hard lesson about women who were ice on top of a vol-
cano—Lisabeth had been that way, and Taylor was too.

Taylor's cool gaze caught his. "But I've decided to
leave in the morning anyway, Jason. I don't think I could
stand much more than another night here...."

Chapter Six

How revealing had her expression been? Taylor wondered while Jason shuffled through the pages of her screenplay. She felt positively sick inside that he'd seen so much of her feelings, then gone ahead and rejected her. She should be grateful, she reasoned, for that rejection, and maybe she would be later. But right now she was wounded and embarrassed and more than a little angry. Jason had fooled her into believing he found her irresistible, and she'd fallen hook, line and sinker for his silken trap. Then again, she thought with self-disgust, maybe she'd only fooled herself.

He was thumbing through the pages as if nothing had happened, but it wasn't as easy for Taylor to turn her emotions off as it apparently was for Jason. She knew she couldn't just shrug off her feelings and start working on her screenplay. She wasn't made that way.

"On second thought," she said, refusing to meet his intent gaze, "I think I'll take a rain check. We can go over it later."

She got up quickly, stepping around the coffee table, but Jason tossed down the screenplay, his hands clamping determinedly onto her arms.

"You have every right to be furious with me," he said tautly, and Taylor's pained eyes lifted at the tone of his voice, "and if you walk now, I can't blame you. But let's not confuse the issues. Your screenplay's good. But it could be great, and you're smart enough to know it."

Taylor didn't take offense at his presumption; she and Jason had traveled too far down this road already for her to treat his advice with anything less than gratitude. But she was currently in no frame of mind to continue. She called on her courage and said with some bitterness, "Somehow I didn't think we were talking only about the screenplay."

Jason laughed, a deep-throated sound that was so unusual it was like stumbling upon a rare and secret treasure. Taylor looked at him in surprise. She couldn't recall ever hearing him laugh like that before.

"I may have been wrong about you," he said, smiling. "You're one of a kind."

Taylor's gaze was fixed on his throat. "What's that supposed to mean?"

He shook his head, unwilling to go into all the reasons he'd had for comparing her—or any woman, for that matter—to his wife.

His hands were still on her arms, and he began to maneuver her backward until her legs hit the edge of the couch and she was forced to sit. "Look," he said, dropping down beside her, "I don't know what's going on, either. I'm not even sure I understand why you came here in the first place. But you've convinced me it wasn't because of this." He gestured toward the screenplay. "If it's because of something Clifton—" he paused and took a deep breath "—or Meredith, seeing as she's in charge, promised you, you're out of luck. I don't give a damn."

"I know." Taylor looked down at her hands. She couldn't help a little prick of conscience when he brought up Meredith's name. What would he do it he ever found out about Meredith's offer? How would she ever convince him it had nothing to do with being there?

"But if, as you keep trying to convince me, you're really here on some misguided mission of mercy, and if the timing on your screenplay is coincidental, then you're one in a million, Taylor."

Taylor's throat was dry. Put in those terms, she could well understand his skepticism over her motives; she didn't need to hear the thread of irony that underscored all his words. "A lot of ifs," she said tautly.

Jason nodded, watching her, as if his own mind weren't entirely made up about her. "Your screenplay's captured my interest, Taylor; I won't deny it. I didn't think anything could at this point, but you've shown me just how wrong I can be."

His low tones dropped to a huskiness that sent a shiver down her spine. But his eyes strayed to the carelessly tossed pages of her screenplay, and Taylor felt an insane jealousy that her work could spark so much interest when she apparently couldn't. She was horrified at her thoughts but was incapable of putting them in perspective.

"If it's possible," Jason said thoughtfully, "I'd like for us to start over."

Taylor got a grip on her emotions, darting him a sharp glance. She knew suddenly that he was regretting the sexual innuendos he'd been making for the past week, and perversely, now that he'd stopped his disruptive attack, Taylor was let down and annoyed. "Start over from where? When we first met? Or when I first came to Whidbey?"

Jason's brows drew together. "It would be pretty difficult to start over from when we first met, wouldn't it? We have a history together, after all."

Taylor thought of all the gossip that had surrounded Jason and her during the filming of the *Diamond Girl* trilogy. Yes, they had a history, all right, but the future loomed hazy and insecure.

"Okay," she said, "from when I first got to Whidbey, then. I guess this means you've decided to quit being an arrogant, insufferable boor."

Jason's lips parted in amazement. "Well, that was the idea, yes," he said dryly. "Unless you'd prefer me that way."

"No. But a little honesty might be nice."

"What do you mean?" Jason's eyes narrowed.

"I can't believe this sudden about-face over my screenplay!" Taylor answered. "You've told me in a thousand ways that you want to get rid of me. All of a sudden you don't. First you lead me to believe it's because you're attracted to me . . ." Taylor paused, gritting her teeth at the memory of that humiliation, "then you bring up my screenplay. It doesn't make sense, Jason. Why don't you say what you're really thinking?"

He was surprised but recovered with remarkable speed. "As you've apparently got it all worked out, I'll let you go first," he offered mockingly.

"I have no idea! I don't know what's going through your head. Maybe you've just got a guilty conscience after all the sexual harassment you've tossed my way.

You don't know how to make amends, so you've decided to praise my work. It doesn't matter, anyway; it's all an act."

After her impassioned speech, Taylor held her breath. She knew she hadn't come close to saying what she really meant.

"You know that's not true," he said tautly. "I would never give you false hope."

"Wouldn't you?" Her chin tilted in challenge and she met his glittering blue gaze.

"I've never lied to you about your talent," he said intensely. "I'm not going to start now."

Taylor pressed her lips together to keep them from trembling. What was wrong with her? She seemed determined to pick a fight with him!

"I'm sorry," she said with difficulty. "I don't know what I'm saying."

Jason just continued to stare at her, and Taylor focused once more on his throat, unwillingly aware of the tanned skin that showed above his shirt, the fine dusting of dark chest hair. For a count of ten heartbeats he didn't move, and Taylor wondered with increasing self-recriminations what he must be thinking of her.

To her consternation his fingers reached out and closed warmly around her chin, tilting her face to his. He looked at her long and hard. "I believe you're upset because I didn't follow through on making love to you," he said softly.

"Oh, Jason!" Taylor squirmed away and tried to get up, but his hands seized her shoulders, holding her down.

"It's true, isn't it?"

"This is crazy." She tried to avert her face, but she'd already seen the amusement lurking in his blue eyes and there was nowhere to hide. "I don't want to talk like this,'' she said stubbornly, and his low chuckle brought a wave of heat to her already inflamed face.

"Ah-ha. Easy for you to psychoanalyze me, but it's not as much fun when the shoe's on the other foot, is it?"

The lazy indulgence in his voice made her want to scream. "I'm beginning to wish I'd never come. There's nothing wrong with you but an overactive imagination," Taylor said tightly.

"Oh, love," he laughed. "You're so funny."

Taylor didn't have a chance to voice her indignation. Before she was quite prepared he'd leaned forward and kissed the slope of her jaw, his tongue probing gently.

"Don't think I don't want you, Taylor, because I do," Jason murmured huskily, "but I'd like to think I have enough sense to know when I'm heading for dangerous territory with a woman."

Goose bumps rose on her flesh as the string of moist kisses slid down her neck, making her pulse pound in her ears. "Dangerous territory?" she repeated, a trifle dazed.

"I like you, Taylor. I like working with you." The pressure of his hands on her shoulders grew more intense. "If I had my way I'd make love to you until dawn. But the last thing I'm interested in is a long-term affair. That's over for me. Do you understand?"

Oh, yes, she understood. There was a warning in his hungry words—one she knew she should heed. Lisabeth had been the one love of his life, and any interest he had in Taylor was purely physical and transitory. She'd suspected as much anyway; now he'd told her.

But even though she'd been forewarned, Taylor found it impossible to ignore the sensual signals flooding through her body. His lips were too knowing, his touch too seductive.

Jason pulled back and looked at her, his eyes dark with suppressed passion. His thumbs moved convulsively over the skin at her throat. "No more game playing, Taylor. I want to make love to you. Now. If you don't want to go on, this is the time to speak up."

Whatever demons had held him back before seemed to have completely disappeared. He laid out the situation implicitly. Nothing to hope for, nothing to gain; all he was offering was an affair that would undoubtedly tear her heart out.

She licked her lips. "I'm not sure."

"Be sure."

His hand moved to her cheek, his thumb probing the corner of her mouth. His concentration on that small movement left her weak. Then, before she could come up with something to say, his tongue touched where his thumb had been.

Rational thought disappeared beneath a tide of sensation. A soft moan escaped her lips, and Jason seemed to take that as a sign of acquiescence. His other hand slid around the back of her neck, tangling in the sun-streaked strands of her hair, and his mouth came down on hers possessively.

She was powerless to avoid the moist intrusion of his tongue, and she slid her hands willingly around his back, bunching the material of his shirt in her fists. The kiss went on and on, and Taylor's fleeting doubts were replaced by certainty as she became used to the new and disruptive way his tongue invited and tormented. Jake Diamond's kisses had never been so primitive, so hungry. She took in a shaking breath of air when he finally released her, but the reprieve lasted only an instant as his lips moved sensuously across the satin curve of her cheek, finding the tiny pulse beside her ear. Then the gentle penetration of his tongue brought a wave of weakness to her lower limbs, and Taylor felt as if she were melting inside.

"Jason . . ." she moaned.

He had unbuttoned her blouse and spread it apart with gentle fingers, revealing the sheer, silken bra that narrowly covered the curve of her breasts. Taylor watched numbly as he unfastened the front clasp, spilling the milky-white fullness of her breasts into his hand.

"Oh, Taylor," he whispered, then he bent his head, putting his hot, moist mouth against the trembling peak of her nipple.

It was impossible to say no. She recognized the fact dimly and accepted his lovemaking with a fatalistic excitement, her own hands working the buttons of his shirt, pulling it down over the taut muscles of his shoulders. She kissed the bare flesh she'd exposed and felt the tremor that ran beneath his skin.

His hands cupped the rounded curve of her hips; his fingers trailed against the skin of her waist, finding the snap of her jeans. Determination was stamped across his features, as was a dark hunger that sent a wave of heat through Taylor's veins. Her lashes fluttered closed, and her head fell back against the couch as his fingers insinuated their way inside her jeans, sliding the material down her hips until she felt the cool air against her bare flesh.

She was letting him do to her things she'd only dreamed of. In a daze, she considered what it was all going to mean in the end. She was quite aware that Jason's attitude had changed; if she wanted to halt this sensual invasion, it was going to be entirely up to her. Yet she was engulfed by a curious lassitude that made the effort to move too great, and instead of drawing back, she opened her mouth to his, her tongue darting between his lips provocatively, a low moan issuing from Jason's throat as he met the sexuality of her response.

His hand had dropped to her knee and was now moving along her inner thigh, starting a trembling within her that Taylor was powerless to control. He looked up once, his intent gaze taking in her slumberous, heavy-lidded amber eyes. Then he began dropping feather-light kisses on her skin, beginning at her throat and the silken curve of her shoulder, moving ever downward, each kiss delivered more slowly and lasting just a hairbreadth longer than the last, the creamy texture of her skin rose-tinged as heat swelled within her.

They had seen a lot of each other's bodies; in their love scenes together they'd worn the barest minimum of clothes. Even so, when Taylor found herself completely undressed, with Jason's head bent to her skin in intimate familiarity, she felt a raw disbelief in what was happening. She watched in fascination as he swiftly removed the rest of his clothing and draped the lean, virile length of his body against hers.

"Don't look like that," Jason muttered tautly, the warmth of his chest pressing against her bare breasts as he propelled her downward, the ribbed texture of the couch meeting the heated flesh of her back.

"Like what?" she whispered, totally conscious of the feel of him where their bodies touched. It was all so new and unbelievable that she found herself trembling against him.

"Like you've suddenly woken from a bad dream," Jason murmured, his lips tugging on the lobe of her ear.

"No...I...that's not it."

His hips were moving against hers sinuously, calling for a response that she found herself giving instinctively.

She'd never been fully naked in a man's arms before, and she was torn between embarrassment and desire. It would help, she realized ruefully, if she could count on Jason's feelings being as deep as her own, but since that wasn't the case, Taylor knew she would have to either accept the situation for what it was, or change things right now.

His mouth was everywhere, now moving in a determined, harrowing line from her neck to her abdomen that left Taylor in a vague panic. "I can't..." she choked, but the movement of her own body made her unwillingly aware that she very well could.

"Shhh," he whispered, bringing his mouth back to hers, and Taylor responded eagerly to his kiss, half-relieved that his sensual foray down her skin had ended.

But it hadn't. His hands touched her softly and possessively, finding secret areas of herself that were ready and anxious for him. The hair on his chest was a soft, sensual abrasion against her breasts, and she was acutely aware of the hands that slid beneath the satin mound of her hips. She felt the hard length of him against her softer flesh and knew with a flash of insight that she was on the brink of an experience like no other.

"I'm not . . . I've never . . ." Taylor gasped at the sensual probe of him against her.

For several seconds Taylor was certain he hadn't heard her, the tide of passion pushing them closer to the edge. She tensed involuntarily, but her legs parted of their own accord, her arms wrapped possessively around his back. She wanted him. Now. No matter what the future brought. She was sorry for the blundering of her own naiveté, but she hoped that Jason would accept the gift of her inexperience and be pleased.

She scarcely realized that he'd stopped moving. Her own flesh was still trembling, her limbs restless beneath him. But Jason had an iron grip on his control. He lifted his head from her breast and stared at her through passion-glazed eyes.

"What do you mean, you've never?" he asked unsteadily.

Taylor's lips quivered. She knew what an anachronism she was: the Hollywood virgin. "I've never been with a man," she managed tremulously.

"Oh, God!" Jason was incredulous. "I don't believe you."

"Well, it's true. I've just never had the time or... inclination."

His brows drew together and he stared at her, searching her eyes for the lie he expected to be there. Slowly the beginnings of belief showed in his eyes—and also, Taylor noted with regret, the beginnings of understanding about what this union might mean to her.

"Why me?" he asked hoarsely, and the look of dismay that crossed his features made it clear to Taylor that he'd hit on the right conclusion.

It was a stunning revelation for her as well. She'd met Jason when she was nineteen, and until that point her only experience with men—boys really—had been childish experiments that Taylor had found slightly distasteful. And then after Jason... well, she'd never even tried to meet another man. She'd known him for seven years, five of which he'd been married, yet she'd never once thought romantically about anyone else. She realized, with a dash of cold insight, that she'd been in love with him for a very long time.

Her pride wouldn't let her admit to loving him, however. She'd already left emotions bare and bleeding, and she couldn't give him the opportunity to wound her even more. "Maybe the time's just right," she said with forced lightness.

He groaned. "For whom?"

"Us. Please don't make too much of this, Jason," Taylor said a bit desperately. "Since I've been here the tension between us has been growing and growing. It's a natural end."

"My God." Jason rolled away from her as the whole truth sank in, but Taylor scrambled to her knees, intent on not letting him get away without understanding.

"I didn't expect this to happen, but now that it has, I'm not sorry."

"Are you crazy?" Jason made a sound of utter disbelief. "A *virgin*? I have no idea in hell what to do with a virgin. I can't...this isn't..." He inhaled sharply. "Tell me, Taylor, have you ever thought about the consequences?"

He was being deliberately cruel, but Taylor supposed the shock was natural. She tried to ignore the humiliation she felt as she pressed on, her eyes eloquent. "Would it be better if there'd been someone else first?"

"Yes."

He looked at her in frustration, then dragged his gaze away from the sight of creamy skin with its faint tan lines, tempting curves and dusky hollows.

"I can't believe I'm having this conversation." Jason reached for his jeans, shaking his head as if he didn't know whether to laugh or give her a piece of his mind.

"Don't you want to make love to me?" Taylor asked with trembling lips.

"No."

Taylor hunched her shoulders and tried to remind herself that he was intentionally trying to hurt her. Jason gave her a sidelong glance, seeing the wide unhappiness and uncertainty in her gold yes. "Yes," he amended heavily, "I do. But damn it, Taylor..."

He couldn't finish, but some of Taylor's confidence returned. "Please, Jason," she murmured, moving to cup his face between her palms.

He closed his eyes and sucked in a long breath. "I'm not Jake Diamond," he said tensely.

Taylor touched her mouth to his. "Don't you think I know that? Who better? My feelings are a lot more complicated than that."

His lids opened, the thick lashes revealing serious eyes that still simmered with a dark hunger. "How complicated?"

"Too complicated to go into right now."

"Taylor, I—"

"Jason," she interrupted firmly. "I'm a big girl. I came here because I wanted to help you. Maybe you can help me too. But let's not psychoanalyze ourselves to death." She smiled. "Phil Walker can do that for us."

To forestall any further arguments, she pressed her mouth to his, rimming his lips with the pink tip of her tongue. He stayed rock still while she explored his chest with her fingers, letting her hands slide through the silkiness of his hair, running the pad of her fingertips over the nub of his nipple.

He managed to withstand her sensual invasion for an incredibly long time, Taylor thought, the only proof of his emotional state the tense coiling of muscles beneath her hands and the rapid beating of his heart. But if he could be determined, so could she, and she worked with sensual touches and impassioned kisses to break through his wall of resistance.

With a groan he pushed her onto her back, and this time Taylor wrapped herself around him in an instinctive and totally possessive way.

"This is crazy," he muttered, but his hands moved almost convulsively down her milk-white curves.

"I know. Don't stop now..."

His breath came in sharply. "I don't think I could."

His knee parted her legs and any last-minute doubts had no time to take root as Jason moved over her, covering her softness with the hard power of his own frame. His hands cradled her thighs, his mouth fused to hers, as he took her in one powerful thrust that caused a sharp cry to escape her own lips.

"Taylor..." He sounded totally unsure and regretful.

"It's all right," she reassured softly, instinctively relaxing. "Love me, Jason. Just love me."

The motion, once begun, couldn't be halted anyway. Taylor was introduced to the world of searing sensuality by the man she loved, her body moving instinctively to the rhythm of desire, feeling a strange and beautiful awareness grow within her that had her reaching toward some indistinct fulfillment.

"I can't—" Jason began.

She didn't want to hear him say he couldn't. She closed her ears and held him tighter. Then everything happened at once. An explosion of pure sensation swept through her, a pulsating tide that made her grip Jason wantonly, wringing a cry of pleasure from her that nearly masked the hoarse groan that followed from his throat. She was still shuddering with a new kind of ecstasy when she realized that the tremors weren't all her own. Jason buried his face between her breasts and pushed within her, passion flooding into a climax that had them both straining for breath.

They lay quiet for long moments afterward, and Taylor let her hand move possessively, tenderly, through the thick hair at the back of his head.

Jason raised his head to look into her eyes, his own glazed with satisfaction. There was humor around his lips and Taylor saw with relief that the last thing they would speak of was regret.

Taylor stretched the aching muscles of her shoulders and tried to think positively about what she had to do. Her fingers were still curled tightly around the steering wheel of her rented Toyota, even though she'd shut off the engine a good ten minutes earlier.

The telephone booth was across the street, and even the slanting afternoon sun couldn't make its dirt-smeared glass walls any more appealing. A brisk wind flattened a newspaper against the phone booth door, pages ruffling wildly. Taylor grimaced and pushed her door open. There was nothing to do but get the telephone call over with.

Puddles from the recent flurry of rain showers stood in the mud and gravel beside the cracked pavement. Taylor stepped gingerly around them, strengthening her resolve. All she had to do was tell Ross her screenplay wasn't as close to being done as she'd originally anticipated, and that she wasn't sure when she would be returning to Los Angeles.

She pulled her jacket collar close around her nape and reflected that the bright, sunny weather was deceptive. The temperature had reached freezing the night before, and the wind of the sound chilled to the bone. If it hadn't been for Jason's vigilance in keeping the fire continually stoked, Taylor was certain she would have frozen to death.

And she'd learned she couldn't rely on Jason to keep her warm by other means, she thought wretchedly. For the past three nights she'd slept alone. After loving him so passionately, she'd just naturally assumed they would spend the night together, but Jason had extricated himself from her embrace with heart-wrenching speed.

"I have to think, Taylor," he'd said to the wounded look on her face.

His sudden soberness had been a depressing blow after the ecstasy of loving him. "Just don't tell me it shouldn't have happened," she'd pleaded hoarsely. "That's something I couldn't bear right now, okay?"

He'd looked pained, running a hand around the back of his neck, reaching for his clothes. "Oh, love." He'd sighed. "I don't know what to tell you."

She hadn't said "You could tell me you love me," but the words had unashamedly crossed her mind, and her face had spoken eloquently of her feelings. Jason had smiled faintly, brushing a finger down the slope of her cheek. "Don't look at me like that. I feel like enough of a heel already."

"Why?" Taylor pushed back the tumbled curtain of her hair and regarded him somberly.

He merely raised his brows, and Taylor bit into her bottom lip. Just because she hadn't actually told him she loved him didn't mean he didn't know. Jason was too perceptive by far, and he'd known her as long and as well as she'd known him. They weren't strangers by any means. They understood and read each other's emotions accurately, and Taylor knew Jason's were far different from her own.

"I'm not the person you seem to think I am," Jason said impatiently, thrusting his long legs into his jeans.

"Oh, Jason..." Taylor stood up and stared at him through frustrated eyes.

"No, Taylor." He turned his back on her allure. "This craziness has got to end. I need some time to think things through."

"For the past week you've talked of nothing but making love to me," Taylor pointed out with tremulous courage, slipping her arms through the sleeves of her blouse. "Now you act as if it were all a bad joke. Did I do something wrong?"

Jason wheeled around swiftly, but one look at her innocent expression and his eyes narrowed. "You're a better actress than even *I* thought," he muttered savagely, but she saw the hint of a smile at the corner of his lips.

"Stop treating me like I don't have a mind of my own, Jason."

"We both have minds of our own. And mine's made up about one thing." He snatched up his shirt and straightened. "We can't get involved any further. I know that's a little like shutting the barn door after the horse is out, but believe me, Taylor, there are...reasons."

The grim tightening of his mouth reminded her of all the problems that still assailed Jason—ones he wouldn't let her help him with.

"I won't ask you what they are," she said softly, buttoning her blouse.

He looked at her with dark, sober eyes. "You won't have to. If I want you to know, I'll tell you."

"That almost sounds like you intend to sometime."

His eyes shifted from hers to some distant point behind her. "Maybe," he answered, his jaw tightening. Then, with a depressing return to the scenario that had plagued Taylor all week, Jason had gone into his bedroom and shut the door with a firm click. She'd had no recourse but to go to hers.

But the events of that night had made it impossible for Taylor just to pack up and leave as she'd intended. In the morning, she told him she'd changed her mind and wished to stay on indefinitely. It had taken a lot of courage, risking a flat-out rejection on his part, but though his brows had drawn together in consternation, he'd made no verbal objection. She was left uncertain how he felt about her, and she'd spent the past three days worrying herself sick about what he must be thinking.

The only evidence that Jason was giving any serious thought to their evening of lovemaking was the way he'd begun to treat her. He was polite to the point of formality, careful to the edge of lunacy, and he made a point not to come anywhere near her in case they might accidentally touch each other. Their conversation, too, had become strained and cautious, centering mainly on her screenplay and what changes they both thought were necessary. Taylor had wanted to scream with frustration, but every once in a while she'd felt Jason's eyes upon her, dark and brooding, and she'd held her tongue, realizing that this was something he had to work out for himself.

As a result, she'd been forced to push thoughts of Jason aside and concentrate on her screenplay, and it had become increasingly clear to her that the few minor changes she'd thought were necessary were really major scene revisions. Jason's ideas, always good, so closely paralleled her own that Taylor had embraced them with enthusiasm. She'd been scribbling notes in the margins and on the backs of the pages, longing for the small home computer she'd left at her apartment.

Then today, after Jason had gone out without more than a curt goodbye, leaving her to slave over the latest changes, Taylor had felt herself wilt from fatigue and depression. To clear her mind, she'd gone for a brisk walk; then, returning to the cabin to find Jason still not home, Taylor had driven into Coupeville, thinking now was as good a time as any to confront Ross.

"Ross Corley Associates," the secretary's cool voice came on the line.

"Hello, it's Taylor Michaelson. I'd like to speak to Ross, please."

"Hold the line."

Taylor leaned her head against the wall. She should be grateful, she supposed, that she'd made as much progress with Jason as she had. The drinking had stopped almost entirely. Whatever else she'd given him, at least she'd offered a pleasant diversion from his dark and dreary thoughts, she reminded herself with irony. And wasn't that why she'd made this trip in the first place?

"Taylor! For God's sake, I've been wondering how in heaven's name to get hold of you.

"There's always the mail," Taylor returned facetiously, thinking with a lift of spirits that at least Ross was always the same.

"I don't have time for mail, hon," Ross said excitedly. "I've been talking to Meredith Maddox about your screenplay. Now get this—she's ready to buy it sight unseen. I told you it was a winner!"

Taylor was stunned. "No, Ross! I can't."

"I think she really wants to have Garrett for the lead, but she's ready to jump in feet first without him. We'll add a contingency that Julie Diamond's got to be played by you—"

"Ross!" Taylor interjected desperately.

"And that you've also got a say in who plays the male lead. I tell you, the woman's so hot for it she won't raise a squeak. The publicity on this thing is—"

"Ross!"

"Going crazy! It doesn't matter what you've written now, darling, it's—"

"Ross, will you shut up and *listen*!"

The silence on the other end accused her. "Well, certainly, Taylor," he said in an offended tone.

"Those few changes I thought I had to make turned into major revisions. I can't get it done when I promised! And I'm not sure I even want to send it to Maddox Productions."

A heavy pause followed. "I don't believe you just said that."

"Ross, please," Taylor said with nervous entreaty. "Jason's helping me on the script and it's a lot better, but it's still got a long way to go. Even he seems to think it has potential, and believe me, coming from him, especially in the state of mind he's in, that's quite a compliment. I can't quit now. It's too important to me."

"Garrett's actually working on the screenplay?" Ross asked incredulously.

"He's offering me advice," Taylor hastened to explain. She smiled wryly. "You know, like always."

"I'm sure this will only make Meredith more anxious to get her hands on it, Taylor."

"I can't make that commitment yet, Ross."

"What commitment? What? We're talking about *your* screenplay, Taylor! *Yours*. Do you know what an opportunity this is for you? Don't throw it away, kid."

As upset as Taylor was, she had to admit that Ross had a point. Why was she being so negative about Meredith Maddox? The woman had shown extraordinary faith in her, yet it made her uneasy to think of giving her the rights to *Diamond in the Sky*.

"Tell her . . . I'll think about it," Taylor said.

"Oh, Taylor." Ross sighed. "How about if I tell her you'll send it directly to her when it's done?"

Taylor bit into her bottom lip and thought rapidly. Where was the harm in that? She was bound to send it to Maddox Productions first anyway—after all, they'd given her her first chance.

"Okay," she agreed reluctantly, "but tell her I don't know when I'll be finished."

"Done," Ross said with relief. "And keep working on Garrett—or has he already decided to do the lead?"

"Hardly." Taylor's tone was dry.

"How are you two getting along, anyway? Has he gotten any more tolerant?"

Ross's inquiry reminded Taylor of the uneasy situation between herself and Jason. "No, he hasn't," she said succinctly.

"Have you called Phil Walker?"

"I tried, Ross, but he wasn't in. Do me a favor, why don't you call him and tell him Jason's alive and well . . . and better," she added as an afterthought.

"Better?" Ross sounded encouraged.

"He's not exactly ready to catch the first flight back to Hollywood, but I don't think Phil should worry about his emotional state too much. Tell him . . . Jason's on his way back from the depths."

Taylor hung up when Ross started asking questions that came too close to the heart of things. She didn't want Jason's friends worrying about him, but neither did she want to reveal her own feelings for him, nor betray any confidences either. She felt like a traitor as it was, sneaking off behind his back to make surreptitious phone calls, reporting on his condition to the people he continually derided. With a fatalistic sigh she pushed open the door to the phone booth and walked back to her car, glad to see no familiar, mud-spattered Jeep standing outside the doors of the Tidewater.

Where was Jason? she wondered. Where had he gone so early this morning? His secretiveness could be a product of her overactive imagination, but Taylor felt there was more to it. She had the uneasy feeling he was up to something, and given the uncertain state of their relationship, she feared it might in some way involve her.

Still feeling restless, Taylor couldn't work up any enthusiasm for going back to the cabin. She spent several hours wandering through some of Coupeville's shops, then drove to Maxine's, luckily finding her at home. She was baking an apple pie, and the pungent smell of cinnamon greeted Taylor as Maxine ushered her inside.

It was obvious to Taylor that Maxine was preparing a special meal, and when the older woman admitted that she was having friends over that evening, Taylor quickly apologized and tried to leave. But Maxine was nothing if she wasn't persuasive; she insisted Taylor sit down and talk to her while she baked.

It was after five before Maxine would hear of her leaving. Taylor drove back to the cabin, a plump apple pie oozing cinnamon and butter balanced on the passenger seat. Taylor thought about how well fed she'd been these past ten days and realized she'd have to go on a diet when she returned to Los Angeles.

Los Angeles. Taylor heaved a deep sigh. She had come to love Whidbey Island, truly enjoying the slower pace. It was going to be difficult to readjust. And if it meant returning home without Jason, it was going to be doubly so.

His Jeep was parked beneath the canopy of fir boughs when Taylor arrived back at the cabin. She carefully gathered up the still-warm pie and walked to the door. Taylor repressed the urge to ring the bell, knowing it was ludicrous after all this time yet unable to shake off the feeling of being an intruder.

"Jason?" she called softly as she let herself inside.

The sight that met her eyes amazed her. The rocker had been removed from the corner of the room, and in its place stood a teak computer table equipped with the same brand of computer she owned in Los Angeles, a high-speed printer and a padded desk chair upholstered in steel blue. Jason was in back of the table, apparently examining the hookup between computer and printer, a manual spread on the floor in front of his knees.

He looked up at Taylor's sharp gasp of surprise and regarded her blandly. "How was Maxine?" he asked, seeing the pie.

Taylor couldn't believe what she was seeing. She knew without asking that he'd bought the equipment for her. "Why did you do this?" she asked, setting the pie on the counter.

"What?"

"This." Taylor gestured to the equipment and empty boxes that littered the floor.

"Oh this." His mouth quirked. "I was tired of hearing you complain about how much you missed your computer."

Taylor shook her head. She realized now why he'd left so early that morning; he had to drive all the way to Seattle to get this equipment.

She stepped around the boxes, moving closer, unable to believe Jason had done this. "But that was just talk," she protested. "Something to say since it's become so difficult . . . to talk to you."

Jason gave her an enigmatic look. "I thought this might make the writing faster," he said easily.

"I . . . I need my disks. And my software." Taylor's heart was pounding. She was overwhelmed by Jason's gesture, realizing now just how much he wanted her to stay. And here she'd thought he was planning new ways to get rid of her! She couldn't believe it.

"I bought your software. Couldn't you just redo the pages that need to be worked on and add them to your disks later?"

Taylor remembered how many questions Jason had asked about her writing—not only the content of the story, but all kinds of technical questions as well. Now she knew why. She was invaded by a curious warmth at this show of concern.

"I suppose I could," she murmured thoughtfully. "Although some of it will have to be typed over." She watched Jason work for long moments. "You didn't have to do this, you know."

"It isn't out of guilt, if that's what you think," Jason replied, examining the back of the printer critically, then straightening, easing himself to the front. "I have a vested interest in you."

"You do?" Taylor looked at him through puzzled eyes.

Jason leaned over the buttons on the face of the printer. "Maybe you should check this out," he suggested. "You probably know lots more about it than I do."

Taylor, who had spent many hours learning all the ins and outs of her equipment, set the printer up for a test and found it worked perfectly. Seated in the cushioned chair, she unwrapped the software, turned on the computer and brought the program up onto the screen.

"Perfect," she proclaimed. "Maybe you've missed your calling."

Jason smiled, his teeth very white in his tanned face. "Think I should give up acting for the computer field?"

Taylor turned off the computer and swiveled to face him. "Seems like you've already given up acting."

"Does it?" Her jab didn't seem to get under his skin as it might have another time.

"What are you saying, Jason?"

He shook his head. "Let's go for a walk and . . . talk."

Everything she'd been striving for seemed to echo in those few words. She glanced at him anxiously, wondering if she could be reading too much into what he'd said. But Jason, actor that he was, wasn't letting his expression give anything away; still maintaining that enigmatic silence, he held the door for her.

Taylor, sensing her future had somehow been decided, had no choice but to precede him through.

Chapter Seven

They walked south along the curve of the sound, the tang of salt air heavy in the brisk breeze. Taylor kept pulling strands of wind-whipped hair away from her face, belatedly conscious of how the breeze then flattened them against Jason's shoulder and cheek, sometimes sliding across his lips. She moved away a bit to avoid the problem, but his hand closed over her upper arm and pulled her back.

"The trail gets narrower here," he explained as Taylor glanced at him, her heart beating at a ridiculously erratic tempo.

The surface of the sound was ruffled by the wind, lights from across the bay making uncertain patterns on the black water. In the evening dimness Taylor noticed the row of yellow buoys she'd seen in the daylight, and when she commented on them Jason remarked, "They're commercial mussel beds. The better restaurants on Whidbey serve mussels fresh daily."

"I'd like to try some sometime," Taylor murmured, intrigued. She was growing more and more at home here, she realized, and being with Jason was a big part of that familiarity.

She couldn't read his expression, but his voice was inviting when he suggested, "Why not later tonight? We can go to the Captain Whidbey and see if they can squeeze us in. The food's great but the dining room's small, and so it's full most of the time." Compared to the armed camp she'd been living in for the past ten days, this friendly attitude was an unexpected about-face and Taylor had trouble readjusting.

They came to the small bench that Taylor had run across on her earlier walk along the sound, and now she stopped. "I don't know how to take this," she said, her gaze casting across the restless waters. "Why are you being so nice to me?"

"God only knows," he said, but there was a smile in his voice.

"I'm serious, Jason. It's nearly impossible for me to keep up with your moods. I thought today when you left so early—"

"What?" he asked, when she cut herself off.

Taylor squared her shoulders. "I thought you were planning new ways to get rid of me."

They were standing in front of the bench, and Jason, his hand still on her arm, eased her down with gentle pressure. He sat next to her, close enough that his thigh and hip touched hers, his arm draping over her shoulders with deceptive casualness.

"Didn't I say I couldn't let you go?" he reminded her gently. As if to punctuate his meaning, Taylor felt his fingers tangle in the hair at her nape. A shiver climbed up her spine and she tried desperately to keep some perspective.

She swallowed. "You also said you had some thinking to do. I was afraid you'd . . . changed your mind."

He buried his face against her neck, and his skin felt cool against her overheated flesh. "Oh, Taylor . . ." he said with a heavy sigh. "You should never have stayed here."

She closed her eyes and whispered, "Why not?"

"Because you're giving so much and getting nothing in return," he muttered hoarsely.

Taylor wanted to deny what she knew to be patently untrue, but Jason gave up talking for kissing, plundering her mouth with hungry urgency. A shudder passed through her, her lips opening eagerly under his, her hands reaching for him. She felt all the pent-up passion in his kiss, and she responded with unrepressed joy. He wasn't as indifferent as she'd believed. His feelings weren't so easily turned off and on. Taylor's spirits soared as Jason groaned low in his throat, and she laid her hand against his cheek, glad she hadn't been the only one in torment, jubilant that their lovemaking had left him, too, only aching for more.

Eventually, with an effort of will, Jason eased back slightly though his arms were still locked possessively around her. "I've been terrible to you," he said roughly. "In every way. I've tried to be, and I don't even have a damn reason."

Taylor smiled, enjoying the feeling of just being held close. "I descended on you uninvited," she forgave him.

"Not good enough." Jason shook his head, and Taylor, responding to an urge that had possessed her since she'd arrived, ran her hands through the silky thickness of his hair.

"Good enough for me."

"Taylor..."

"Shhh. Don't spoil the moment. I just want to be cuddled."

It was all she'd ever really wanted, she realized, as Jason's arms tightened around her: to have someone hold her, keep her warm, enjoy her for the person she was. She snuggled against his chest and heard the hard beat of his heart, smelled his clean, male scent, felt the rise and fall of his deep breathing. His chin was against her crown, and her scalp tingled where his breath stirred the burnished strands of hair. She had never felt such overflowing love for another human being, and she wished she could stay this way forever, part of him, her soul fused to his.

The night air was cold and chilling, dampness crept up from the wooden slats of the bench, but Taylor didn't want to move. She could abide the small discomfort in the greater joy of his enduring embrace.

"You ask for so little," he murmured musingly, his fingers methodically sliding, then sliding again, through her long, sun-streaked tresses. He kissed the top of her head and added in a more distant tone, "My wife was a totally different kind of person."

Taylor's brain marked time, too disbelieving to accept what she had actually heard. Jason had never brought up Lisabeth voluntarily! Her pulse leaped at the prospect of what this could mean. Her eyes opened, all senses suddenly on alert, waiting with such intensity that she was certain he could feel it.

But when minutes went by and he didn't continue, she reminded him quietly, "You said you wanted to talk."

"Mmm. Yes." His reluctance was plain.

"About . . . Lisabeth?"

Jason's arms tightened briefly. "No, I was really more interested in discussing us, but maybe one follows the other." He sighed. "Do you remember, on Madeira, when you came to my hotel room and asked for help?"

Taylor nodded her head against his warm cotton shirt. She was holding her breath, sensing she was about to learn something important about the past, half-afraid she didn't want to know now that her emotions were so irrevocably involved.

"Clifton and I were having a fight," Jason went on. "I imagine that was pretty obvious. You showed up in the middle of it."

"I remember." The scene was indelibly printed on her mind.

"He was furious at me because I'd told him I was quitting Hollywood. I think I told you the same thing later."

Taylor nodded again. She sensed how difficult the words were becoming for him; she could feel his heartbeat quicken. But he seemed determined to go on, and realizing he was doing it for her, as a recompense for what she'd given him, made Taylor mute with gratitude.

"I never told Clifton why, though I'm sure he guessed my motives. Lisabeth was the reason I moved the family to Whidbey." Taylor felt him inhale a slow breath. "Lisabeth, herself, was dead set against the move, and we had one of our worst fights ever over my decision. I told her she didn't have to go, but I was taking Kerri. In the end motherhood won over martyrdom, but just barely."

Bitterness seeped into his voice—bitterness Taylor was certain he was unaware of. He hesitated for so long she was afraid he was going to stop, but in a colder voice, he said, "Lisabeth had taken up with a fast crowd those last few months. Right before we left for Madeira I accidentally found a packet of cocaine in her purse."

Taylor closed her eyes. For the first time she got a glimpse into his nightmare.

"Things went from bad to worse very fast. We fought horribly. Then I came home several times to find Kerri alone in the house." At Taylor's gasp, he said, "She was asleep both times, and when Lisabeth returned she tried to assure me that she'd just run out to get something. I was furious and scared. I told her you don't leave a two-year-old alone—*ever*—but she resented my interference. I hired a governess, who Lisabeth promptly fired, and it got to be such a problem that I couldn't go to work without being sick with worry. As far as I could see Lisabeth had lost all sense of responsibility.

"About this time," Jason said grimly, "I tried to back out of *Queen of Diamonds*, but my leaving would have cost Maddox Productions millions of dollars. I sent Kerri to stay with Phil Walker's family while I was gone, and Lisabeth, for once, didn't object. It should have been a red flag, I suppose, but I couldn't back out of my commitments."

Jason shifted his weight, his recollections making him acutely uncomfortable. Taylor had never heard him say so much about his past; remembering his state of mind when she'd arrived on Whidbey, she worried that bringing it all up again might have adverse effects. But she was mesmerized by his revelations and too curious to try to make him stop—something she wasn't certain she could do now anyway.

"I called Lisabeth every night, but she was rarely home. When she was, she wasn't alone. I could hear other people's voices. And Lisabeth was high on more than one occasion, but not from alcohol." There was an ominous tone in his words. "I'd confided Lisabeth's problems to Meredith and she suggested I blame Lisabeth's so-called illness on drinking. I knew better by then; so did Meredith."

It crossed Taylor's mind that Jason's own drinking seemed odd considering what had happened to his wife. He clearly hadn't forgotten the agony of her drug abuse, and though it was the only conclusion, Taylor found it hard to believe that the accident had forced him down a similar path. Unless, she realized with a shiver of unease, Jason was somehow blaming himself.

"Anyway, as soon as I got back from Madeira I moved from Hollywood to here. End of story."

Not quite, Taylor thought, but as Jason's tone didn't invite further discussion, she didn't bring up the accident or ask about the events leading to it. It was enough that he'd confided as much as he had, and she could sense the emotional tremors running beneath his calm facade. She knew the deaths of Kerri and Lisabeth were preying heavily on his mind.

Taylor stirred. "You said once that you hadn't spent the past two years grieving. That's not true."

Jason inhaled sharply. "I don't think *grieving* is exactly the right term. You know as well as I do that I've been trying to self-destruct."

"Because of losing them?"

He shifted, and suddenly she was being held at arm's length. But his tense expression was also full of longing, and as her heart trip-hammered painfully, his hands came up to caress the sculptured planes of her cheeks. "I thought I could never look at another woman again," he said with emotion, "but I was wrong. Ah, Taylor... your therapy is unorthodox but it works."

She smiled tremulously. "Does this mean our relationship has changed?"

His thumb found her mouth, tracing her lower lip. "It's been changed since the night we made love," he admitted, his thumb continuing its sensual foray. "Good Lord, Taylor, you don't know what it's been like!"

She waited breathlessly. "Tell me."

Jason laughed seductively. "You've been complaining about your damn screenplay right and left, about how you need your computer. I've been living in a state of fear that you intended just packing up and leaving after all. I had to think of a way to chain you down."

Taylor blinked. "Is that why you bought the computer?"

"Would anything else have been as effective?"

"Why didn't you just tell me?" she asked softly. "Oh, Jason, I wouldn't have left."

"Why?" he asked hoarsely. "Why wouldn't you have?"

Taylor looked down at her hands. It hurt to be so honest. "Isn't it obvious?"

He tilted her chin up to face him, scrutinizing the planes of her face. "I've learned not to trust the obvious. God, Taylor, I wish things were . . . different."

His last words were spoken against her lips, his warm breath filling her mouth with suffocating intimacy. She understood the meaning behind his words only too clearly: he didn't feel the same way about her as she felt about him; he didn't love her. His feelings for Lisabeth hadn't died with her, and though it hurt, Taylor forced herself never to forget that undeniable truth.

A blast of wind howled in from the sound, chilling Taylor to the bone. She couldn't help the way she shivered as she clung to him, and he was finally forced to let her go.

"Damn wind," he muttered, pushing back unruly locks from his forehead, his face split by a rakish grin.

"Maybe we should go back," Taylor suggested, and the gleam that came into his eye made her pulse pound. There would be no more putting their desire for each other on hold.

"After you," Jason said, helping her to her feet. "And I haven't forgotten my promise of dinner, either...at least not completely."

Taylor tucked the hem of her magenta blouse into her black wool skirt, then reached into the closet for her matching black sweater vest. It was warm in the cabin, so she slung the vest over her arm, glancing in the tiny mirror over her dresser for a last-minute check on her appearance.

Her face was still flushed from the cold wind, and her excitement turned her eyes to amber jewels. She wrinkled her nose at the idiocy of her feelings and vainly tried to bring some order to her hair by raking her fingers through it. With a sound of exasperation she tossed the sweater vest on the bed, searched through her purse for her brush and comb, then brushed through the golden strands until they crackled.

She leaned forward and stared at herself, unused to the way she looked. The billowing sleeves of the blouse added a soft femininity she didn't normally connect with herself, and she shook her head at the foolhardy way loving Jason was making her feel!

By the time they had made it back to the cabin it was already half past seven, and by mutual consent—and regret, she thought with a smile—they'd decided to go directly to dinner. Since the Captain Whidbey's reputation as a fine restaurant precluded jeans, Taylor had had to search through her closet for something appropriate to wear. She was lucky she'd had the foresight to pack one nice outfit, and was even luckier it had survived her careless packing when Jason had tossed her out the first time. She pulled on black dress boots, her mouth quirking humorously, as she wondered if Jason had anything decent to wear. In the cursory examination she'd made of his clothes the day she'd gone into his bedroom, nothing had been evident.

Taylor looked in the mirror once more, decided she'd done all she could, grabbed her vest and walked into the living room. She waited several minutes, but Jason didn't appear, and on impulse she walked to his bedroom door and rapped lightly.

"Come on in," she heard him say, and she twisted the knob.

He was standing in front of his own small dresser and mirror, head bent over one stubborn cuff. His pearl-grey shirt was still unbuttoned down the front, and Taylor glimpsed the dark chest hair that arrowed to his waist where a pair of darker grey cords were slung low on his hips.

"I think you need food," Taylor observed, realizing the slackness of fit was because of the way he'd abused himself these past years.

"I've gained ten pounds since you arrived," Jason responded without looking up. "If I continue eating the way you and Maxine would like me to, I'll end up—"

His sardonic monologue ended when he finally glanced her way. He didn't actually whistle, but the appreciative stare that swept her from head to toe spoke volumes.

Taylor, to her intense embarrassment, felt her cheeks growing warm.

"I'd forgotten what you look like dressed up," Jason said softly, amused at her discomfiture.

Taylor shrugged off the implied compliment. "You probably haven't seen a woman dressed up for a long time."

"I don't think I'd have the same reaction if Maxine came in dressed that way," Jason said dryly.

"You never know."

"Yes. I do."

With long, unhurried strides he walked across the floor to meet her, and Taylor, senses acutely attuned to his lean masculine appeal, felt her pulse flutter wildly almost against her will.

"Want me to do that for you?" she asked, indicating the button at his cuff, but the husky tenor of her voice was a revealing glimpse into her inner feelings.

Whatever Jason's intentions had been, a look into her darkened eyes made it impossible to ignore her sensual appeal. "God, you're beautiful," he murmured, and Taylor smiled at him uncertainly, trembling as his fingers spread around the waistband of her black skirt, his thumbs massaging her hipbones in a way that made her want to press his hard angles against her yielding curves.

He kissed her lightly, almost experimentally, and Taylor's lips parted in abandon. She had no resistance where he was concerned; their one night of lovemaking had left her tantalized and hungry for more. Distantly, she knew she was setting herself up for a colossal fall, but she was too absorbed in the present to worry about what could happen later.

She moved closer to him, their bodies touching in strategic places, her hands tentatively sliding beneath his shirt. Her own skin was unusually sensitized, and even through her clothes the feel of his hands made her weak with longing.

The kiss deepened, and his grip at her waist intensified. Taylor moaned softly, low in her throat, and Jason's hand slid around her nape beneath the heavy cascade of hair.

"We'll never make dinner if this continues," he said unsteadily.

"I know," Taylor sighed, her breath shallow. She felt cool air against her skin as Jason undid the tiny buttons down the front of her blouse.

His fingers found the catch at her waistband, and he knelt down in front of her, pressing hot kisses against her bared abdomen. Taylor's hands unconsciously wound into his hair.

"I want to kiss you everywhere," Jason murmured.

"Everywhere?" she asked tremulously.

It was more than she could stand as he put meaning to his words. Her limbs trembled uncontrollably, and when she was certain she would fall, his arms came around her to lift and carry her to the bed.

He came down beside her instantly, kissing and touching her in ways that made her bones turn to liquid. She reached for him, eyes slumberous, lips parted in disbelieving wonder. Jason quickly removed his clothes, and Taylor felt the heat of his flesh against hers.

This time their union was quick and wild, but then Jason's movements became slow and deliberate, lighting a smoldering fire within Taylor that raged through her veins like an inferno. Her fingers dug into his shoulders, but he appeared not to notice, and as she scaled the heights of passion a lusty cry erupted from her throat. She strained against him, wanting to draw him within her, be as close to him as she could, and as she reached the peak she felt the shudder that went through him, an answer of passion as old as time itself.

The Captain Whidbey was a split-log inn reputed to be over a hundred years old. The dining room was warmed by a blazing fire at one end, and its eastern wall was a row of paned windows that had a commanding view of the sound. It was dark and intimate, with an atmosphere that invited the kind of sultry mood that had infected Taylor ever since she and Jason had made love.

He was sitting across from her, looking at the menu, but his arm reached across the table and his fingers methodically caressed her hand. Taylor sensed a possessiveness in his touch that made her fears about the future dissolve. It was as if he were afraid of losing her, as if he'd come to depend on her, to live again through her. Well, maybe that was more her hope than the reality of the situation, Taylor conceded, but whatever the case, she was glad she'd come to mean as much to him as she had.

The dining room was practically empty by nine o'clock at night, and they'd been regretfully informed by the maître d' that many of the evening's entrées were no longer available. Taylor was too absurdly happy to care, and even Jason had exhibited an easygoing nature that Taylor had never witnessed before.

But, the waiter had informed them, fresh mussels from the sound were available in abundance. Now, as Jason set down the menu, he told the waiter, "We'll both have the mussels," and with a perfunctory nod, the waiter disappeared into the kitchen.

"Would you like some wine?" Jason asked, but Taylor shook her head.

"I'm fine," she said with a slow smile, and Jason's mouth quirked with humor.

It seemed incredible to her that such a short time had passed since her arrival; Taylor felt as if she'd been on Whidbey for months. Her life in Hollywood was distant and remote, a blur of people and appointments that had relatively little to do with the real person she was inside. She was in love. Wildly, madly, foolishly in love, and the sense of well-being within her pushed aside even the slightest twinges of uneasiness.

The mussels proved to be delicate and delicious, their small, shiny black shells steamed open and served in small cast-iron pots. Jason and Taylor made quick work of them, now and then playfully feeding the tender morsels to each other.

There were only two other tables occupied at that late hour. Taylor had been oblivious to them throughout the meal, but finally she noticed a teenage girl who had been turning to stare at them every few minutes.

"That *is* Jake and Julie Diamond," she said insistently in a loud whisper to her parents when Taylor accidentally caught her eye. "I told you so!"

The man and woman seated across from her saw Taylor watching them and smiled apologetically. It was the first time it had occurred to Taylor what the public might make of her relationship with Jason, and she realized with some regret that if she and Jason should return to Hollywood together, their affair would be splashed across the front pages of the tabloids.

Jason turned to follow her gaze, and to Taylor's surprise, he gave the family a wide smile. Then he looked at Taylor and said suggestively, "Jake and Julie never had it so good."

Neither have I, Taylor thought, but she didn't say it aloud.

Rain began pouring from the skies just as the waiter was clearing their table. It ran down the paned windows in swirling rivulets and made the atmosphere within the dining room seem even more intimate. When their waiter asked if they would like anything else, Jason looked questioningly at Taylor, and on impulse she ordered a Spanish coffee. She wanted to prolong these moments out of time; she was certain the rest of the evening would be spent lying in Jason's arms, yet there was a certain excitement in putting off that pleasure—just knowing it was waiting for her.

Jason ordered plain black coffee, and when the glass mugs arrived, Taylor touched the rim of hers against his. "Thank you," she said.

"For what?"

"For bringing me here. For—" she shrugged charmingly "—changing your mind about me, I guess."

Jason stared into his coffee. "I haven't changed my mind about you, Taylor. I've always liked you."

Why did the word *like* suddenly sound as if it were an insult? Taylor fought against her own reactions. She sipped the hot drink, then licked some grains of sugar from her lips.

"You have a way of doing that that destroys my equilibrium," Jason drawled in a dry tone, and Taylor's doubts disappeared.

"You should have ordered one." She smiled. "I feel warm inside and out."

Jason regarded her quite seriously. "I know this may sound hard to believe, but usually I stay away from alcohol."

Taylor blinked, confused. "Really?"

"Really."

She had a sudden memory of that night in Madeira, when he'd offered her some wine to take the chill off but had taken none for himself. As she cast her mind back, she could not recall ever seeing Jason with a drink until she'd shown up on Whidbey.

"I've never been diagnosed as an alcoholic," Jason went on thoughtfully, "but I don't like myself very much when I drink."

"Then...why...?" Taylor's voice trailed off as she realized how obvious the answer to her question was: Jason had started drinking after the accident because he hadn't wanted to go on living without Lisabeth and Kerri. She'd known it all along, yet now, as she thought about it, it bothered her in a way it never had before. Taylor knew a moment of self-hate as she realized what she was feeling was jealousy. She was jealous of Jason's deep feelings for his dead wife.

Jason sighed. "You've made me take a hard look at myself," he admitted. "Something I didn't want to do."

Taylor played with the handle of her mug, feeling nervous. She was certainly glad she had helped him, but it made her feel like little more than a necessary—but temporary—prop.

His next words only increased her anxiety. "But I never really planned on getting sexually involved—no matter *what* I said to the contrary!" he added with a self-effacing grin. "And, my God, to find out that you had never even had a lover..." Jason inhaled deeply.

"It's not important," Taylor put in hurriedly.

"It's not?" Jason looked at her in disbelief.

Taylor shook her head. She didn't think she could bear to explain her feelings for him when he so obviously didn't return them. A small, hopeful part of her believed that in time those feelings might be returned, and that was what she lived for. But this emotional postmortem was something she wasn't ready for now.

They left the restaurant in silence, Jason's gaze touching her thoughtfully from time to time as he drove her Toyota back to the cabin. Taylor wished she could recapture the dreamlike euphoria she'd felt earlier, but she couldn't quite meet Jason's eyes. She was certain he could see inside her heart, and she felt she had to keep some part of herself private—a reaction she didn't entirely understand.

He was quiet until they were both inside the cabin; then he asked soberly, "What did I say to receive the silent treatment?"

"Nothing."

"Come on, Taylor. Something happened at the restaurant and you just shut me out. I want to know what it is."

The determination in his voice made her feel impatient. "You're being too sensitive."

"No, I'm not." His tone was crisp. "What the hell's going on? If you're having second thoughts, just say so."

Taylor turned her eyes on him in time to see him rake his hand frustratedly through his hair. Her eyes spoke eloquently of her feelings. "It's not second thoughts," she said quietly.

"Then *what*, for God's sake! Don't make me guess. I've had enough game playing to last me a thousand lifetimes."

There was nothing she could say without leaving herself more vulnerable. But she saw the uncertainty in his eyes and wanted to assure him that her detachment was only self-preservation. She crossed the room and wrapped her arms around his waist, laying her cheek against his chest. "Believe me, Jason, I'm not having second thoughts. I just...want you."

He groaned and buried his face in her hair. "Don't do that to me again," he said unsteadily. "I'm not that secure."

Taylor squeezed her eyes shut. Maybe not. But his insecurities were vastly different from her own, and they were gradually disappearing with every passing day. Someday he would wake up and realize he didn't need her anymore; that was the day she dreaded, because even when he stopped needing her, she would still be in love with him.

Chapter Eight

Taylor ripped off the last sheets of paper spewed from the printer, tore off the perforated edge, separated the pages and put them in numerical order. She glanced at Jason's closed face as he read through the sheaf of papers he already had; she was anxious to know what he thought of the changes. Her revisions were all but done now, and she was waiting for his final word. If Jason approved she could consider the screenplay finished; after all, who knew the exploits and characters of Jake and Julie Diamond better than he?

A silky lock of hair kept falling in his eyes, and he kept brushing it back distractedly, a line of concentration furrowing between his brows. Taylor had the urge to brush the hair back for him, but she stifled it—just as she'd stifled similar urges all week long.

Just because she'd made headway with Jason in certain areas didn't mean the war was won. His attitude toward her, though distinctly less hostile and sometimes openly indulgent, was still constrained, and Taylor had learned that even their lovemaking couldn't break down all the barriers.

During the day Jason left her almost completely alone, departing in the early morning and returning after sunset. She'd ventured to ask once what he did with his time, but apart from a noncommittal, "I've got some things to take care of," Jason hadn't offered any explanations. Taylor did manage to work when he was gone, and she had to admit that it was probably for the best since having him around would have been distracting. Still, she yearned for more certainty in their relationship, and impatience and anxiety gnawed at her stomach every minute he was away.

At night, even though Taylor could feel his eyes on her when her back was turned, Jason made no direct moves to initiate any further intimacy. It was as if he were still wrestling with it in his mind, and though Taylor chafed at the pointlessness of it all, she had no choice but to accept Jason's pace. Then, just when she wanted to scream from the tension, he would reach for her and they would spend the night in each other's arms—only to start the next day the very same way, distant and ill at ease. Taylor knew she couldn't stand it much longer, but every time she tried to voice a complaint Jason skillfully turned the discussion to her screenplay. It was clear he thought her time on Whidbey was only temporary—and so it was—but Taylor wouldn't let herself believe that was all there was to their relationship. It couldn't be! She wouldn't let it be!

She tried hard to crack through his shield of implacability, but it was impossible. Despite their continued passion and intimacy there were no more revelations about his past, and there were certainly no plans made for the future.

Taylor handed Jason the last pages, and he took them without looking up. *And now your last excuse for staying is over,* she reminded herself, mentally biting her nails as he slowly read through her changes. Part of her anxiety was over what he would say about her screenplay, but most of it was much more personal. What were his feelings for her? His innate caution made Taylor want to tear her hair out.

But every time she was sure she was at the end of her rope, she remembered how he'd treated her at the Captain Whidbey, the possessive way he'd looked at her and touched her. "I'm not that secure," he'd said, and Taylor realized he was trying now to keep their relationship in perspective. Remembering what he was like when she'd first come to Whidbey, she reasoned she should be grateful for the progress she'd made so far; Jason's wariness about falling into a complicated relationship with her was understandable, probably even commendable.

Taylor sighed inwardly. She could rationalize all she wanted; it still hurt to know how little his emotions were truly involved.

"Well?" she asked, as he stacked the pages of the manuscript together, a thoughtful line sketched between his brows.

Jason pinched his bottom lip between his thumb and forefinger. "There's only one scene I would change," he said slowly.

"Which one?" Taylor's heart plummeted as she envisioned another lengthy rewrite, but her defeat was tempered with hope: she might be able to stay longer than she'd imagined.

"You're not going to like it," he warned with a faint smile.

"Lay it on me." Taylor moved closer, attempting to look over his shoulder and see which scene had captured his attention. "I've learned to take my lumps and bounce back."

Jason glanced sharply at her when she said these double-edged words, but he didn't rise to the bait. "I think the first scene still needs work. It's not quite right, and since it sets the wheels in motion for the whole story, you need to give it some power."

Taylor wasn't certain what showed in her face, but she could feel her shoulders droop. There *was* something wrong with the first scene; she'd felt it too. But for the life of her, she couldn't seem to see her way around it.

"Don't get panicky," Jason said quickly, separating the pages he was concerned with. "I'm not talking about a major rewrite here. I think it just starts at the wrong point."

Taylor peered over Jason's shoulder. He wore a blue work shirt, the sleeves rolled up to expose muscular, tanned forearms sprinkled with dark hair. His collar was open, and Taylor couldn't help the constriction of her heart at the sight of his dark-skinned throat. It amazed her, the way she reacted to him, and she determinedly dragged her eyes away and concentrated on the printed pages held in his long-fingered hands.

The first scene was where the fortune-teller approaches Jake and Julie's café table and makes her startling prediction. It was the key to the entire story, and Taylor was too tired and confused to imagine changing it. "I don't know what you mean," she said, discouraged.

Jason shifted uneasily, his arm accidentally brushing Taylor's breast. "If it bothers you that I'm playing critic, let me know, Taylor. This is your work and I'd probably resent—"

"No, no—I know you're right." Taylor was quick to assure him that she agreed with him. She was not, by any means, suffering from a bruised ego where Jason was concerned; hers was a different malady entirely. "I just don't know what to do to change it. Got any suggestions?"

"A few."

Taylor met his narrowed gaze, and her pulse leaped as she saw the flash of hunger in his silvery blue eyes. He couldn't look at her that way and really expect her to walk out of his life after her screenplay was finished, could he?

Jason looked away first, took a deep breath and locked his jaw determinedly. Then, in a distance lecturer's voice, he said, "The fortune-teller just pops onto the scene without any fanfare. One minute Jake and Julie are alone; the next, there she is."

Taylor nodded. That was all part of the surprise.

"What would you think about starting the scene with her instead of with Jake and Julie?" Jason suggested. "Maybe outdoors. Have her looking over her shoulder so the mood would be set by her uneasiness."

Taylor's attention turned to the screenplay. She felt faint stirrings of interest. Then she glanced at Jason and caught him searching her face for a reaction.

"Go on," Taylor said softly.

"The action starts on Madeira, so this scene could be filmed in Funchal, the capital, maybe along one of those black-and-white mosaic-tiled squares. It's broad daylight. There are lots of people. The fortune-teller is walking down the street. She has a sixth sense that something's wrong—that she's being followed—and her steps quicken. She glances around, more urgently this time. Nothing. But she knows there's something there."

Jason's soft words raised goose bumps on Taylor's flesh. She was amazed at his vivid imagery.

"While the action's happening," Jason went on, "the noise of the square recedes until it's almost as if she's alone, cut off from the people she sees. The only sound is her rapid shallow breathing in counterpoint to her quickening steps."

"Wow!"

The corner of Jason's mouth lifted. "You like it?"

"Of course I like it." Taylor took the sheaf of papers from Jason's hands. "It adds another dimension that the story needs. It'll work great." Taylor's voice grew in conviction as the idea took root. "Fantastic! It'll keep the people riveted to their seats. There's something really scary about the threat of danger in the midst of a normal, bright sunny day."

"Exactly."

Taylor's thoughts were tumbling one after another. "Then we could shift to Jake and Julie—show them having a carefree vacation, never suspecting the disaster that's heading straight their way."

"We?" Jason smiled.

"Yes, *we*." Taylor gave Jason a brilliant answering smile of thanks. "I think this screenplay has become something of a collaboration, don't you?"

"No." Jason was adamant. "This is your work. I'm no writer. Now go ahead," he added as Taylor turned to the computer, "finish it."

She was divided between putting his idea on paper and seizing this opportunity to become closer to him. She could sense his indulgence; she yearned for him just to give in willingly and let her love him. "You sell yourself too short," she said softly.

As if sensing her conflicting desires, Jason abruptly turned away, reaching for his hat. "Hardly," he said, just loud enough to be heard. Defeated by the implacable stand he'd taken once again, Taylor let her shoulders droop. She knew it was ridiculous to feel this way, but every time Jason left so she could work, she felt as if he were deliberately pulling something away from her.

She stood motionless, trying not to let him see how miserable she felt, knowing she was making too much of what was to him a simple courtesy.

Jason jammed the Stetson on his head. "I'm one of the worst egotists you'll ever run across."

"I've met some terrible egotists in my time," Taylor responded in an attempt to keep him from leaving. "You're not even close to the worst."

His jaw tensed. "You don't know me all that well, Taylor. Not really."

"You don't give me a chance," Taylor answered.

She had the sense that he was working up to telling her something she didn't want to hear, and she instinctively braced herself. But she couldn't have prepared herself for his next words if she'd planned for a year.

"Did you plan for me to play Jake Diamond in your screenplay?"

Taylor blinked rapidly several times. "Well . . . I can't deny that the thought's crossed my mind, but I never imagined you would do it." She peered closely at his face, shadowed by the wide brim of his hat. "Would you?"

He merely shook his head, as if he couldn't find words to answer her; then with a mumbled, "I'll be back later," he walked through the door, leaving her with a last, quick impression of his fist tightly gripping the handle as he shut the door quietly behind him.

The Jeep sputtered to life instantly when Jason turned the key. He backed around, grinding the gears mercilessly, before swinging the nose in the direction of the road. Rattling like the piece of junk it was, the Jeep splashed through standing pools of water left from the rain that had drizzled down on Whidbey for the past few days. Jason kept his hands firmly on the wheel and, with muttered imprecations only he could hear, tried unsuccessfully to thrust Taylor Michaelson from his thoughts.

He was fast becoming a desperate case, he realized with a rueful scowl. Unless he started exorcising her from his life now, he would find it impossible later on.

"Damn," he muttered through clenched teeth.

How had everything gotten so crazy? He hadn't imagined any woman could get to him so thoroughly, and fool that he was, he'd just let it happen! And now...now...

Jason drove with savage intensity, the wheels of the Jeep bumping over familiar roots and stones, water splashing halfway up the battered doors. Where should he go today? he wondered, automatically turning south when he reached the highway.

Whidbey Island, he'd discovered, had suddenly become too small for him. He'd spent every day this week exploring its southern end, and he'd even crossed to the Washington mainland several times, caught ferries to the other San Juan Islands and one day even gone as far as Vancouver Island. But there was nowhere he could go to escape himself, and he was forced to face the issue that was causing him such inner turmoil.

He wanted to go back to Hollywood with her.

Jason did a sudden U-turn and drove back to the lane to his cabin. He stopped at the head of the lane, just past the mailbox, jerked on the emergency brake and let the engine run. Then he slowly lowered his forehead to the steering wheel and considered what returning to Hollywood meant.

Hollywood. Just the idea of the place had made his skin crawl a bare two weeks ago. He couldn't think of it as just a location; it held too many memories of Lisabeth and Kerri and what had happened since.

So how could he be contemplating returning now?

It was Taylor's screenplay that had changed him; her screenplay and herself. He still hadn't trusted her motives until he'd actually sat down and read what she'd written—then everything had changed. He'd been stupified by her work! Absolutely incredulous that Taylor had written such a wonderful script! He'd had a vision of her slaving diligently for the past two years, agonizing over every word, trying to survive after the brutal end he'd put to her career as an actress. Her effort had made him understand what a pointless waste his own life had become.

Reading Taylor's screenplay had given Jason the uncanny feeling he was opening the door on his own future. He hadn't realized how numbed his senses were until he read her story; it was like being grabbed by the throat! He'd felt dazed by a suffocating kind of exhilaration. He knew that Taylor had given him the vehicle for his return to Hollywood: he was Jake Diamond. What he hadn't known was that he wanted to go back so badly...

And what about Taylor herself?

Jason lifted his head and stared at the ceiling of the Jeep. He was involved in a tricky situation with her that defied rationality. If he did go back with her, what then?

Jason was in touch enough with his feelings to know that his own emotional problems hadn't just evaporated. He still couldn't drive north, for instance, he realized, his teeth on edge. Even the thought of passing the site of Lisabeth's and Kerri's accident caused him to break into a sweat, and he swiped at his forehead angrily.

Putting the past behind him was going to take some time—a lot of time. He didn't want to find himself hurting Taylor in the process, but he was selfish enough not to want to give her up now that he'd found her.

He swore beneath his breath, kicked open the door, then walked around the back of the Jeep to the mailbox. He was crazy to be thinking the thoughts he was thinking, making the plans he was making. But Taylor's screenplay was almost done; something had to give soon.

Jason reached inside the rusted box. He had no answer for the future, but he knew the moment of decision was fast approaching. Taylor, herself, was not the most patient person in the world, and considering the whole incredible series of events that had led to their current situation, Jason couldn't say he blamed her.

The box was full of its usual junk mail. Jason flipped desultorily through the advertisement, his mind far away. He had a vision of himself and Taylor that wouldn't quite go away. It was a companion to him during his days and haunted his nights, hovering in the back of his mind when he was with her, making love to her, touching her, helping her. It made him hate himself that, after all his condemning words, he should be the one to want Taylor, her screenplay and a second chance in Hollywood. What kind of man was he? Jason railed at himself. Everything he'd accused her of trying to set up was coming true—*but it was his fault!*

At the bottom of the stack was an envelope addressed to Taylor. Jason, immersed in self-recriminations, stared at it uncomprehendingly for several moments. When the meaning penetrated his brain, he was filled with rising dread. The return address was printed in clear blue letters: Ross Corley Associates.

Jason felt as if he'd been hit in the gut. He'd thought it was his fault. *His* fault! But what was Taylor's agent doing writing to her *here*, unless the whole thing had been a setup all along?

Taylor dipped a tea bag into the steaming cup of hot water, her mind still on her screenplay. She was excited about it. Even with her tendency toward self-doubt she had to admit it: it was really good! For the first time since she'd started on this venture she realized there was a possibility of a sale because of—and *only* because of—her screenplay's actual worth.

The printer was running off the new pages she'd written for the first scene. She couldn't wait for Jason to get back and read them; she was dying to know what he thought. But she instinctively knew he would like what she'd done, and inside she was bursting with a beautiful excitement that could hardly be contained.

Where was Jason? Taylor glanced at the clock and realized he'd been gone for several hours. Did he intend to make this another all-day excursion to parts unknown? If so, she had a long wait ahead of her; it was only a little after three o'clock now.

The sound of footsteps on the porch, followed by two familiar raps on the solid panels of the front door, heralded Maxine's unexpected arrival. "Sorry I'm late," she said, shrugging out of her heavy coat.

"Late?" Taylor smiled. "Your timing was perfect. I just finished my screenplay."

Maxine's face split into a broad grin. "Completely?"

"If Jason gives his approval, yes."

"Well, that's cause for celebration."

Maxine turned and picked up her coat again, heading for the door. Taylor stopped, her cup halfway to her lips. "Where are you going?"

"Into town. Tonight I'm cooking something special."

"Oh, no. It's not that big a deal." Taylor followed ineffectually after the older woman. "Really, Maxine. There's no need—"

"Oh, hush. I'll be right back."

Taylor watched in dismay as Maxine trudged back up the path to her house. The last thing she wanted was to turn the finishing of her screenplay into a big event, she thought sinkingly. There were too many issues as yet unresolved between Jason and herself, and somehow planning a special evening didn't seem the best way to approach Jason about the future. He would undoubtedly react better if things were kept low-key.

She bit her lip. Maxine had been wonderful to her during her stay; in fact, she'd been Taylor's only contact with humanity besides Jason during this past week. Taylor couldn't bring herself to charge after Maxine and appeal to her to put off the celebration; it would be showing the worst kind of ingratitude. She realized she would just have to make the best of it and hope that Maxine's plan for a big night of celebration wouldn't end up in disaster.

Taylor was giving her revisions a last critical look when the cabin door suddenly swung inward and Jason, hair tousled from wind and face flushed with cold, strode inside. He was carrying a packet of mail in his hands, and he tossed it unceremoniously on the counter, holding back one letter.

"This one," he said expressionlessly, "is for you."

If Taylor had had more warning she might have been more prepared, but now she just regarded him blankly. "Me?"

Jason inclined his head, blue eyes colder than the eddying wind that had followed him inside.

As it occurred to Taylor who might be sending her mail, the blood drained from her face. What if it was from Meredith? Or even Ross? How would she explain to Jason that although they knew where she was, her trip to Whidbey had been solely her idea?

Jason stretched out the envelope toward her, and Taylor read the return address. Ross Corley Associates. Her throat went dry.

"Why don't you open it?" he suggested in a dangerously soft voice, and Taylor knew then that the letter had become a test of loyalty. Her heart sank. As long as she and Jason had been insulated from the rest of the world, he'd let himself believe in her. But any word from Los Angeles was, to Jason, a stab in the back. She wondered, as she opened the letter with shaking fingers, what he would think if he knew about her telephone calls.

Taylor unfolded the single page, praying silently. If Ross had written anything damaging, anything to make Jason feel as if he'd been right about her after all, anything to prove her reasons for being on Whidbey weren't entirely altruistic, then she might as well kiss her sunny future goodbye.

The message was brief: AT&T provides telephones for the public to use. Use one. Love, R.

Taylor nearly collapsed with relief. Good old Ross. He'd understood enough from her phone calls not to break the fragile trust between herself and Jason.

"What," Jason asked evenly, "does that mean?"

"It means that I promised Ross I would call him and tell him when I was coming home." Taylor folded up the letter. "He's been awfully eager to get me to test for several prime-time shows. I think he's growing impatient."

It was the perfect time to tell Jason about Meredith Maddox's offer on her screenplay, but the words stuck in her throat. She thought of several different openings to ease into the truth but couldn't bring herself to utter a sound. She had too much to lose if he should take it the wrong way—and Jason was notorious for taking things the wrong way.

"A prime-time show?" Jason repeated, brows drawing together. "You never told me that."

Taylor laughed shakily. "You haven't been exactly eager to hear about Hollywood happenings."

"Is that what you want to do?"

Taylor glanced toward the counter where her revisions waited. She picked the pages up, tapped them together, then held them out to Jason. "I want to do *this*," she said. "Nothing else. And I want to do it with you!"

She practically stopped breathing, hearing the strength of her own words echo around them. She knew she'd crossed the line, but she didn't care. Just how long could she tiptoe around the issue, anyway?

Jason accepted the pages. "You're done?"

"Yes, and when Maxine found out she decided we were due for a celebration. She's at the store now, planning something special for dinner."

Taylor smiled faintly. All these plans could be premature if Jason decided he didn't like her revisions. Watching his face with anxiety, Taylor searched for some sign of his thoughts, but apart from a thoughtful crease between his brows Jason's expression gave nothing away. Then his eyes lifted, and a slow smile spread from one corner of his mouth to the other as he said, "You're really good at this, you know."

Taylor was afraid to believe him. "You think so?" she questioned anxiously.

"Mmmhmm. This is better than *Queen of Diamonds*—maybe better than all of the *Diamond Girl* films."

Taylor flushed with pleasure. "Well, I wouldn't go that far."

Jason laughed at her modesty, and Taylor watched in awe at the transformation of his face. When he laughed it was as if the years of pain and disillusionment fell away and once again he was the Jason Garrett she'd first met.

"'...like a diamond in the sky,'" he quoted with a grin, then added urgently. "The screenplay's great. Don't test for the prime-time show, Taylor. Do *Diamond in the Sky*. I'll do it with you."

After so many days and nights of praying for just this impossibility, Taylor could hardly believe her ears. "Do you mean it?"

Jason nodded gravely, but his eyes glinted with mirth. Giddy with delight, Taylor flung her arms around his neck and hugged him without restraint, the excitement of the moment carrying her away. Jason's whole body froze, but before Taylor could regret her impulsiveness he suddenly hugged her back with a bone-crushing squeeze that left her breathless.

"I'll even go one step further," he said in a harsh whisper near her ear. "I want to produce it—*we* could produce it, you and I, Taylor, together. What do you say?"

Taylor was too caught up in the joy of expressing her love to pay much attention. Jason's arms, taut as steel around her, the late-afternoon roughness of his cheek scraping against hers, the hard muscles of his thighs, his earthy scent—Taylor's senses were already on overload.

But the expectancy with which he waited brought Taylor back to reality. Produce it? *Produce it?* Taylor let her arms slide down his neck, tilting her face to look at his.

He was utterly serious, she realized, and swallowing with difficulty, she said, "I can't produce anything on my own, Jason. I don't have that kind of money."

"But I do. You've done all the work, love. Let me put up the capital. It won't be hard, and with your story and our track record together, we'll have our pick of studios to choose from."

Taylor stared. She thought of Ross, eagerly anticipating a sale to Maddox Productions. She thought of Meredith, promising Taylor she would read her screenplay if Jason could be lured back to Hollywood. And she thought of Jason, blissfully unaware of the wheels that were already turning, the steps that had already been taken to ensure that her screenplay was produced.

Her heart thudded with dread. "Jason..." she said faintly.

"Mmmhmm?"

"Ross knows about the... screenplay." Nothing had ever been so hard to say. Taylor struggled onward before she lost her courage. "He's already talked to Maddox Productions—to Meredith—about producing it."

Jason looked at her long and hard, his blue eyes narrowed on her ashen face. "I see," he said slowly, though what that meant Taylor was afraid to ask.

"I never dreamed—" Taylor added unsteadily, "—that you would really be interested in accepting the lead." She emitted a short, odd laugh. "Let alone *producing* it! Coming here was a gamble, Jason, but even I wouldn't have gambled on talking you into that."

"What kind of arrangement do you have with Maddox?" he asked distantly.

"Nothing—at least nothing firm. I haven't even finished the screenplay, or at least I hadn't before I left." Sensing she hadn't lost the battle yet, Taylor refrained from mentioning the phone calls between herself and Ross since she'd arrived on the island.

"Then give Maddox a flat, unequivocal no," Jason said firmly, gripping her upper arms, pushing her back to look at her more closely. "It's simple."

Simple? He had no idea what kind of hornet's nest she would stir up. Ross and Meredith Maddox would fight her all the way; having Jason produce *Diamond in the Sky* would fit into neither of their plans.

"I—I don't know."

Jason's fingers tensed perceptibly around her arms. "Why don't you?"

"The money—the risk! Oh, Jason," Taylor appealed to him, "what if it didn't work?"

He chuckled softly, guiding her toward the couch. "It'll work, Tayor. Believe me." He let go of her when she was sitting down beside him, but then his hands returned to her shoulders, thumbs rubbing sensuously against the sides of her throat. "Ever since I read your screenplay the idea to produce it has been an obsession; I can hardly think of anything else. I haven't felt that strongly about anything in years, Taylor."

She heard the underlying emotion in his voice and understood. Inadvertently she'd done exactly what she'd set out to do: give Jason a reason to get on with his life. Why then did she feel so used and abused?

"It's up to you what you want to do with your screenplay," he went on while Taylor studied her clasped hands, "but don't let the cost of coproducing frighten you into accepting another offer. Let that be my problem. I want it to be my problem."

"It's not . . . just that."

"Then what?"

What indeed? Her own guilt, perhaps. Or maybe the suspicion that Jason's feelings for her would never amount to anything more than a professional interest in her. And whose fault was that anyway? Taylor knew she had no one but herself to blame if falling in love with Jason turned into emotional disaster. He'd never promised her anything; in fact, he'd warned her more than once not to get involved with him.

As she considered it, the idea of coproducing with Jason truly began to sink in. It could be wonderful, she realized with dawning recognition. Just Jason and herself, and a new production company that could conceivably make one film after another, not just this single venture.

"What would we have to do?" she asked tentatively.

"To start production?" Jason's keen gaze discerned the change in her, the sparkle of anticipation that began to displace the worry. "Well, first," he said, pulling her close until her head leaned against his shoulder, "we need to call Ross and nix any deal with Maddox. Then we've got to start packing; I'll need to close the cabin."

"So soon?" Taylor buried her face in the soft cloth of his shirt, feeling a pang of regret that her time alone with Jason was about to end.

"Right away, love. We'll put off talking to Meredith or Clifton, or whoever's in charge at Maddox, until we get there. Then I'll have to figure out my finances and drum up some extra backing. It shouldn't be too tough. With you, me and *Diamond in the Sky*, how can we lose?''

Taylor closed her eyes and didn't respond to his rhetorical question. She was afraid, very afraid, that she could too easily find an answer.

Chapter Nine

Taylor awoke slowly. As consciousness returned she felt the weight of a masculine leg thrown possessively over hers, saw deeply tanned arms clasped around her. For a moment she lay languidly in Jason's arms, a sleepy smile crossing her lips; then her eyes flew open in remembrance. They were no longer at his cabin. This was her apartment—her bed!—in Los Angeles.

She snuggled closer to his enveloping warmth, and Jason complied by mumbling sleepily and drawing his arms tighter around her. But with wakefulness came that feeling of anxiety that fluttered continually in her stomach. Since Jason had put his plan to return to Hollywood in motion, Taylor had been seized by an irrational case of nerves that had begun during Maxine's special celebration dinner.

Maxine had prepared roast leg of lamb stuffed with garlic while Jason worked out the details for returning to

Los Angeles. Maxine's enthusiasm was easy to see, and when Jason casually asked Maxine to bring her family to the meal, too, Taylor realized that it was his way of saying thank you and goodbye.

Maxine's husband had been working, but she and Sarah joined Taylor and Jason for dinner. It was ironic that, although Taylor had worried about how Jason would react, it was she who found it difficult to join in the celebration.

"Don't worry," Maxine had said when she had a minute with Taylor alone. "Jason's a strong man. He just needed a push in the right direction, and you gave it to him. He won't fall apart when he gets there."

Taylor had smiled and returned Maxine's hug of friendship, never letting on that the older woman had misread Taylor's fears. It wasn't that she felt Jason couldn't stand the pace; she knew that if he ever set his mind to anything, he wouldn't fail. It was her own insecurities that kept her awake all that night and the next few as well.

The call to Ross hadn't been a huge success either. With Jason standing just outside the open phone booth, her conversation was tense and stilted.

"What do you mean you want to produce it yourself?" Ross bellowed incredulously. "Are you out of your mind?"

The muscles in Taylor's face ached from the strain. "Probably, but that's my decision, Ross."

"You and Garrett? Taylor, for God's sake, don't do anything rash! Wait until you get back to Los Angeles to make a decision."

"Sorry, Ross, we're coming back tomorrow, and I won't change my mind."

She'd hung up before he could harangue her further. Jason had given her a tight squeeze of reassurance, but Taylor had been unable to shake the image of Ross calling Meredith Maddox with the stunning news.

The butterflies in Taylor's stomach just wouldn't settle down, and they had gone into full flight when she and Jason had stepped off the plane at Los Angeles Airport yesterday—straight into a battery of press people. Ross, after nearly coming apart at the seams at Taylor's news, had alerted the world that Jason Garrett was coming back to Hollywood.

A semicircle of reporters with cameras and microphones were waiting at the gate, and there was no way she and Jason could avoid them. Taylor instinctively moved to deflect the questions, but Jason, with a slight shake of his head, told her he was perfectly able to handle the impromptu press conference.

Despite a drawn look around his eyes and the tension that appeared off and on to stiffen his jaw, he was polite and informative, and even self-effacing about his two-year absence. The press loved it, and luckily for Taylor, they zeroed in so exclusively on Jason that her own relationship with him was, at least for the moment, forgotten.

"What made you decide to come back?" a smiling blond-haired woman asked him. "Or maybe I should ask, what sent you away in the first place, and what's now changed to bring you back?"

"There were lots of reasons why I left," Jason answered with a slight shrug. "Mainly I needed time alone with my family."

Taylor had been amazed that he'd purposely brought up Lisabeth and Kerri, but moments later she understood that he was anxious to leap that hurdle now before the questions got too close to home.

"Unfortunately, things didn't quite work out the way I'd planned," Jason went on a bit grimly. "And I'd rather not go into all the details."

A murmur of sympathetic understanding swept through the room; this particular group of newspeople wasn't out for blood. "What changed, then," asked a man in an expensively tailored suit, "to bring you back?"

Jason slid a sideways glance toward Taylor, and the line of microphones swiveled to include her. "My costar here showed me a screenplay she's written—a sequel to the *Diamond Girl* trilogy. It's a great story and, with some convincing, she talked me into coming back and doing it with her."

"There's a rumor you plan to produce it, too." This was from the blonde.

"We'd like to turn that rumor to fact," Jason admitted.

"We? Does that mean you're involved in production, too, Taylor?"

Taylor pinned on a confident smile. "Yes, Jason and I plan to coproduce if everything works out."

"What does Maddox Productions have to say about all this? They did produce the *Diamond Girl* trilogy, after all, and I'd imagine they would want to continue the series."

Taylor saw strain tighten Jason's jaw. "We haven't spoken to them yet," he said evenly.

A disheveled-looking reporter with shrewd eyes put in, "But weren't there hard feelings between you and Maddox Productions when you broke contract after *Queen of Diamonds*? Clifton Maddox had some harsh words to say after you left town."

"I didn't break contract." Jason shifted his weight, and Taylor sensed he'd had about all he wanted to take. "I just didn't sign for the next picture."

"And consequently it wasn't produced." The man was persistent. "How do you think they'll feel about you branching out on your own?"

Jason's jaw knotted. "I imagine we'll find out soon enough."

Jason made a move to skirt the newspeople, but they pressed in closer and Taylor was unable to escape the blond woman.

"What about the two of you?" she asked. "Can we expect an off-screen liaison as well as on-screen?"

It was the kind of question Taylor least wanted to answer. "I've already said we plan to coproduce," she countered.

"Are you saying there's no romance brewing between you?"

Taylor smiled enigmatically and squeezed her way past them, following rapidly on Jason's heels down the concourse.

"Thank God that's over," he exhaled fervently, and Taylor knew just how difficult those few minutes had been for him.

But their run through the press gauntlet hadn't ended there. To Taylor's dismay more reporters were camped outside her apartment block, and when she and Jason tried to sneak inside they were thwarted by a crowd of about ten. She hadn't realized what terrific copy Jason's mysterious flight from, and then sudden return to, Hollywood made.

This group of reporters went straight for the jugular, and as she and Jason bent their heads and tried to walk past without answering, the questions flew after them like bullets.

"Jason, was it true your wife didn't want to leave Hollywood because of a dependency on drugs?"

"When your wife and daughter died, weren't you first at the scene of the accident?"

"Taylor, what made you decide to go stay with Jason on Whidbey Island? Is there an off-screen romance flourishing...or is it just a continuation of where you left off?"

"Jason, we understand the reason you didn't come back before was because you had a nervous breakdown. Could you confirm that? It's wonderful to see you looking so well now..."

Now, thinking back on the ghoulish digs into Jason's private life, Taylor shuddered and burrowed closer to him. When they'd finally reached the security of her apartment they'd both been uncommonly silent; neither one of them had imagined his return would be the sensation it was.

Taylor let her eyes droop closed and tried to think positively. Maybe it hadn't been wise to have Jason stay the night with her, she thought with a pang; it had probably just added more grist to the rumor mill. But after the emotional upheaval of their return, Taylor was more eager than ever to feel the security of Jason's arms around her. Jason, too, seemed to need her support, so they'd barricaded themselves in her apartment, snacked on frozen food thawed in the microwave oven and spent the night nestled warmly together.

"Don't think about it," Jason's deep voice murmured as he felt the quiver of revulsion that swept through her.

It was comforting to know that he understood her so well. "It's hard not to. I never imagined it would be like this."

"Didn't you?" Jason sighed, and Taylor felt his warm breath against her nape. "I suppose I didn't give it enough thought."

She turned in his arms, sun-streaked tresses fanning like spun gold across her pillow. "You held up remarkably well," she said softly. "Especially when they brought up the accident."

Jason looked at her solemnly but without the flash of remembered horror that had invaded his soul for so long. "Some day I'll tell you all about that night."

Taylor's heart jerked. She laid a hand against his beard-roughened cheek, struck silent by the commitment he'd shown her in those few words. He rubbed his jaw against her palm, the soberness of his gaze being replaced by a devilish light. Then he scoured his beard against the soft skin of her neck, getting a howl of protest from Taylor that quickly turned to out-and-out laughter as he moved down her throat to scratch against her breasts.

"You fiend," she accused, giving the hair on his head a sharp tug.

"Only for you, my dear," Jason growled against her flesh, and Taylor found her laughter dying as his playful attack became a searing, sensual invasion.

"I love you," she whispered, not knowing what she was going to say until the words hung between them.

Jason didn't halt his assault on her senses, but neither did he answer in kind. Taylor was too seduced by the loving touches of his hands and mouth and body to worry unduly, and she let herself be swept into the wine-dark world of sensuality without a breath of regret.

Taylor's apartment lacked any touch of her personality, but it had never bothered her much before. However, with Jason as her guest she couldn't help looking at the walls and rooms afresh, wondering how she could have locked up her own feelings so tightly that her own home didn't give a clue to the type of woman she was. It was as if when Jason left for Whidbey, she had lost a vital part of herself as well. And, she thought, shaking her head in disbelief, she hadn't even known.

She stepped out of the shower, thrust her arms into the apricot-colored robe she had hung on the bathroom door and toweled the ends of her hair dry. Jason had already dressed, and she could hear him searching through the cupboards in the kitchen, intent on getting the coffee started while Taylor finished getting ready.

She'd told him she loved him, she realized now, but it hadn't sent him scurrying for emotional shelter. It was a relief to know that she could at least be honest without bringing dire consequences down on her head, and even if Jason didn't feel the same, well, the future held endless possibilities.

The future. It stood before her like a long, straight road; the twists and kinks had already been worked out. With a feeling of joy Taylor squeezed her arms around herself, controlled the urge to pinch herself out of this beautiful dream, then went into the kitchen to find Jason.

He was, as ever, in a pair of jeans and a faded shirt, the sleeves rolled up to his elbows. But for some reason he seemed different now that they were back in Los Angeles, more self-assured and confident, more like the man he'd been before. Absurdly, it gave Taylor a moment of unease, like the nurse that sees her patient outgrowing her.

"You found the coffeemaker," she observed.

"And the coffee, and even the sugar if you so desire."

She smiled. "You know I drink it black."

"Yes." He gave her a quick, loving look. "I do. But if you think there's anything else to eat in this place, you'll have to think again. We've got to go grocery shopping before we starve to death."

It made Taylor feel good that Jason seemed to think of everything in terms of "we." She perched on one of the counter bar stools, tucked the lapels of her robe around her throat and didn't comment that it was great to see his appetite had returned in full.

The doorbell suddenly buzzed, and Taylor nearly fell off her stool in surprise. She looked askance at Jason, and he raised his brows and shook his head.

"Want me to get it?" he asked, glancing pointedly at her attractive dishabille.

"I guess we can't hold them off forever," she murmured, sliding off the stool as Jason walked to the door.

Taylor had just turned into the hall, intent on dressing before facing the press, when she heard Jason open the front door, followed by his sharp intake of breath.

"Lisabeth?" he whispered hoarsely, dazedly.

Taylor whipped around, her heart accelerating in panic. Then she saw Meredith Maddox standing in the doorway, the expression on her face impossible to describe. It took Taylor three pounding heartbeats to remember how closely Meredith Maddox resembled her sister.

"I probably should have called first," Meredith repeated herself, looking at Jason. "It was more of a surprise than I'd expected, seeing you again; I can't imagine what it must have been like for you."

Jason's gaze was not on his former sister-in-law; his blue eyes were fixed on Taylor as he half-sprawled, half-sat on her couch, his arms stretched out across the back.

"It was," he said in a deceptively normal voice, "a shock."

He'd realized almost immediately who Meredith was, and the shadow of regret that passed over his eyes showed he remembered what he'd said, but by then the damage to Taylor's sense of well-being had been done. If she'd ever believed Jason was over his love for Lisabeth, she couldn't believe it now.

He'd recovered himself remarkably, however, and now lounged lazily on the couch, listening to Meredith bring him up to date on what was happening at Maddox Productions.

"...since Clifton's stroke, that is, but I'll probably have to give up the seat of power to him soon. He's been recovering by leaps and bounds, though the pressure of being head of production is certainly beyond him at this point."

Taylor felt superfluous and completely underdressed. Meredith had done a classic double take upon seeing Taylor in her robe, and her face had darkened in disapproval. Taylor was quite aware of how she must feel; after all, Lisabeth had been Meredith's sister and this was the first time she'd seen Jason since the accident. It stood to reason she wouldn't appreciate being confronted with another woman in his life.

"I'll get us a cup of coffee," Taylor murmured, torn between the desire to get dressed and the need to do something useful. She poured the coffee first, set three cups on a serving tray and returned to the living room.

"Ross called and told me you weren't interested in letting Maddox produce your screenplay," Meredith said a trifle coolly as Taylor handed her a cup.

"Er...no." She darted a look at Jason for confirmation.

"We want to produce it ourselves," Jason supplied easily. "I'm sure you've already heard it from Ross, if not from the morning papers."

"I heard, but I didn't believe it." Meredith's lips tightened and the look she sent Taylor was full of censure. "Have you talked to Phil Walker?" she demanded, swinging her attention back to Jason. "I bet he doesn't think you're ready to tackle such an all-encompassing project."

Jason leaned forward slowly, dangerously. "Phil Walker—and you—are going to have to learn that I can make my own decisions."

"Oh, Jason, don't get so upset." Meredith's face relaxed, lips curving into a wry smile. "You've been gone a long time and things have changed. There are new techniques, costs have risen, the whole scope of production has changed. How can you expect to compete without the current know-how?"

"I'll find a way," Jason retorted dryly.

"Really."

Jason's eyes were a cool challenge. "Really."

Meredith flicked a considering glance at Taylor. "How do you feel about all this?"

"I'm with Jason all the way."

Out of the corner of her eye Taylor saw Jason's mouth quirk in approval. Meredith, faced with the strength of their convictions, seemed stymied for a moment. It was a good thing that Meredith couldn't read minds, Taylor decided; hers was filled with second thoughts and anxieties.

"You both seem awfully definite about this," Meredith said after a long moment.

"We are." Jason was positive.

"What would you think about cutting your costs in half and going into production with Maddox? We could ensure production and split the profits fifty-fifty."

Taylor held her breath. That was quite a concession for the head of Maddox Productions to make, and it was indicative of how much Meredith wanted to produce Taylor's screenplay.

Jason looked as if he were going to turn her down flat, but Meredith forestalled him by adding, "You two, of course, would have the leading roles, and Maddox would sign a contract with you both, guaranteeing you'll star in another two films as yet unscripted. If Taylor wants to do the screenplay for those, so much the better."

"You haven't even read Taylor's screenplay!" Jason stated in amazement. "How can you gamble so much?"

Taylor squirmed in her chair, hearing the challenge to Meredith's business sense beneath Jason's words. But Meredith was unperturbed.

"Because Ross Corley let me see a copy of Taylor's outline," she explained. "The story has all the elements a good Diamond film needs. And—" she turned up a realistic palm "—your own interest in it says a lot, Jason."

Taylor had forgotten about the outline; she should have known Meredith wouldn't make such wild promises without at least a glance at the story. She realized guiltily that Ross had probably shown her the outline because Taylor had practically agreed to let Maddox produce *Diamond in the Sky*.

And what would be wrong with having Maddox Productions in for half? To Taylor's way of thinking it would solve a whole host of problems, not the least being that she could pacify Meredith. She didn't want to alienate the woman if she could help it.

Jason's reaction to Meredith's proposal was harder to read. The muscles of his face were set; his eyes narrowed on Meredith's sculptured features. Or was he seeing Lisabeth sitting there? Taylor asked herself with a pang.

"You certainly know how to make things attractive, Meredith," he said with a smile that didn't quite touch his eyes. "But we'll have to think it over."

"What's to think over? I'm offering you a deal I wouldn't offer to anyone else, Jason. I'm sure you realize that."

Taylor glanced from Meredith to Jason and back again. There was something about the way they were looking at each other that raised the hair on her arms. The undercurrents in the room were palpable, and Taylor knew she was missing something important.

"I'll call you, Meredith," Jason said tersely, rising. Meredith, given no choice, reluctantly followed suit. She shook hands briefly with Jason, nodded curtly to Taylor, picked up her purse and walked to the door, hesitating at the threshold.

"Don't take too long," she said to Jason, then raised a hand in goodbye and left.

Jason shut the door softly, his palm resting on it a shade longer than necessary. He eased his shoulders back and turned sober eyes on Taylor, who was standing tensely on the other side of the room. "You didn't tell me about the outline," he said.

"I didn't know Ross had given it to Meredith. I only gave it to Ross so that he could see I was serious about writing. He'd been giving me a lot of grief about it," she added dryly.

Jason inclined his head and exhaled deeply. "Well, it doesn't matter now anyway. The decision's made and Meredith is just going to have to get used to it."

"You mean, you're not even going to consider her offer?" Taylor tried to keep the anxiety out of her voice.

"Does it matter so much to you?" Jason frowned. "I thought we'd settled all that."

Taylor hunched her shoulders. "I still don't like the idea of you shouldering all the costs. Maddox could cut the risk in half."

"And the profits," Jason reminded her, long strides bringing him closer to her.

"So who cares? I'm not dying to be super rich. I just want to work, and hopefully keep you from losing all your money in the bargain."

Jason smiled into her earnest face. "I'm not going to lose all my money," he assured her. "I'm not going to lose any of it." He brushed back the silky tumble of her hair from her forehead. "Stop worrying," he said softly.

"I can't help it. I don't like it that you're the one taking all the chances. Are you sure you don't want to accept Meredith's offer?"

In lieu of answering, Jason clasped her hand, guided her to the couch and pulled her down beside him. He meditatively traced the bones on the back of her hand as he said, "Look, there's something I need to tell you."

Taylor suddenly felt cold. "What is it?" she asked in a low voice.

"There's a reason I don't want to get involved with Meredith and Maddox Productions." Lines formed between his brows. "Lisabeth, of course, is part of it—" his jaw tightened "—but that's not all of it. I'd just like to keep some distance from both Meredith and Clifton."

Remembering his reaction when he'd first seen Meredith, Taylor was sure she knew the reason. But she was shocked into silence when Jason's blue eyes looked somberly into hers and he said with a trace of bitterness, "Meredith made a pass at me once, Taylor."

Taylor's lips parted in disbelief, and Jason sighed, his lips tightening. "It was a very determined effort on her part, too," he admitted. "While we were on Madeira. Clifton was furious—"

"He *knew*?"

Jason grimaced in remembrance, and he leaned back against the cushions, every muscle tense. "He had the bad luck to catch Meredith—undressed—in my room." He shook his head, inhaling between his teeth. "Believe me, I wasn't interested, and I was explaining as much to Meredith when Clifton arrived. You can't imagine the scene that erupted. To make a long story short, Clifton and I had a row to beat all rows, and when I told him I was leaving Hollywood he nearly came apart. I told him a little bit about Lisabeth's problems, enough to make him see I wasn't trying to flee the scene of the crime, but he was still furious. He threatened me with a breach-of-contract suit, but I'd never signed any contracts so it was all a big smokescreen." He smiled faintly. "I couldn't wait to get out of Los Angeles and back to someplace sane."

Taylor slid her arm around his waist. "Oh, Jason," she murmured, "I didn't know."

His fingers ran under the curtain of her hair, caressing her nape and the slope of her throat. "You were the only solid thing left in my life. I used to watch you—how hard you worked, how much you wanted to do it right, be the best you could be—and I'd think, if only everyone was like Taylor." He buried his face in her hair. "I used to look at you and wish—"

"What?" Taylor whispered when he broke off.

Jason kissed her lightly on the temple, ruffling the sensitive hairs near her ear. "Let's just say it would have been a lot more difficult to say no to you than it was to Meredith."

Taylor twisted to search his face. This was the first indication she'd had that he'd ever felt something more for her than friendship before she'd come to Whidbey.

He was regarding her from beneath lowered lids, watching her as closely as she was watching him. "I would never have been unfaithful to Lisabeth—and you would never have had an affair with a married man—so the question of 'what if?' is academic. Besides," he added lightly, trying to dispel the mood of solemnity that had dropped over them, "I got to take you to bed several times while we were on Madeira."

Taylor smiled. "Jake took Julie to bed, as I recall, and Jason Garrett concentrated very hard on remembering his lines."

"It wasn't all that tough," he said lazily. "The words just came."

She felt the knot slip on her robe as Jason's fingers started a dangerous foray across the warm skin of her abdomen. She looked at him through mysterious amber eyes and murmured, "What's it going to be like playing a love scene together now?"

She saw his rakish grin before his head dipped to taste the triangle of skin exposed by her spreading robe. "We won't have to worry about motivation, will we?"

"No…" Taylor's eyes fluttered closed as his tongue left a moist trail across her skin. Her hands clenched in his hair and her limbs trembled, her body sliding weakly down the cushions in utter capitulation.

"And practice makes perfect," he added thickly, just as the robe parted completely and his mouth found the eager anticipation of hers.

Taylor had barely gotten over the scorching headlines in the Hollywood tabloids, when the phone rang for the umpteenth time, followed by the buzzing of her doorbell.

"Oh, Lord," she muttered, flinging down the paper. "What now?"

Jason had managed to sneak past the reporters and meet with one of the major studio heads, and Taylor had filled her time—between phone calls—by making lists of what to do next. She knew she was in way over her head as far as production went, but she believed implicitly in Jason's business acumen. They were a team, she realized, in more ways than one, and what he couldn't do, she could, and vice versa.

She told the production person on the line that Jason wasn't in right now, then she hung up and went to open the door. If it was another blasted reporter...

The short man with the trim beard was definitely not a reporter; he was Phil Walker.

"Hello, Phil." Taylor ushered him in with a smile.

"Taylor."

"Jason's not here right now," she said as he looked slowly around her apartment. Taylor wondered if he saw the same lack of personality that she had, and what conclusions he was drawing if he did. "He's out looking for studio support and financing."

Phil's dark brows rose. "Already?"

"He's not a man to sit and wait for it to find him."

Phil cleared his throat. "No, he's not." He looked at Taylor thoughtfully. "So you got him to come back. I must say, I'm surprised."

"That I was successful, or that he came back at all?" Taylor asked, her smile widening.

"Both. I was worried about you, you know."

Taylor nodded. She hadn't forgotten Phil's well-meant advice for her not to go to Whidbey—but she was glad she hadn't taken it.

"So, how is he, in your opinion?"

Taylor shrugged. She didn't like talking about Jason behind his back, and she felt especially uneasy where Phil was concerned. "Maybe you should talk to him. He seems okay... to me."

"Hmm." Phil's gaze was sharp. "Has he talked to you about the accident?"

"He's mentioned it, sort of—in passing." Taylor heard the uncertainty creeping into her voice, and added, "But I haven't pushed him about it."

"Has he brought up the events of that night at all? What caused the accident? What frame of mind Lisabeth was in, what frame of mind *he* was in?"

"Look, Phil—" Taylor made nervous motions with her hands. "No! I don't know. You'll have to ask him yourself."

"You really think he'll talk to me?" Phil asked with weary humor. "Ah, Taylor, I think Jason would rather sleep on nails."

She couldn't help laughing at his comic defeat, but Phil was enough of an expert on human nature not to take offense. He smiled and accepted her invitation to join her in a snack of cheese and fruit, and by the time Jason arrived they had cemented a firm friendship.

Jason walked in just as Phil was saying to Taylor, "You may be the best thing that's happened to Jason Garrett in years."

"Is that another expert opinion on your part?" Jason asked without rancor, but his expression was closed as he pulled up the chair next to Taylor and across from Phil.

"Hello, Jason." Phil was remarkably at ease as he added, "And yes, that is my expert opinion, although I admit I was against Taylor going up to Whidbey in the beginning." He stroked his beard again, and said thoughtfully, "You certainly look a lot better than the last time I saw you."

In a dark suit and white shirt, his tie loosened around his neck, Jason seemed a different person from the one Taylor had first encountered at the Tidewater. Still, beneath the trappings, he'd changed very little—except that he seemed to be getting over Lisabeth's and Kerri's deaths.

"You look remarkably the same," Jason answered dryly.

Taylor could tell Phil was impressed by the change in Jason when he responded with a half smile, "I hope that means you're not going to throw me out again."

"Not yet." Tiny laugh lines drew together at the corners of Jason's eyes. "But watch your step."

It was another hurdle jumped with relative ease, and after Phil and Jason had finally broken the ice, Taylor heaved an inward sigh of relief. If only all their problems could be so easily solved.

Jason explained that he'd had good luck with his meetings and expected to sign a distribution deal with one of the major studios soon. In the meantime, he was looking around for office space, somewhere to headquarter Whidbey Productions, the name Jason had whimsically given their production company. Everything seemed to be going perfectly.

If there was a cloud on the horizon at all, Taylor felt, it was Jason's inability to shake the past—evidenced by his reaction when he first saw Meredith again. Taylor didn't need to question him about it to know what his feelings were: he was still in love with Lisabeth and it was simply going to take time for him to put his love for her to rest. It bothered Taylor more than she liked to admit, but it was just part of Jason's overall makeup, one piece of a fascinating whole, and she was determined not to let that fragment spoil her love for him.

Ross Corley's swank offices were in Westwood, not far from Wilshire Boulevard but thirty miles and several income-tax brackets away from Taylor's southern Los Angeles apartment. As Taylor stepped from the elevator and walked down a wine-carpeted hallway to the glass doors embossed with Ross's name, she reflected that Ross had shown unusual restraint in not offering unasked-for advice about what a mistake she was making by producing *Diamond in the Sky* herself.

"Taylor," he said, rising from behind his desk and clasping her hand. He was as impeccably dressed as ever, and his sharp eyes traveled over her from head to toe, missing nothing. Taylor resisted the impulse to smooth her taupe skirt, or tug on the hem of her jacket.

"So you're really going into production on your own," he mused with a doleful shake of his head. "Unbelievable."

"It's good to see you, too, Ross," Taylor said dryly, then more seriously, "You think I'm making a mistake, don't you?"

Ross was pragmatic. "No. Maybe not. Everyone seems to have a great deal of confidence that Garrett will pull it off. Tell me, how in the world did you get him to do it?"

"It was his idea."

Ross laughed. "Oh, Taylor, you can't con me like you did Garrett."

"I'm not kidding," she said with asperity, seating herself stiffly in one of Ross's soft leather chairs. "It was Jason's idea to produce. I wanted to go with Maddox Productions but I was overruled."

"Uh-huh." Ross was barely holding a smile in check.

Taylor hadn't come all the way to his office to listen to veiled insinuations about her relationship with Jason. She gave him a mock glare that fell just short of furious, and said, "I just wanted to touch base with you. Jason's found some offices and he's putting together a production crew right now. They're going to start casting right away, so if you know anyone right for the other parts...?"

Ross snapped back into professionalism. "I've got lots of talented actors perfect for those parts. Let me give you a few names."

As Ross called his secretary to bring him some files, Taylor leaned back in her chair and crossed her legs. She'd told Jason she wanted to check with Ross before making a casting announcement because, whatever else Ross was, he was a terrific agent and had a knack for casting. Jason had been more than willing; he also knew Ross's reputation.

"You know," Ross said, after giving Taylor the details on several actors and actresses, "your father stopped by the other day."

Taylor looked up in surprise. "My father?"

"He wanted me to represent him, said he's been testing for that prime-time soap I told you about and is pretty certain he'll be cast."

Taylor didn't know what to say. She loved her father—rake that he was—but she knew better than anyone how poor he was at making commitments. "What are you planning to do?" she asked cautiously.

"I don't know," Ross mused. "I was thinking about giving him a try. I've seen some of his work and I know the part he's trying for. If he can get his act together, so to speak, he's got a chance at a part that's perfect for him."

Taylor felt a surge of excitement that she instantly quashed, remembering all the other times he'd thrown away chances for a perfect part.

"Would you hire him for *Diamond in the Sky* if you had the right part for him?" Ross asked.

The question made Taylor drop her eyes, and she fingered a frayed corner of one of the files Ross had given her. "I don't know," she prevaricated, when in actual truth she was certain she wouldn't take such a chance. She ached inside, calling herself the worst kind of ingrate, yet she knew she wouldn't sabotage Jason's efforts with such a high risk as her father.

"That bad, huh?" Ross murmured sympathetically.

Taylor's eyes were clouded with regret when she met his gaze again. "My father's a great actor, but he has no ambition. Sometimes I think it would have been better if it were the other way around."

"Perseverance counts for a lot," Ross agreed. "Just look at where it's gotten you."

As if embarrassed by his unexpected compliment, Ross got back to the business of convincing Taylor to cast several unknowns in her production. Taylor, however, had been given something to think about, and as she drove back to her apartment that evening she considered her talents and ambition in a new light.

It was ambition and perseverance that had put her where she was today, and a certain unfailing stubbornness. Going after Jason had been just the type of challenge she couldn't resist—refused to fail at.

As she drove into the parking lot she felt a swift rush of confidence and excitement. How could she and Jason fail, with the two of them working together? Jason was terrifically talented, but he was also ambitious and knew how to persevere. They were, and always had been, a remarkable team, an unbeatable team; only when they were apart did disaster seem to strike.

With a new sense of identity Taylor climbed the stairs to her floor. As long as she and Jason were together, the production was sure to be a success, she told herself happily. And there was nothing that could break them apart now.

Chapter Ten

Production began as a trickle of jobs attended to mainly by Jason, but it fast became an avalanche that had both him and Taylor inundated. Every day new people were hired to help, and as sets, locations, scenes and cast members were changed, then changed again, the pace became even more hectic. Taylor became a gofer for anyone who needed something done right away, and in the process learned more about preproduction than she'd ever imagined.

The press paid them more attention than they really wanted. The fact that on-screen lovers had turned off-screen lovers was a source of interest to all the tabloids. It added an extra element of adventure and romance to Jason and Taylor's project, and every time Taylor turned around she saw another headline about herself, Jason and *Diamond in the Sky*.

She hoped, after the big buildup, that the film would be a success.

"You," Jason told her after an especially exhausting day, "are a natural-born worrier."

They were seated in Jason's makeshift office, Jason behind a massive desk with his feet propped on top, Taylor on the leather couch that rested against a side wall. It was one of the few quiet moments they'd been able to share in days.

"Well, I never would have called you an optimist," Taylor said, smiling, "but I think I'm beginning to change my mind."

Jason shook his head. "I'm a realist. Everything's going to be fine, you'll see." He reached into his desk drawer and pulled out a bottle of bourbon tied with a bright red ribbon. "Want a drink?"

Taylor was a little surprised. She hadn't seen Jason drink anything since his days at the Tidewater. "Are you going to have one?"

Jason gave her an odd look. "Hell, no. We start shooting tomorrow and I'm not going to screw that up. This was a gift from the crew, sort of a precongratulations for a job well done."

Taylor's anxieties melted away and she stretched languidly and yawned. "Then I won't either. Besides, you don't have any glasses and I'm not hard core enough to drink straight out of the bottle."

"You underestimate me," Jason retorted, pulling out a stack of Styrofoam cups.

For some reason they both laughed, the giddiness of success going straight to their heads. When the moment of hilarity passed, Taylor saw Jason looking at her with such desire and love that she caught her breath.

"I take back everything I ever said about Phil Walker," Jason said huskily, "because he was certainly right on one thing: you are good for me."

Taylor felt her eyes fill with unexpected tears. "We're a team," she said unsteadily, trying to blink them away.

"Yes. We are." Jason's expression was grave.

A knock on the door broke the tension that had developed, and at Jason's hollered, "Come in," the door opened to admit Meredith Maddox.

Taylor looked at her in surprise. Meredith was dressed in a smart black business suit and looked as if she'd just come from some special meeting. But her features were drawn and pinched, and she was shaking with emotion.

"I need to talk to you, Jason," she said in a strained voice.

Jason exchanged a puzzled look with Taylor, then said, "Sit down, Meredith," as he came around his desk, tucked a hand under her elbow and guided her to the couch. She clutched the fingers on her arm with a kind of desperation that made Taylor feel uncomfortable. Wondering if she should leave, Taylor looked questioningly at Jason, but he gave a quick, almost imperceptible shake to his head and Taylor sat back tensely, unnerved by Meredith's frantic state.

When Jason tried to straighten after depositing Meredith on the couch, her hands reached up and captured his wrists. "You won't believe what's happened," she said in a hoarse whisper, her eyes huge. "Clifton's usurped my power! He's taken over as head of Maddox Productions again!"

Taylor's shoulders instantly relaxed. From Meredith's state she'd feared disaster had struck, not just some top-level infighting.

"I'm not surprised at all," Jason told her gently, easing himself away from Meredith's grasping hands. "Clifton isn't the kind of man to take a back seat for long, especially now that he's recovered."

Meredith clenched her teeth together and shook her head violently. "You don't understand! We had a huge argument over company procedure and he just took over! I was furious; I *am* furious. I—I told him I wanted a divorce."

Jason's brows drew together in a dark line as he gazed down at his ex-sister-in-law. He rubbed a hand around the back of his neck, and Taylor could sense how uneasy he felt. Meredith's emotional state was taking a toll on him as well, and with a primitive rush of protectiveness, Taylor suddenly wanted to shield Jason from what Meredith could do to him. Did she remind him of Lisabeth? Taylor wondered with an inward grimace. Something about the white-lipped way Jason was looking at her made Taylor think she did.

"You know what Clifton said?" Meredith asked disbelievingly. "He said okay. Just like that, as cool as you please. 'Okay, Meredith, you've got your divorce.'" Her hands trembled as she nervously fingered the dark strands of her hair. "My God. I can't believe this is happening."

Jason glanced at Taylor, his expression unreadable; then his eyes fell on the bottle of bourbon. "Let me get you a drink," he told Meredith. He poured some into one of the plastic cups and placed it in Meredith's shaking palms.

"Wait!" Meredith's hand plucked anxiously at Jason's sleeve as he attempted to walk back to his desk. "I came over here for a reason, not just to lay this on you," she said with a short, mirthless laugh. "I've given my heart and soul to that company. I've made it what it is today!''

"Clifton knows that, Meredith," Jason said in a taut voice. Meredith had risen and was standing right next to him, not releasing his arm. Taylor's throat felt constricted. She wanted to alter the course of the conversation but was powerless to do anything but stand by helplessly.

"Does he? I don't think he does," she said bitterly. "That's why I've come here. I want to work for you. I want to make your production company the best, and believe me, I can. You know I can, Jason."

She was looking up at him appealingly, but with a slant of determination to her jaw. Taylor saw Jason swallow hard. With frightening insight she realized he was reliving some other scene.

Taylor was furious with Meredith for not seeing what was so plain to her. Was the woman so self-absorbed that it never dawned on her how fragile Jason's emotions still were over Lisabeth? Had she forgotten how much she looked like her sister?

"Meredith," Taylor said into the uncomfortable silence, "are you certain that's what you want?"

Meredith turned to look blankly at Taylor, as if she'd forgotten she was even in the room. Then the simmering resentment Taylor had always known existed blazed from her eyes. "What do you mean?" she asked distinctly.

"I mean, as far as Clifton's concerned, mightn't that be the last straw? Your coming to work for us?"

"What are you talking about?"

Taylor now had Meredith's full attention, and she began to feel sorry she'd ever ventured into the fray. There was something about Meredith's frozen stare that made

Taylor hesitate, want to back down. Only her love and need to protect Jason kept her going.

"I don't know what you really want, Meredith, but if you're interested in saving your marriage, coming to work for Jason is about the worst thing you could do."

Taylor hadn't meant to give away that she knew about Meredith's attempt to have an affair with Jason, but from the way the blood drained from Meredith's cheeks, leaving them a sick gray, Taylor realized she'd inadvertently done just that. Even Jason's brows lifted in surprise, but before he could say anything Meredith sprang into action.

"Who the hell are you?" she demanded, her voice shaking with rage. "I don't need advice on my marriage from *you*!"

"I wasn't giving advice. I just meant—"

"I know what you meant." Meredith's lips drew into a tight line of anger.

Jason sighed and tried to get Meredith to sit down again, but her body was rigid with animosity. "Meredith—"

"Don't patronize me, Jason." She tossed her head back and glared at Taylor, her voice trembling with suppressed fury as she asked coldly, "If you're so knowledgeable about relationships, why haven't you been straight with Jason? Why haven't you told him about our little deal, Taylor? The one you broke when you got a better offer?"

Taylor's eyes widened in shock at the pure venom in Meredith's tone.

"Oh, don't look so innocent," Meredith went on scathingly. "Go ahead, Jason." She looked into his impassive face. "Ask! Ask me all about Taylor Michaelson. I know you're dying to."

"Meredith." Jason's voice held an element of danger. "I think you should leave."

"She didn't tell you, did she? About what I offered her in exchange for bringing you back? No . . . I can see she didn't."

Once started, Meredith seemed compelled to pour out the whole story, and Taylor, who felt incapable of any kind of defense, listened to the fury and frustration that had been festering inside Meredith. She realized she'd misunderstood Meredith's motives where Jason was concerned.

"Oh, I didn't really have much hope that she'd succeed," Meredith continued, her mouth bowed scathingly downward, "but just in case, well—" she lifted a dismissive shoulder "—I decided to give her some added incentive. I told her Maddox would produce her screenplay if she could get you to come back. We had a deal, a pact. Isn't that right, Taylor?"

Taylor couldn't speak. The web of tiny lies she'd strung, one after another, to ensure Jason's trust in her made it impossible for her to deny the black picture Meredith was painting.

"Get out, Meredith," Jason ordered savagely. "Get the hell out, and don't come back."

Meredith's lower lip quivered. "You'll learn the truth soon enough, Jason. Just ask Ross Corley. He knows about Taylor's intentions; she called him from Whidbey several times with reports on you." She shot a rancorous glance at Taylor and said in a sugary tone, "We were all so glad to hear how well you were progressing."

Jason didn't believe a word of Meredith's vindictive accusations; he'd known her too long to accept anything she said on face value, and she'd proved more than once that her motives weren't always what they seemed. "Get out!" he roared, and Meredith took a step back.

"Wake up, Jason," she muttered. "Just take a look at your lady love and you'll know I'm right."

Taylor could have been a statue, her face was so pale, her features so immobile, her eyes transfixed. Jason took in another sharp breath, considered hustling Meredith out of his office bodily if she said one more spiteful word, then hesitated, constrained by something in Taylor's reaction.

Meredith stood by, silently triumphant.

"Taylor?" Jason asked in a low voice.

Taylor blinked several times and took in a shaky breath, but she still couldn't speak. Her eyes filled with awesome regret, and Jason's stomach turned inside out, the bitter taste of gall filling his throat.

"So." Meredith's voice was curiously subdued. "Now you know."

Seeing she'd wreaked enough damage, Meredith walked woodenly toward the door, casting a yearning glance over her shoulder at Jason. "You know, I'd hoped things would be different for us, once you got your head together over Lisabeth," she said quietly, regretfully.

Jason's head turned slowly to look at Meredith, but he didn't say anything. Meredith, understanding the silence for what it was, gave him a weak smile and left.

Taylor hadn't noticed the unearthly quiet of the room before, but now it seemed to press upon her, suffocating her.

"You lied to me," Jason said flatly.

"No, I didn't lie. I told you the truth from the beginning about why I went to see you." Taylor held his gaze. In this, at least, she could be completely honest.

"The hell you did," he growled. "God." He threw back his head in disbelief. "My God."

Taylor was squeezing her hands together so tightly they were bloodlessly white. "I love you, Jason. Believe me. You know that's true."

"Shut up!"

His thundering voice made her capitulate instantly. She was shaking all over, trembling uncontrollably. She waited with drowning eyes while Jason visibly reined in his rage.

"You did strike a deal with Meredith, didn't you? And you did call Corley, didn't you? *Didn't you?*"

"I called Ross. That much is true. But I didn't go to Whidbey because Meredith wanted—"

"What did she offer you on your screenplay? How much?"

Tears pooled in the corners of her eyes. "No amount," Taylor whispered. "She said she'd read it if I..." She couldn't go on without breaking down completely, but Jason waited with a stone-cold implacability that made her insides fill with pain. "But I never asked her to," she managed unsteadily. "I went to see you because I...loved you."

The expression on his face was part disbelief, part loathing. Taylor's hopes of explaining herself died a quick death and tears tracked silently down her cheeks.

"I thought...I was smart enough...not to get tricked by a woman again." Jason's voice was strangled. "But, oh, Taylor, how you've proved me wrong."

She shook her head, hair tumbling in tawny waves around her ravaged face. "I never tricked you."

"You used me! You used me as a means to sell your screenplay! And, sucker that I am, I went all the way with it. I begged you to let me produce it."

"Jason..." Taylor rose on unsteady legs, a hand reaching out to him in entreaty. "If you think about what you're saying, you'll realize I'm not like that."

"Sorry, Taylor." His blue eyes were as cold as winter lakes. Taylor shuddered involuntarily as he snarled, "I know exactly what you're like...now."

"You don't know me at all, then," she whispered, squeezing her eyes closed against the welling tears.

"Yes. I do." Jason was savage. "You're even worse than Meredith because you stung her and Maddox Productions along the way too!" He moved sharply, violently. "God! And I made it so easy for you to get everything you wanted!"

Taylor sensed she'd already lost him, but he was too important to her just to hang her head and give up now. "The only thing I've ever wanted is you," she said with trembling conviction. "You. I didn't even know it when I first went to Whidbey, but I know it now. I love you. I'll always love you."

Jason's laugh was harsh and cruel. "Always is a long time, Taylor. I don't think your 'love' for me is going to last another five minutes." She looked at him with a complete lack of understanding until he said, "I'm going to recast the role of Julie Diamond. You're out. I'll pay you for your screenplay and even something for your work so far, but you're out as far as production goes. Take me to court if you want, but you'll lose. I guarantee it."

"Jason..." Taylor felt weak. Her legs could hardly hold her.

"In the end you got exactly what you wanted." His voice lashed at her like a whip. "Congratulations. You should be a happy woman."

In dim misery Taylor saw him stalk to the door and fling it open. It crashed against the wall with shuddering force. "That's all, Taylor," Jason said, his face filled with the kind of white tension she hadn't seen since Whidbey. She tried to say something, but the only sound that issued from her throat was a gurgling sob. Jason's stony features showed no remorse, and Taylor was forced to stumble from the office, her head throbbing with an intense pain that was as much of the spirit as it was physical.

She turned back, her lips parting in a yet unformed plea, but the door slammed shut in her face, a last volley in the terrible battle.

Time was a slow healer of wounds, Taylor concluded a week later. She felt more miserable now than she had after that awful fight, and she knew she was going to feel a whole lot worse before she felt better. She'd tried to talk to Jason several times, once when she'd made the mistake of going to his office, and then again when he'd come to pick up his clothes from her apartment. That had been the worst, watching him collect his possessions, knowing he hoped never to see her again. She'd followed him disconsolately to her bedroom, watching him rip his clothes from her closet and toss them on the bed.

"Stay out of my way," he'd warned coldly when Taylor made an involuntary move to help. "And stay out of my life."

Taylor hadn't been able to choke back the gasp of desolation his cruel words evoked. She was utterly shattered. She'd hoped—no, prayed—that he would have had time to come to his senses and realize she wasn't the avaricious woman Meredith had proclaimed her to be.

"I need to talk to you," she'd said faintly. "I need to explain."

Jason's back was to her. He didn't bother turning to face her as he continued stuffing his clothes inside his suitcase. "There is nothing you can say that will change my mind about you. Nothing."

His cold refusal to listen had burned inside her, firing her blood, making it impossible for her to let him walk so unjustly out of her life. "Damn you, Jason! You're so certain everybody's ready to sell you out. Well, you're wrong!" Taylor's anger made her reckless. "And you're taking the easy way out—just like you did before!"

He swung around with such swift force that Taylor was momentarily alarmed. "You don't know anything about that," he snarled.

"How could I?" The muscles of Taylor's face ached from her effort to maintain control. "You keep it all bottled up inside. You won't let anyone in!"

"Well..." He turned to snap the suitcase shut, giving her a view of his broad back. "Seeing how things turned out, it looks like I was lucky I didn't confide in you."

"You wouldn't have anyway." Taylor's chin lifted stubbornly though it trembled with the effort. "You can't trust anyone. You're so ready to believe the worst in someone that you overlook the obvious."

"My problem is I *didn't* believe the obvious, Taylor!" Jason muttered savagely. "I knew why you came to Whidbey. My mistake was letting you in in the first place!"

It was the feeling of knowing that everything that mattered to her was slipping through her fingers that goaded Taylor on. She loved Jason. She needed Jason. And the more he refused to believe in her, the more determined she became to prove her love.

"Your mistake, Jason," she said harshly, fists clenched, "was closing your ears and mind to the truth. I love you. I've said it before and I'll say it again: *I love you*. You're just too blind and stubborn to believe it!"

She saw the muscles tense beneath his shirt and had to control the urge to throw her arms around him, capture him, shake some sense into him.

He swept up the case and tried to bulldoze his way past her, but she blocked the doorway like some dramatic heroine, her tawny gaze waging a desperate war with his ice-blue one. The knuckles around the handle of his suitcase whitened, the muscle along his jaw jumped to life, and with a deadly kind of determination, Jason pushed her aside with his other hand.

She wanted to kick and scream and yell. "You damn fool," she choked on a sob, striking his shoulder with an impotent fist, and in an instant Jason's suitcase had fallen to the floor and she was suddenly held against the wall by his full weight.

"Yes, I'm a fool," he ground in her ear. "A damn fool!"

Her shoulders were being pressed mercilessly against the wall, the pressure becoming painful, but she didn't care. She could feel the hard, wild beat of his heart and the hidden emotions that ran like tremors within him.

"Oh, Jason..." She lifted her palm to his face and for just a moment he stared at her through pain-filled eyes. Then he wrenched himself away, grabbed his case and slammed out of the room, out of her apartment, and out of her life.

Taylor had flung herself on the couch and cried huge, wracking sobs into one of the pillows, telling herself she hated him, knowing that in part she'd brought this down on her own head.

Over the week she'd tried to pull herself together and think about the future, but without Jason she was only half a person. All her ambition, all the fire and inspiration that had made her the person she was, seemed to have vanished with Jason. She felt empty and hollow inside, and the future was bleak and gray.

When the phone started ringing with reporters abuzz over the news that Taylor no longer worked for Whidbey Productions and that she would not be playing the lead character, Julie Diamond, Taylor unplugged it. Whole parts of herself seemed to be dissolving and shifting, disintegrating within her, and she couldn't take hearing any more. How could Jason do it? What right did he have? If he was purposely setting out to hurt her, he couldn't have picked a more effective way.

When Ross gave up trying to reach her by phone and came over to her apartment, beating on the door and calling to her until she finally let him in, Taylor was at a very low ebb.

What he thought when he saw her he didn't say, but he gave her some quick, sharp advice.

"Get yourself together, Taylor, and we'll get you a job with another production company. We'll sue Garrett for the right to *Diamond in the Sky* and we'll make his life so miserable that he'll wish to hell he was back on that godforsaken island!"

"I'm not a vindictive person, Ross, you know that," Taylor said later, in his office. "I'm not interested in a lawsuit."

Though Ross's words had brought her somewhat to her senses, Taylor had no intention of trying to get revenge. Jason could have *Diamond in the Sky* for all she cared; it had been forged out of her love for him anyway.

"It's not like you to give up, Taylor," Ross said flatly. "I say, sue him! Don't let him ride roughshod over you. You pulled him back from the edge, and this is how he pays you back?"

There was no explaining to Ross about Jason's paranoid certainty that people always used one another to their advantage, about how she'd assured him she was different, about how she'd inadvertently proved herself wrong. As far as Ross was concerned, it was her screenplay and she had every right to demand it back from Jason—period.

"The bastard!" Ross said indignantly. "Who the hell does he think he is? That's your screenplay! That's your part!"

Taylor wearily pushed her hair away from her face. Ross's unrelenting attack on Jason's character had at first helped bounce her back, but now it just added to her crushing desolation.

"I'm not going to sue him," she said firmly. "To be honest, I really don't give a damn about the screenplay."

Ross was incredulous. "Are you kidding? All that work, Taylor! You can't let Jason Garrett steal it from you!"

Taylor stood up and crossed her arms beneath her breasts. She walked across the lushly carpeted floor to the wide window at the back of the room. The view was of buildings and traffic and afternoon haze, and Taylor yearned for the clear crisp air of Whidbey Island. "He's not stealing it. He's paying for it, and I'm sure he'll be generous," she murmured with some bitterness.

"The press has had a field day with this," Ross commented dourly.

"Don't I know it." Taylor sighed, remembering.

The telephone calls had begun again as soon as she'd plugged her phone back in the wall. Speculation had been rife, and though she'd hoped interest would have diminished, it seemed with every passing day there was a new wrinkle in the story. One account had it that Jason had tossed her out when he caught her with another man. Another suggested that he'd finally realized how untalented she was and had simply paid her off. A third stated that she hadn't written the screenplay at all and had been found out and consequently fired.

Several reports simply blamed the breakup on a lovers' quarrel, and Taylor wasn't certain she liked that any better than the other stories, even though it was the closest to the truth.

Incredibly, with all the notoriety, she'd suddenly found herself in hot demand professionally. Ross had several offers for her to wade through and he'd insisted she get down to his office to go through them. But his anger at Jason had ruled the morning, and so far he'd been able to discuss little else.

"They're casting for someone to replace you as Julie Diamond," Ross said quietly. "I suppose you know that."

A sharp pain lanced Taylor's heart. "Yes, I know."

"It's not fair, Taylor. Jason Garrett used you."

That was just what Jason had accused her of doing. Taylor winced as she remembered Jason's angry words. But if she'd used him, what had he done to her? And how could he think she'd been motivated by pure avarice? She'd given him so much of herself—the most a woman can give. How could he think so little of her? *How?*

Suddenly the answer was obvious, and as Taylor stared blankly out the window she considered it carefully, knowing she'd simply been unable to face it before. Jason's need of her was over. He'd gotten through the worst of his loss over Lisabeth and Kerri and had found a way to his future. Meredith's revelations had just given him the means to break off with Taylor painlessly—at least for him.

Except that he'd really been hurting when he came to her apartment that last time. That had been real emotion, not acting.

"You're grasping at straws," she reviled herself beneath her breath.

"What?" Ross came over to her, looking down at her with concern.

"Nothing. It just . . . hurts." She gave him a quick, artificial smile. "That's all."

Ross placed an arm around her shoulders and guided her back to her chair. "We've got things to go over, decisions to make. Put the abominable Jason Garrett out of your mind for a while and start thinking about yourself."

Marshall Durnley cleared his throat and grimaced inwardly at the task facing him. As director for *Diamond in the Sky*, he really had no authority to call Jason Garrett on the carpet, but if someone didn't say something soon the whole film was going to go down the tubes.

"Are you going to test with this new actress?" Marshall asked a bit sarcastically. "Or should I send her packing right now?"

"What does she look like?" Jason asked somewhat distractedly.

Marshall dutifully handed Jason the same photographs he'd shown him the night before. The packet of photos had been sitting on Jason's desk all day, yet somehow he'd never managed to open it on his own. "If you don't test with her, you're going to have to do it with someone else. Either that or bring Taylor Michaelson back."

"No."

Jason's flat refusal was the first spark of life Marshall had seen in him in days, and though it was probably a good sign, Marshall gave an exasperated snort. "You're going to ruin this picture with plain apathy, stubbornness and ego!" Marshall hit his fist lightly on Jason's desk and stalked to the door. He looked back at the drawn features of the man who'd hired him, shook his head, then slammed out.

Jason stretched his shoulders, grimacing. Damn Marshall! Damn Taylor! The whole production was in jeopardy because of her deceit.

Jason closed his eyes and leaned back, the chair squeaking under his weight. Honesty made him admit that that wasn't totally true. The production was in jeopardy because *he* couldn't make a decision. If they didn't cast the lead soon they'd run over budget before filming even began.

The trouble was, every actress looked the same. It didn't matter what color hair she had, what shade her eyes were, what she wore, said, did—they all looked the same!

And none of them were right for Julie Diamond.

Jason sighed. He'd always abhorred the egotists and incompetents in this business who held up production, but look at him—he was doing the same thing. Marshall Durnley was right, Jason thought grimly, rubbing a hand across his face. If he didn't decide something soon, he could kiss *Diamond in the Sky* goodbye.

He was going to have to dissociate his feelings for Taylor from the actress who was to be Julie Diamond and get on with it. Taylor had made her bed, as far as he was concerned, and now she could lie in it. Production was going to go on successfully without her.

Decision made, Jason got to his feet. He walked down the hall to the room they had rigged up with special lighting for the screen tests. Tomorrow, or the day after, or the day after that if it took that long to find the new Julie, production would move to the studio sound-stages, and then they would go on location to Madeira.

He put his palm flat on the panels of the door and paused, fighting back a surge of memories that were all mixed together: Lisabeth, the squealing tires, a scream, Taylor's amber eyes full of betrayal . . .

Jason shook his head. It was a reflection of his current mental state that he couldn't get Taylor out of his mind any more than he could the accident that had taken the lives of his wife and daughter. He suddenly longed for the cabin on Whidbey and the drifting life he'd led until Taylor had come for him.

Taylor. Jason clenched his fists and tried not to be consumed by black rage. Why in God's name couldn't he get over her? Why did thinking of her make him feel more desolate than he'd imagined possible?

He pushed open the door and strode purposefully into the room full of people, determined not to let anyone see his feelings. *Feelings!* Jason thought scathingly. *What are feelings?* His own had been trampled into dust, and he was glad that he didn't have to deal with them anymore.

Chapter Eleven

Okay now, Taylor. You and Craig are just going to read some lines together—nothing fancy. Don't be nervous." Allan Parman dropped a fatherly hand on Taylor's shoulder and handed her the script, pointing out the section of dialogue he wanted her to read.

Taylor nodded and smiled, hoping her fragile veneer didn't crack into a thousand pieces before she got through the scene. The actor she was working with, Craig Grassle, was friendly and eager, and though not as quick and talented as Jason, he seemed to be less mercurial.

"Go ahead," Allan said, and out of the corner of her eye Taylor saw the red light flash on that indicated the cameras were running.

She took a deep breath and blanked her mind to thoughts of Jason. This screen test could be important; it was for the part of Maggie Templeton, willful daughter of rich oil magnate and sometime adventurer,

Charles Templeton, of *Templeton's World*, National Broadcasting System's latest prime-time adventure-drama. Craig, the muscle-bound actor who'd already been hired to play Nick Raphael, Maggie's on-off, thorn-in-her-side lover, had the dark good looks of a typical television heartthrob.

Taylor tossed back her mane of streaked blond curls and said with a trace of biting sarcasm, "You can plot and cajole and work yourself into a heated frenzy but I'm not going with you. I'd rather die a thousand deaths than spend ten days alone with you."

Craig glanced at his script, then at Taylor. "You're a terrible liar, Maggie. You can't wait to go." He drew his lips back in a triumphant smile.

"For all your macho prowess, you don't know a damn thing about what a woman wants!" Taylor returned coldly.

Craig looked down at his script once more, his features tense. Then he lifted his head and regarded Taylor through heavy lids, his index finger coming up to slowly trace her lips. "I know *you*, Maggie," he said huskily, a split second before Taylor thrust his hand away. "I know what you want."

Templeton's World lacked the thread of humor that had been the mainstay of the *Diamond Girl* trilogy and also *Diamond in the Sky*, and personally, Taylor didn't feel she was quite right for the part. Maggie was to be cool and ruthless with emotions seething underneath—a character type in direct contrast to Julie Diamond. And, she realized wryly, Craig Grassle was no Jason Garrett, either in style, talent or manner.

Yet there was something to be said for having a bird in the hand, and since Jason hadn't given up his private vendetta against her, she would be foolish to sit around and dream of the perfect part.

If she really wanted to be an actress at all . . .

Taylor continued with the script for another page or two before the test ended, ironically aware that in this case, she was the far more seasoned performer. Craig could use someone like Jason Garrett to take him under his wing, Taylor thought with a pang of remembrance.

"We'll call you soon," Allan Parman said as she was leaving the studio. "It was a great test."

Was it? Taylor wondered as she drove back to her apartment. She knew her performance had been head and shoulders over Craig's, but in this case, since Craig had already been hired and needed someone of compatible presence and ability, her performance might work against her.

Not that it was that great, she reminded herself with a sigh. But it was okay.

Taylor wondered if she would ever get over this feeling of insecurity about her acting. Jason had always been there before, picking up the pieces, showing her the best way to work, giving her insight into her character. She worried about what kind of actress she would be without him.

Writing was really where her talents lay, Taylor concluded as she slipped the key into the lock of her apartment door. She had an idea percolating in her brain for another story—another *Diamond Girl* story. She bit her lip and wondered if she'd ever get out of this self-destructive phase. Writing about Jake and Julie Diamond seemed to be all she wanted to do these days, and she feared it was because she wouldn't give up on Jason. This was her way of hanging on to him, through the character he played, and she was almost obsessed with the scenes she created in her mind for Jake and Julie.

Taylor flipped on the television for company and went into her kitchen, trying to work up some enthusiasm for dinner. She ended up making a cheese omelet, then curled up on the couch, feet tucked beneath her, eating without enthusiasm.

Images flicked across the TV screen but Taylor barely noticed. She was too self-absorbed and her heart felt leaden. Not enough time's passed yet, she reminded herself in an effort to put her feelings in perspective. You ought to congratulate yourself on how far you've already come!

But Taylor had spend enough tear-filled nights the past several weeks to make a mockery of her days. And she was afraid there were a lot more in store for her.

She set the half-finished plate aside, pulled out a blanket from the wicker chest next to the couch and tugged it around herself. There was one rather incredible thing that had happened because of all the notoriety over her and Jason's breakup: Taylor's mother had called to offer sympathy.

It had been several nights earlier, when Taylor was at a particularly low point. The telephone had rung and Taylor, after a moment of worrying if the press was after her again, had placed the receiver next to her ear, her voice as lackluster as her whole future seemed to be.

"Hello?"

"Hello, Taylor. It's Loretta."

It was typical of her mother to identify herself by her first name, but Taylor had been too shocked to resent the purposeful detachment. "Mother?" she said faintly.

"Yes, darling. I've been reading about you all week and I just wanted to make certain you're all right."

Since when do you care?

The mean thought surfaced once then sank into oblivion. Taylor had long ago realized her mother was one of those people who simply couldn't relate to their children. "I'm fine," she assured her in a voice a good deal stronger than she felt. Her mother wouldn't expect any other answer, and if given one, wouldn't know how to handle it.

The conversation had gone on for several minutes, as brief and unrewarding as their relationship had always been. Even so, after Taylor had hung up she'd felt better. Infinitesimally better, but better nevertheless. Her mother had reached out to her in the only way she could, and for that, Taylor was grateful.

She was lost in her memories when suddenly her attention was riveted to the television screen. There was a picture of her and Jason on Madeira, one of the old posters! Taylor's heart beat faster as she saw the azure sky and ocean shading into each other, wispy strands of golden hair reaching across the distance between their two faces, eyes locked upon each other, smiles of utter happiness curving their lips. She had memorabilia from *Queen of Diamonds* herself, but seeing the poster suddenly brought a tightness to her throat she couldn't control.

She paused only an instant before turning up the volume.

"...only a few years ago posters like this one were everywhere, and they're destined to be again since production of *Diamond in the Sky* began and the screenplay's author, Taylor Michaelson, was unceremoniously booted out of Jason Garrett's new production company."

Taylor groaned. She should have guessed the thrust of the dubbed-over voice, but her eyes were frozen to the screen, seeing every contour and line of Jason's beloved face, seeing clearly for the first time the love shining innocently from her own face—love for Jason.

"...have selected a new actress to play Julie Diamond, the part vacated by Taylor Michaelson, and we're waiting for confirmation."

The picture disappeared from the screen, and the news changed from entertainment to sports. Taylor's face was a portrait of dismay. She didn't want to believe what she'd just heard; it seemed the final nail in the coffin. Jason had found another actress to play her part!

"Damn," she whispered. "Damn, damn, *damn*!" Her hands clenched impotently. How could he? In all truthfulness, she'd never fully believed he would have the audacity to take her screenplay and cast someone else as Julie Diamond. She'd subconsciously expected him to admit he was wrong and go back into production with her.

How could he do this to her? *Diamond in the Sky* was her work! She'd spent two years creating it, using it as a method to put her life back together after Jason's abrupt departure. All her brave words to Ross turned to ashes, and she suddenly realized she was in a blazing rage, more angry now than hurt. She wanted to kill him!

Acting on impulse alone, Taylor grabbed her sweater and her purse and left the apartment, practically running to her car. She wanted to see Jason before this glorious anger faded. She wanted to kick and scream and pound his chest with her fists.

How could he!

By the time she reached his office, most of the lights were out and a tug on the door handle proved it was indeed locked. Taylor rattled the handle with savage impatience, this last barricade only adding to her frustration. Suddenly the door swung inward. One of the crew members that Taylor knew was standing on the other side.

He looked at her in surprise and Taylor said with an attempt at a smile, "I've come to see Jason. Is he here?"

"Yep. In his office."

"Thanks."

She didn't offer any explanations and the crew member apparently didn't expect any. He watched her walk down the hallway, then shrugged, letting himself out.

Taylor's bravado began to slip when she was faced with the hard practicality of Jason's office door. She had a picture of herself twisting the handle and sailing into his room, all majestic fury and righteous anger, but she couldn't follow through. After a tense hesitation she lifted her clenched hand and rapped lightly on his door.

Jason didn't answer, but the door had been only partially latched and now it swung slowly inward, revealing him tilted back in the chair at his desk, eyes closed, hands locked behind his head.

His eyes opened as soon as she walked in, and he stared at her in silence for several heart-stopping moments, long enough for her to see the half-drunk bottle of Scotch, the glass balanced on his stomach, the total disorder of his office. A look of jaded weariness etched strong lines down his face from nose to mouth. Papers were scattered everywhere, overflowing from his desk to the floor, and as Jason shifted his weight in the creaking chair, his feet, crossed on the top of his desk, knocked a few more papers to the floor.

"Well, Taylor," Jason said magnanimously. "What brings you by?"

She wasn't fooled by his friendly tone; his eyes were a cold, icy blue. But just the sight of him constricted her throat, and she blinked several times before she could answer.

"I could say I was in the neighborhood, but that would be a lie," she said, straightening her shoulders.

Jason lifted a sardonic brow. "Another one?"

Taylor winced. She'd known it wasn't going to be easy, but she had hoped Jason would at least be in a more receptive mood than last time. "If I lied, it was only by omission. You were hardly in the frame of mind for me to admit that I'd had a talk with Meredith before I came to see you on Whidbey."

Jason smiled faintly and reached for his drink. "I see. Better to wait and spring it on me later."

Taylor's lips tightened. "Something like that, yes. I wasn't about to blow my chances with you by confessing to something that had *no* bearing on the real reason I came to see you!"

"Ah...yes..." Jason raised a pensive finger to his lips. "Refresh my memory. It was something about how much you cared for me, right?"

"Why are you being this way, Jason?"

Taylor stared at him through pain-filled eyes. She couldn't stand much more of this. He held her gaze and a terrible longing crossed his face, but then he looked away.

"You must have a reason for being here. State it, then get out."

Taylor's knees wobbled, and she had to sit down on the couch before she collapsed. "I came because... because..."

His silence and unrelenting expression made it nearly impossible to continue. Taylor heard her pulse beat in her ears like a slamming piston. "Because I love you," she said in a voice that sounded far away and weak. "Because I've always loved you, and because I keep hoping, praying, that you'll realize it soon before it's too late."

"It's already too late." His tone held no animosity; it was only a cruel statement of fact.

"Only because you've made it be!" Taylor said with a return of spirit. "I gave you myself, Jason. I'd do it again, even knowing how things have turned out. If you can't see that—"

"All I see," Jason interrupted fiercely, "is that by a smooth trick of timing you found a way to have it all— and damn the consequences to anyone else!"

"Then you're blind." Taylor's voice shook. "As blind as you were on Whidbey."

Jason's feet dropped to the floor with an ominous thud. "I don't need another scene with you," he said through his teeth.

"Well, you're damn well going to get one!" Taylor's cheeks flushed. "I've spent these past few weeks in utter misery—waiting, *waiting* for you to come to your senses. But you never have. For some reason you won't let yourself see what's staring you right in the face: *I love you!*"

As Taylor was speaking, Jason had walked around his desk and now stood directly in front of her. Taylor met his gaze and fought the trembling of her chin. Their eyes duelled for dreadful moments, and then Jason's gaze altered, narrowing on hers.

He inhaled deeply and silently, then said coldly, "Lisabeth used that same excuse once or twice, Taylor. 'I love you, Jason,' she said after the cocaine episode. She said it again after the first time I caught her in bed with someone else, even after the second time. And then she said, 'I'm sorry, Jason. I'm so, so sorry.'"

He watched Taylor's eyes widen with shock, then asked quietly, "Are you going to be sorry, too?"

Her lips formed a soundless protest. She looked at Jason helplessly.

"I thought taking Lisabeth to Whidbey would be a way to get her out of the fast lane, but it didn't quite work out that way. She told me she was dying of boredom and begged me to bring her back to Hollywood over and over again, but I wouldn't listen."

Jason was still watching her, so closely that Taylor felt a curious sense of what was to come. With cold waves of premonition running down her back, she murmured desperately, "I don't think I want to hear this."

Jason's hand lashed out to capture her wrist, and he pulled her to her feet. "Oh, you'll hear it. You've been begging me to tell you from the moment you turned up wide-eyed and eager on my doorstep."

"Jason..." Taylor twisted her wrist but she was shackled by the full strength of his hand. Her heart pounded. Her head ached. She tried to yank herself free but his hard grip bruised her to the bone.

"The night they died," he said tensely, "Lisabeth had been with another man; she'd found a lover on Whidbey, too. Only this time she was proud of it. No more 'I'm sorry, Jason.' That had long since passed. Now it was a punishment, the ultimate 'I told you so,' and though I'd convinced myself by that time that she couldn't hurt me anymore, I found out I was wrong."

Taylor ceased fighting completely. She felt as if she were in a dream, and she waited for it to be over.

"She told me she was going back. She already had the car packed. I think I realized at that point what a mistake I'd made believing isolation would help, and so I gave in with as much grace as I could manage." His mouth twisted bitterly. "Which wasn't much. But I was relieved, almost glad, that the decision had been made, until she told me she was taking Kerri with her. I wouldn't let her. I told her the only way I'd give up Kerri was after I was dead."

Taylor made a sound of protest but Jason was oblivious to it. Whatever he was remembering was so vivid that he'd forgotten the present, and Taylor realized it was as terrible as she'd ever imagined.

"She managed to trick me," Jason whispered hoarsely, "and get Kerri in the car with her. I screamed at her, but she tore out of the driveway and headed north...around the bend...."

"Jason, please!"

"Don't move, Taylor." His voice was steel, his fingers tightening painfully, punishingly. "Don't dare move."

"I don't think this is good for either one of us!"

"No?" The look in Jason's eyes was anguished. "They say confession's good for the soul, and you've wanted me to confess for a long, long time."

"Not this way," Taylor's voice was a thready whisper.

"Then what way? How would you like it? I can't think of any way to dress it up."

"I don't want to hear it at all," she moaned.

He pulled her very close, but it was not a lover's embrace; every muscle in his body was tense, and Taylor was no different. "I want to tell you now, Taylor," he grated in her ear. "Don't stop me."

Taylor's lips trembled but she stayed mute, listening.

Jason took a deep breath. "I followed Lisabeth in my Jeep, driving like a maniac because that's what she was doing. And around the last curve of the bay I saw it happen. One moment there were taillights, the next a rapidly sinking car. I watched while the lights went out under the water.''

"Jason!" Taylor was horrified.

"I don't remember diving in, but I did. I couldn't get there in time. I saw Lisabeth's face behind the windshield. She was alive, beating on the window. I fumbled with the door but it was too late. I just…couldn't…get her out."

Taylor was trembling from head to foot. She wanted to faint but fought not to, knowing how much Jason needed her at that moment. She hugged him very tightly, holding on, holding him, hearing the rasp of his ragged breathing, tasting the salt of her own tears as they ran into her mouth. His recollection was horrifying; she offered solace in her own silent anguish.

"I didn't see Kerri, thank God," Jason said, his voice breaking, "but I have dreams…"

"Oh, love. Oh, love, love…" Taylor had no words of comfort other than the soft, flowing croon that rose from her throat of its own volition.

She kissed him and held him and wondered how he'd remained sane at all. She didn't think she could have.

She buried her face in his chest, and felt his hands convulsively clench her hair. She wrapped her arms around his neck and kissed his throat, loving him, sharing his misery in the only way she knew how. His head bent to hers and their mouths touched, hungered, fused. It was a heated emotional moment and it shook Taylor to her soul, offering hope and love and the chance to forge something beautiful from the ugly ashes of his past.

But then his hands were suddenly on her upper arms, pushing her away. Taylor looked at him uncomprehendingly.

"Jason…?"

"I didn't think I could ever hurt like that again," he rasped, "but lady, you've done a damn good job. I don't ever want to hear 'I love you' from your lips again. I don't want to hear anything from you."

Taylor's eyes were drowned in her own tears. "Oh, Jason...please..."

"Go away, Taylor." He took in a shuddering breath and turned his back on her, fists clenched at his sides. "I can't stand the sight of you."

She believed him. She hadn't before, but she suddenly believed him now. Now she knew how he could hire another actress to take her place. Now she realized what seeing her did to him.

Through a haze of tears, stumbling, sobbing, she managed to get outside his office to the silent hallway. She felt hot all over, as if with fever, and she was sick to her very soul. She understood now; to Jason she represented the worst of what Lisabeth had been.

She ran to her car, jerked frantically at the handle, crying uncontrollably. It finally opened and she sat down heavily behind the wheel, chest heaving, tears streaming. She had no defense. There was nothing she could do. Not now. Had she known about Jason's lack of faith in Lisabeth, she might have done something to prevent this awful reckoning, but now she was a victim of her own naiveté.

Taylor cried until there were no more tears, until she was completely empty of feeling, numb to the bone-deep misery that consumed her. Then she drove herself home, crawled between the sheets of her lonely bed, and fell into a deep, exhausted slumber.

Chapter Twelve

I think it's time for us to go out and celebrate," Ross said, the smile in his voice reaching Taylor's ears across the telephone line. "Congratulations, Taylor. You got the part!"

"Of Maggie Templeton?" Taylor was astonished.

"Yup. Craig Grassle thinks you're the sexiest woman alive, or so he's telling the press."

Taylor rubbed her fingertips against her temple, trying to soothe the headache that had been her constant companion for days. She tried to work up some enthusiasm. "That's great, Ross. I really... can hardly believe it."

She could hear Ross laughing quietly to himself and demanded, "What's so funny? Is there something you're not telling me?"

"Oh...." Ross sighed in a thoroughly pleased way. "You know me too well, Taylor Michaelson. Craig isn't the only one who's glad you're in the series. There are others who love you even more."

Taylor went completely still. Ross's unfortunate choice of words echoed painfully in her heart. There were no "others" who loved her; she'd never truly been loved by anyone.

"What do you mean?" she asked, trying not to destroy his ebullient mood with her unhappiness.

"Your father's in the series, too. He plays your lovable, debauched uncle." Ross laughed. "Yes, he's a Templeton, too."

"I don't believe it!" Taylor was stunned.

"He hasn't told you yet? Well, that's because he just found out himself. Let's all go out and paint the town red."

"Ross..." Taylor protested faintly.

"Are you upset?"

Ross's voice had changed instantly, and Taylor sought to assure him that everything was fine. "Heavens, no. I'm just so pleased that Dad is...has a job." Taylor shook her head in amazement. She *was* pleased. Terribly pleased, and she realized she'd been wrong when she thought she would never take a chance on her father. She would. Even with all his faults, her love for him had always been strong.

"Then what's the problem?" Ross asked gently.

The sudden lump in Taylor's throat had no reason to be there. Nothing Ross had said should have put it there. But it swelled so huge that it took her several moments to pull herself together.

"There's no problem," she whispered. Except that I'm dying inside. Except that I have no interest in the series. Except that I don't want to work with any man but Jason.

"Then we'll celebrate?"

Taylor slowly clenched and unclenched her fist and said brightly, "Why not?"

"Good. I'll pick you up at eight and we can meet your father at the restaurant. Oh, and Taylor, if it helps at all, I understand Jason Garrett took an unexpected leave from work and went back to Whidbey Island. Maybe we'll be lucky and he'll give up on the project and you can finally get your screenplay back."

Taylor looked around the eclectic humbleness of Phil Walker's office and concluded it was fashioned the way it was to put his clients at ease. There were pictures in warm colors, comfortable leather chairs and magazines overflowing in a cluttered jumble from a rack beside a standing bookcase.

"Stop pacing, Taylor," Phil said for the third time. "There's nothing you can do."

"He wouldn't walk out of production unless something was terribly wrong. He wouldn't."

"So what do you think's wrong?" Phil questioned, lifting a palm.

Taylor darted a glance at him and wondered just who was being analyzed here. She began to understand Jason's impatience with the man and could well imagine why Phil had been bounced out of his cabin.

"I told you what he said about the accident," she reminded Phil shortly. "What if he's...back to being...like he was?"

Phil sighed. "Telling you about the accident was probably the best thing Jason could have done. He's never told anyone, you know, though we'd all pretty well guessed something like that must have happened. Jason's not the kind to let something eat at him unless it was too terrible to face.''

''Then why's he gone back up there?'' Taylor demanded, her face white.

''Look, Taylor.'' Phil leaned forward and motioned for her to take a chair, but she remained stubbornly on her feet. ''Don't get any ideas about chasing after him again. This time, he needs time *alone*. He's probably just coming to terms.''

''You don't understand,'' Taylor said miserably. She hadn't yet been able to tell Phil about her own betrayal of Jason.

Phil rubbed his knuckles across his salt-and-pepper beard. ''I understand enough to know you've had some major falling out and that Jason blames you for it.'' He shrugged and gave her an encouraging smile. ''It was bound to happen.''

''Why do you say that?''

''Because Lisabeth nearly ruined his life! He's transferred those feelings to you.''

Taylor peered at Phil thoughtfully. ''You really are a shrink, aren't you?''

He laughed. ''Not really.''

''I can see why Jason barely tolerates you, but—'' Taylor's lips curved almost against her will ''—I have to admit, I do feel a little better.''

''Wait for him to come back. I'm sure he will. He's just got to put some ghosts to rest.''

Taylor looked down at her hands. ''But there are no guarantees for the future—for me. He could come back and still not want to see me anymore.''

''I won't lie to you, Taylor.'' Phil was very serious. ''You were there at a time when he needed you. He might not feel the same now, or ever again. But then again, he might."

"Then all I can do is wait," she said, and Phil nodded soberly. "Okay," Taylor whispered. "I'll try."

Production for *Diamond in the Sky* was suspended, and Taylor, who'd never heard the confirmed report of who would take over the part of Julie Diamond, found herself waiting in a kind of breathless limbo, half-believing, yet afraid to believe, that Jason might have had trouble finding someone to take her place. If, as Phil Walker seemed to think, he was getting himself together at the cabin, then there was a chance he would have a whole new perspective on her as well.

It was Clifton Maddox, surprisingly, who unwittingly killed that hope for her. He called her one afternoon and asked if she'd have lunch with him. Taylor accepted, foolishly longing to be with anyone who reminded her of Jason, although she couldn't imagine why Clifton would want to see her.

Clifton had aged considerably since she'd seen him on Madeira, his shock of hair nearly completely white, his skin still a bit gray and papery. But he smiled when she walked into the small café, and gallantly helped her to her seat.

"You look as lovely as always, Taylor," he said.

In a pale lemon jump suit just a few shades lighter than her hair, Taylor looked as bright and fresh as the anticipation welling within her. Clifton must have called her regarding something about Jason; he was the only interest they had in common.

"It's good to see you up and around again, Clifton," she said, watching as he poured her a glass of wine from a crystal carafe.

"It's great to be up and around," he said fervently, frowning slightly at something in his memory. He gave her a quick look. "I suppose you know Meredith and I have split up. She's gone to work for one of the studios."

Taylor nodded. She had heard about Meredith's decision. Though she understood some of the reasons, it seemed such a shame that, after years of working together and building a successful production company, Clifton and Meredith hadn't been able to save their marriage.

"Let me get right to the point," Clifton said after the waiter had taken their order. "I asked you to meet me because I have a proposition for you—one I wanted to deliver personally."

Taylor raised her brows, unable to imagine what that proposition might be.

"I was wondering if you'd be interested in writing another *Diamond Girl* sequel—this time for Maddox Productions."

Taylor couldn't hide her surprise. Whatever she'd expected from Clifton, this wasn't it! She'd toyed with the idea of writing another screenplay, but she hadn't imagined anyone would take her seriously after the fiasco with Jason.

"Meredith showed me the outline of *Diamond in the Sky* and I was really impressed with your work," Clifton went on. "Show me another outline as good and I'll buy your next screenplay."

Taylor recovered herself slowly. "I—I don't know what to say."

"Have you ever given any thought to writing another?" Clifton asked curiously.

"Well...yes, as a matter of fact..."

"But . . . ?" he urged gently.

Taylor sighed and lifted her shoulders. "I've been offered the role of Maggie Templeton in NBS's new adventure-drama, *Templeton's World*. To be honest, I don't know if I'll have the time to write."

"Ahhh." Clifton rubbed his nose. "Have you signed the contract already?"

"No, but I'm considering it."

The meal came at that moment, interrupting whatever Clifton was about to say. Taylor tried to do justice to her salad but ended up by moving pieces of lettuce around her plate, barely tasting those she managed to eat.

Over coffee Clifton observed, "I don't think it really matters whether you take the part or not, Taylor. You have enough ambition and drive to play Maggie and write too—if that's what you want."

"You give me too much credit," Taylor murmured, fingering her spoon.

Wasn't that what Jason had said to her—that she gave him too much credit? Taylor's features unconsciously tightened and she felt that familiar ache inside—the one that came to life every time she thought about Jason.

"No, I don't. I've worked with you enough. Tell me, why haven't you signed for *Templeton's World* yet?"

"I don't know. I guess I'm just thinking over all the ramifications."

Clifton Maddox hadn't got where he was by being obtuse. He regarded Taylor through narrowed eyes for several moments, then said, "This doesn't have anything to do with Jason Garrett, does it?"

Taylor straightened in her chair. She wasn't about to discuss Jason with Clifton. "Why would you say that?"

"Well, he's got your other screenplay. I wondered if maybe you were expecting him to call now that he's back, and put you back in as Julie Diamond. After all, it's *your* part."

Taylor hadn't heard anything past the revelation that Jason had returned from Whidbey. "Jason's ... back?" she asked disbelievingly.

"He hasn't called you, then?"

Clifton wasn't trying to needle her; he just wanted to get the facts. But Taylor felt as if she'd been delivered a blow. Jason was back and nothing had changed.

"No." She smiled faintly.

Clifton sighed and poured them each another glass of wine. "I'm sorry, Taylor. I don't know what's happened, but it's obvious that Jason's at the root of it." His mouth pulled down at the corners and he said, "Jason and I have had our differences, too, but he generally has a good reason for what he's doing. Do yourself a favor and stop thinking he'll call. When Jason makes up his mind, it's not likely to be changed, and I have a feeling he's made up his mind about you."

Taylor was hardly able to keep herself together long enough to plead a headache and make a polite exit. But back at her apartment she gave a lot of thought to Clifton's words, and she continued to think about them day after day. A week later, she was finally able to convince herself that she should put Jason and *Diamond in the Sky* out of her mind and sign with *Templeton's World*.

Ross had sent the contract over days earlier, but Taylor hadn't been able to work up the enthusiasm to look at it. Now, as she flipped through the pages, she realized that what Clifton had suggested was true: she'd put off signing on the off chance that Jason would call and offer her the role in her own screenplay.

Taylor's lips tightened. It was galling, the way he'd wrangled her screenplay out from under her. Maybe, she thought defeatedly, she should have listened to Ross's advice and fought him for it. Maybe she should take him to court.

Picking up the pen, she clenched it tightly between her fingers, determined to write her signature and sign away her future. If she chose to go with *Templeton's World* there would be no chance for her to do *Diamond in the Sky*, even if Jason called; she wouldn't have the time.

But he wasn't going to call and she was foolish to even think he might.

With a sound of frustration directed solely at herself, Taylor tossed down the pen, grabbed her sweater and walked outside to the mailbox. She took in a deep lungful of air and exhaled slowly, wishing she could find an easy way to get over Jason. He'd been back from Whidbey for over a week and hadn't called; he wasn't likely to now.

Wait, Phil Walker had told her. She was just beginning to find out how difficult that was proving to be.

She picked up her mail and flipped through it on the way back upstairs, her steps faltering as she recognized the logo of Whidbey Productions.

It was from Jason! For a moment Taylor's heart leaped with excitement, but as she stared through the window of the envelope in her hand, it slowly dawned on her that what she saw was her name printed across the face of what could only be a check.

Jason had paid her off.

The morning's lack of decisiveness evaporated in a flash of anger. Taylor ran up the rest of the steps, jerked open her door and slammed it behind her. She picked up a pen and slashed RETURN TO SENDER in a bold scrawl across the front of the envelope. Then she drove to the nearest mail drop and thrust the envelope inside, her heart beating in rapid double-time.

Damn him! Damn, damn, damn him! He'd really gone all the way with this. Taylor could scarcely believe it. She'd pinned all her hopes on his changing after his trip to Whidbey, she realized sorrowfully. And he'd let her down...again.

With an intensity of purpose she hadn't had before, Taylor drove back to her apartment. The contract was still waiting for her where she'd left it, and this time she carefully wrote her signature on the line.

Then she dropped her head in her hands and fought back the tide of anguish that swept through her.

Two days later, Taylor had finally worked up the conviction to take the contract to Ross. She was in the process of pulling on her sweater and getting ready to leave when her door bell rang. She opened it warily, and was surprised to see a uniformed messenger on the other side.

"Taylor Michaelson?" he asked.

"Yes."

"I have a letter for you."

She knew what it was even before she saw her own furious scrawl, and as he stretched it out toward her she shook her head. "I'm sorry. I can't accept." At his look of bewilderment, she said with a smile, "You'll have to take it back."

Shrugging, letting her know by his silence that he thought she was a crazy lady, he started back down the steps. Taylor found herself grinning like an idiot. It felt good to thwart Jason, even it if was something of a hollow victory. Let him stew about that! He'd probably think she'd changed her mind about letting him have the screenplay, and in a way she had.

She dropped the contract off that afternoon, dodged an invitation from Ross to go to lunch, spent some time desultorily shopping in some expensive boutiques and arrived back at her apartment around twilight.

She'd just set her purchases on the kitchen table when she heard the slam of a furious fist against her door. She didn't need to be clairvoyant to guess who was on the other side. To her disgust she felt a decided trembling all the way to her knees and a flutter in her pulse.

Taylor allowed herself a moment to pull herself together before she faced Jason, running nervous palms down her slacks and trying to remember all the techniques Jason had taught her about being an actress. She was going to have to give the performance of her life, she reckoned, because she had a sense that this meeting with him was her last chance. If he suspected any weakness in her, there was no telling what kind of damage he could do to her self-respect.

She put a pleasant and slightly baffled mask across her face and opened the door.

"Jason!" she said in surprise.

He was in the jeans, shirt and boots he'd worn on Whidbey, and Taylor noticed that he filled out his clothes a lot better than he had when she had first seen him up there. Apparently this trip hadn't reduced him to the emotional cripple he'd been before, and Taylor took some measure of comfort in that.

Jason stalked past her into the center of the room, all masculine aggression and lithe muscular grace. "What the hell do you think you're doing?"

If he'd reacted differently, Taylor would have dropped her act and flung herself at his mercy. She loved him too much to want to pretend, but his cold attitude forced her to keep up pretenses. Even so, she had to curb the impact he had on her senses; there was something about his long limbs, steely blue eyes and determined stance that played havoc with her hard-won self-control.

"I'm not sure what you mean," Taylor said blankly.

Jason swore under his breath, ripped the familiar envelope from his pocket and tossed it in the general direction of the coffee table. It sailed across the top and drifted gently to the carpet, landing halfway between Taylor and the couch.

"You know exactly what I mean!" he rasped. "What stunt are you trying to pull this time? It's a little late to change your mind about our deal."

Taylor leveled cool amber eyes at him. "I don't remember making any deal."

"So you *do* want to renegotiate." Jason was scathing.

She regarded him helplessly. Couldn't he see what really mattered to her? Couldn't he see her love for him staring him right in the face? Or was it that he just didn't care?

"I don't want anything from you!" Taylor said tautly, her temper suddenly reaching flash point, surprising both her and Jason. She snatched up the envelope, grabbed his hand and crumpled the letter into his palm, closing his long fingers around it. "I won't take a dime of your money! And I don't give a damn about renegotiating! When is it finally going to penetrate that thick skull of yours that all I ever wanted was *you*?"

Jason looked down at the envelope, tossing it furiously aside. "I won't make out another check," he said tensely.

"Don't! Don't make one out!" Taylor felt all the wild, helpless feelings she'd tried to contain well to the surface. "I wouldn't accept it if you did! I don't want anything from you—especially money. What I gave you of myself, I gave as a gift. Don't cheapen it by trying to pay me money!''

His blindness to her feelings drove Taylor to desperation. She curled up her fist and hit him in the chest, twice, before Jason's fingers pressed cruelly into her wrists.

''Would you listen to me?'' he demanded. ''I'm trying to pay you for your screenplay, for God's sake!''

''The hell you are. You're trying to buy me off. It's your conscience money, Jason, and you can damn well keep it!''

''Crazy woman,'' he muttered.

Tears burned in Taylor's eyes, distorting her vision. ''I've had all I can take, Jason. If you can't believe in me, then leave.'' She laughed brokenly. ''You're so good at telling people to get out. How does it feel to be on the other side?''

''Oh, Taylor...''

She heard the anguish in his voice, but she'd had more than her share of misery. If he couldn't see her love for what it was now, he never would. ''All I ever wanted for you, Jason, was the best. You can keep *Diamond in the Sky*. I don't want it. I don't want a penny from it.''

''My God... my God...''

All of a sudden he was embracing her, holding on to her like a drowning man. Taylor felt tears run down her cheeks, but she didn't make any attempt to return his embrace. He could come to *her* now; she'd more than met him halfway.

''What am I doing with you?'' he murmured, the words muffled as he buried his mouth in her hair.

''You're making me miserable. You're cheating me. You're transferring all the weaknesses you saw in Lisabeth onto me.''

She felt the shock wave that ripped through him. *"What?"*

"Well, I'm not Lisabeth," Taylor said in a heartfelt whisper. "I'm not."

Jason pulled back to look at her, his expression unreadable. "I never thought you were. Who put that idea in your head? Phil?"

The hostility she'd begun to expect from him had all but disappeared, and Taylor realized with a pang of pure joy that at last he was listening to her.

The rakish grin that had made Jake Diamond famous flashed across his lips. "You did talk to Phil," he said disbelievingly. "You actually bought that stuff!"

"Well, yes, I did." There was no use denying it.

"Taylor..." Jason shook his head, opened his mouth to prove her wrong, then hesitated. After a moment of thought, he shrugged and admitted, "Maybe there's a grain of truth in there somewhere, but in actuality you and Lisabeth are very different kinds of women."

"It's certainly taken you long enough to figure that out," Taylor said with a cautious smile. She didn't want to risk alienating him again.

"No, I've known." He grimaced and looked somber. "I just haven't let myself believe in you. I couldn't take a chance on being hurt like that again."

"And now?" Taylor's heart was beating fast.

His hand cupped her chin, the look on his face one of torture. Taylor's heart did a steep nosedive, but then he whispered hoarsely, "I've put you through hell, Taylor. I don't know how you've stood it!"

"You're the one who's been through hell," she argued quietly. "I never really knew what you'd been going through until you told me about the accident. I'm amazed you've remained sane, Jason. I don't know if I could have."

His strong arms squeezed her close and she wound her arms around his neck, pressing her damp face against his warm skin.

"If you had accepted that check, I don't know what I would have done," he said on a heavy sigh.

"You were testing me?"

Jason shook his head. "Not consciously, but subconsciously... yes, I suppose I was a little."

Taylor kissed his throat, tasting the salt from her own tears. "What a rat!" she said, smiling. "I might have taken that money just to prove you couldn't hurt me anymore!"

"But you didn't."

His lips found hers, and for a moment no more words were necessary. Taylor clung to him with all the pent-up love she'd saved since the day they'd broken up.

"I'm sure you know I went back to Whidbey," he said unsteadily when the kiss ended and Taylor began raining a string of little kisses down the side of his neck.

"Mmmhmm..."

"I wanted to get you out of my mind and my heart," he admitted. "I couldn't find anyone to recast as Julie Diamond; there was no one like you, and I went to Whidbey as a kind of purge."

Taylor understood very well about purges. She'd tried to purge herself of Jason and the past by writing *Diamond in the Sky*.

"But it didn't work. Although I did find I could think about Lisabeth and Kerri in a totally different way. I even drove past the accident site without feeling I was going to pass out."

Jason's arms tighened convulsively. "I can even look at my daughter's picture again," he admitted.

"Oh, Jason..." She was so glad for him that new tears burned behind her eyes.

Jason tucked a strand of streaked blond hair behind her ear. "The one thing I *haven't* been able to face is losing you."

Taylor blinked in bafflement. "Then why didn't you call me when you got back?"

"I don't know. I'd been terrible to you—always expecting the worst when all you gave was the best. I guess I sent the check as a way of making some kind of contact, and then you had the nerve to send it back. I told myself I was furious, but inside it gave me some hope. So I sent it back to you, and you sent it back again."

"So you decided to hand-deliver it."

"Yes, and there you were, so cool and uncaring. My whole world came apart, Taylor."

She gave him a look of pure disbelief. "Well, what did you expect? You specifically told me you never wanted me to say 'I love you' again. How was I supposed to react? With open arms?"

Jason groaned in self-disgust. "I must have been out of my mind to say that."

She peered at him closely. "You mean that?"

He tilted up her chin, his eyes lovingly tracing every curve and contour. "I love you, Taylor. I have for a long, long time. I'm only half a person without you, and I'd do anything to win you back."

It was almost more than she'd hoped for. Her fingers gently followed the line of his jaw, and she said softly, "You can't win back what you never truly lost." Then she added with a grin, "Like it or not, Jake Diamond, we're a team."

"Marry me, Taylor."

She was struck speechless. The urgent tone of his voice told her this was no light-hearted request; it came straight from his soul.

"Taylor . . . ?"

His anxiety over her long silence echoed in his voice, and she said simply, "Yes. When?"

The tension in Jason's body relaxed, and she heard the relief in his voice as he said, "Right away. Before we start filming *Diamond in the Sky*." He snapped his fingers and asked, "How would you like getting married on Madeira?"

"That would be wonderful," Taylor murmured, overwhelmed. "I can't imagine a more beautiful—" She inhaled a sharp breath and moaned. "Oh, no . . ."

Jason froze. "What?"

"I just signed to play Maggie Templeton in *Templeton's World*. I won't be able to do *Diamond in the Sky*!"

"Call Ross." Jason had spun her around and was pushing her toward the phone before she could think of anything else to say. "Tell him you have to break contract and explain why."

"Maybe . . . maybe the contract's still in his office." Her voice gathered conviction. "I'm sure it is, I just dropped it off."

"If they want you badly enough, they'll wait until you're done with *Diamond in the Sky* anyway."

Taylor picked up the phone with shaking fingers, her happiness and excitement making her weak. "Ross is going to scream."

"Let him." Jason nuzzled the back of her neck, his arms wrapped around her possessively.

Taylor felt as if she were dreaming. All she ever wanted was coming true. She waited in a beautiful delirium while the secretary connected her to Ross.

"Ross?" she asked, as Jason's hand undid the buttons of her blouse. She couldn't stifle a laugh as she slapped it away.

"Yes, what is it, Taylor?" He sounded impatient. "I'm just on my way out."

"Tear up the NBS contract for *Templeton's World*."

"What? Why? Taylor, have you lost your mind!"

"Mmm . . . probably." Jason was nothing if he wasn't determined, and he continued his assault on her buttons.

Thinking she'd better get off the phone as quickly as possible, Taylor said, "Ross, I can't explain everything now, just trust me. Jake and Julie Diamond are about to become Jason and Taylor Garrett. I'll call you later with the details."

She hung up and twisted in Jason's arms, looking up at him with all the love expressed in that poster from long ago. And Jason's love was evident, too, as he bent down to meld his lips to hers.

AMERICAN TRIBUTE

Where a man's dreams count
for more than his parentage...

*Look for these upcoming titles
under the Special Edition
American Tribute banner.*

LOVE'S HAUNTING REFRAIN
Ada Steward #289–February 1986
For thirty years a deep dark secret kept them
apart–King Stockton made his millions while
his wife, Amelia, held everything together.
Now could they tell their secret, could they
admit their love?

THIS LONG WINTER PAST
Jeanne Stephens #295–March 1986
Detective Cody Wakefield checked out
Assistant District Attorney Liann McDowell,
but only in his leisure time. For it was the
danger of Cody's job that caused Liann to
shy away.

AM-TRIB-1

AMERICAN TRIBUTE

RIGHT BEHIND THE RAIN
Elaine Camp #301—April 1986
The difficulty of coping with her brother's
death brought reporter Raleigh Torrence
to the office of Evan Younger, a police
psychologist. He helped her to deal with
her feelings and emotions, including love.

CHEROKEE FIRE
Gena Dalton #307—May 1986
It was Sabrina Dante's silver spoon that
Cherokee cowboy Jarod Redfeather couldn't
trust. The two lovers came from opposite
worlds, but Jarod's Indian heritage taught
them to overcome their differences.

NOBODY'S FOOL
Renee Roszel #313—June 1986
Everyone bet that Martin Dante and Cara
Torrence would get together. But Martin
wasn't putting any money down, and Cara
was out to prove that she was nobody's fool.

MISTY MORNINGS, MAGIC NIGHTS
Ada Steward #319—July 1986
The last thing Carole Stockton wanted was to
fall in love with another politician, especially
Donnelly Wakefield. But under a blanket of
secrecy, far from the campaign spotlights,
their love became a powerful force.

COMING NEXT MONTH

RIGHT BEHIND THE RAIN—Elaine Camp
The difficulty of coping with her brother's death brought reporter Raleigh Torrence to Evan Younger, a police psychologist. He helped her deal with her emotions, including love.

SPECIAL DELIVERY—Monica Barrie
Five years ago, the man Leigh knew only as Jared helped her through childbirth and disappeared as mysteriously as he'd arrived. Now he was back . . . but this time she wanted some answers.

PRISONER OF LOVE—Maranda Catlin
When Alexandra hired Joe to work on her ranch she got more than she bargained for. His qualifications didn't list "ex-con," and the shackles of the past threatened to destroy their new love.

GEORGIA NIGHTS—Kathleen Eagle
When the band Georgia Nights had a gig in Massachusetts, Connor met Sarah Benedict. How could he win the heart of a dark-haired, dark-eyed enchantress who wanted nothing from him?

FOCUS ON LOVE—Maggi Charles
Judith found that when she photographed Alex the camera revealed a truth that only pictures could capture. Could Alex forget the ghosts of the past and zoom in on a new love?

ONE SUMMER—Nora Roberts
Shade and Bryan were working together, traveling across the country, recording two views of one American summer. They were complete opposites, but passion was destined to draw them together.

AVAILABLE THIS MONTH:

THIS LONG WINTER PAST
Jeanne Stephens

ZACHARY'S LAW
Lisa Jackson

JESSE'S GIRL
Billie Green

BITTERSWEET SACRIFICE
Bay Matthews

HEATSTROKE
Jillian Blake

DIAMOND IN THE SKY
Natalie Bishop